Date: 1/2/18

LP FIC EASON
Eason, Lynette,
Chasing secrets

CHASING SECRETS

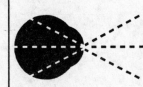

This Large Print Book carries the
Seal of Approval of N.A.V.H.

ELITE GUARDIANS, BOOK 4

CHASING SECRETS

LYNETTE EASON

THORNDIKE PRESS

A part of Gale, a Cengage Company

Farmington Hills, Mich • San Francisco • New York • Waterville, Maine
Meriden, Conn • Mason, Ohio • Chicago

LIBRARY OF CONGRESS CIP DATA ON FILE.
CATALOGUING IN PUBLICATION FOR THIS BOOK
IS AVAILABLE FROM THE LIBRARY OF CONGRESS

ISBN-13: 978-1-4328-4214-7 (hardcover)
ISBN-10: 1-4328-4214-5 (hardcover)

Published in 2017 by arrangement with Revell Books, a division of Baker Publishing Group

Printed in the United States of America
1 2 3 4 5 6 7 21 20 19 18 17

Dedicated to my family.

I love you more than you'll ever know.

PROLOGUE

Rock Moran Castle
County Mayo, Ireland, 1991

Five-year-old Aileen Burke crouched in the small hidden room in the big castle she called home. Terror caused her little heart to beat in her chest like the wings of a hummingbird. More gunshots rang out and Aileen ducked her head and covered her ears. She pressed back into the warm body behind her. "Mam," she whispered. "I want me mam."

"Shh, child, yer mam canna be here. I'll keep ye safe. Just don' say a word."

Aileen shuddered and clamped her lips shut. She'd seen the big red stain that grew on the front of her dad's chest after the man with the gun had yelled at him. It had scared her, so she'd run to her favorite hiding place. The place where Nanny Iona had found her and crawled inside with her.

"Da's hurt, Nanny, that bad man shot

7

him. He's bleeding." She kept her voice low, barely above a whisper, as the screams and shouts and loud noises echoed around them. "Make it stop, please."

"Shh, say no more."

Aileen fell silent. Tears leaked from her eyes, and someplace deep inside her, she knew she would never see her dad again.

A loud thud just outside the small door made her jump. More screams raked across her ears and she shuddered. Nanny's arms tightened around her and she felt the woman's lips touch the edge of her forehead. "May the God of peace bring peace to this house," she whispered.

The siege seemed to go on forever as the castle, her home, shook with violence. She must have fallen asleep, her ear next to Nanny's heartbeat, because the next thing she knew Nanny was shaking her, whispering that they needed to go. "Close yer eyes, *leanbh*. I'm goin' to carry you out of here. Promise me. Promise ye won't look."

Aileen didn't answer and Nanny opened the small door that was barely big enough for the woman. If she'd been any bigger, Aileen figured she'd have gotten stuck just like her dog Henry did when he tried to come in the doggy door. Her mam had had to open the door and pull him out, then her

8

da had made the door bigger for Henry. But no one had been able to convince Henry to use the doggy door after that.

She yawned. She wanted to go back to sleep, but mostly she wanted her mam and da. But Da was hurt . . .

Aileen swallowed the lump in her throat and grimaced at the gritty feeling. She tried to be brave. She wished she'd gone to school today. She was supposed to have gone on a field trip to the zoo with all of her friends, but Nanny had kept her home because she had a little fever and a sore throat. Aileen had been very upset about missing the trip, but when Nanny had brought her chicken broth and let her watch her favorite cartoon with a promise to take her to the zoo as soon as she was well, Aileen had cheered up and then fallen asleep.

And then the loud bangs had awakened her and scared her. She'd heard running footsteps, mean shouts, and lots of bad words. So she'd hidden.

Nanny slipped past her and out the door. She turned and held out her hands. Aileen let Nanny help her out of the hiding place and pick her up. "Close your eyes, love."

Aileen obeyed. Her nose twitched. Her home smelled funny. Bad. Like the time her dad had killed a deer and let her watch him dress it. She hadn't liked it then and she didn't like it now. But she kept her eyes shut.

Nanny moved quickly, her steps sure and steady. "Are yer eyes closed?" she whispered.

"They're closed, Nanny, they are."

Nanny walked and Aileen bounced against her shoulder. The woman pressed a hand against the back of her head and shoved Aileen's nose into her neck. Too hard. She couldn't breathe. "Can I open them now?"

"Not yet." Nanny's voice sounded thick, like she had something in her throat and was trying to talk around it. "Not yet." Nanny's chest heaved and Aileen heard her sniffle. She struggled against Nanny's hold and broke free. She leaned back to look at Nanny in spite of Nanny telling her to keep her eyes closed and was shocked to see her face wet with tears. "Nanny, I want me mam."

Nanny renewed her grip on the back of her head and pushed her back into her shoulder, trying to keep her from seeing. "Don't look. Don't look."

But Aileen struggled free of the hold and looked. She saw her da on the floor, the stain on his chest still a bright red, his eyes empty yet staring at the ceiling. "Da! Da!" She reached for him, but Nanny was moving her farther and farther away.

"*Leanbh,* don't look, don't look."

"Daddyyyyy — !"

[1]

Present-Day Ireland
Rock Moran Castle, County Mayo
September

The knock on the door jerked ninety-year-old Ian Burke out of his afternoon nap. He sat up and blinked at the shadow moving toward the foot of his bed. It took him a moment to realize it was Hugh McCort, his faithful assistant. They didn't call themselves servants these days. "What is it?"

"How is your headache?"

Ian pressed a hand to his temple. "It's eased a bit. Is that why you woke me?"

"Of course not. There's a visitor here to see you."

Ian frowned. "I don't do visitors, Hugh, you know that."

"I do know that, but I'm making a judgment call on this. He's a member of the Gardaí."

"The Gardaí?" The Irish police. "What

13

does he want with me?" Ian slid out of bed and pulled on the robe Hugh held out to him. He might be ninety years old, but he still commanded respect, with his straight shoulders and razor-sharp mind.

"I believe it has something to do with your granddaughter."

Ian froze. "Aileen?" he whispered.

"Indeed."

"What kind of news does he have?"

"I don't know, he wouldn't tell me. He said he would only speak to you. I allowed him to wait in your office. I hope that's all right."

"Of course." Curiosity and old grief ate at him. Ian threw off the robe that covered the lounge pants and T-shirt that he found himself wearing more often than not. "I need to dress."

Fifteen minutes later, Ian stepped out of his bedroom, dressed in his favorite pair of khakis and a crisp collared shirt, to walk down the stone-lined hallway to the other end of the house. He stopped at the entrance to his office to whisper a prayer. *Please let this be good news.* He breathed in, then out, and entered his office.

A young man dressed in full Gardaí uniform set down his tea and stood from his perch on the love seat. He pulled his cap from his head and gave a slight bow. "Thank you for seeing me."

Ian motioned for the man to sit. "I hear you have news of my granddaughter?"

"I think so."

"She's been dead for twenty-five years. What kind of news could you possibly have?"

"Let me start with an introduction. My name is Duncan O'Brien. I work in the cold case department and I've come across something that I thought you might find interesting."

"So my dear Aileen is a cold case." He sniffed. Of course she was. Her murderer had never been found.

O'Brien cleared his throat. "And I asked for this case in particular because I've had an interest in it since I was very young."

"Why is that, lad?"

"Because I was supposed to be on the bus for that field trip."

Ian felt himself pale but stood statue still.

The young officer cleared his throat. "The flu had been going around me class. I'd fallen ill with it the night before the trip and Mam kept me home. I remember Aileen clearly. She was my friend."

Ian fell silent for a moment as he felt the emotions of that long-ago day wash over

15

him. It had been twenty-five years since the bus carrying his granddaughter and her nanny had exploded and killed all twenty-seven people on board. Twenty-one five-year-olds and six adults. Yet right now, it felt as though it had happened yesterday. Like he was reliving the news of that horrific moment all over again. He drew in a deep breath and tried to ignore the renewed pounding in his head. "I see."

"My sergeant honored my request to work the cold cases. 'Tis the one I'm most interested in. The one I'm most desperate to solve."

Ian made his way over to the wingback chair next to his desk and seated himself. "What do you have on the people who killed Aileen?"

O'Brien reached into his pocket and pulled out a plastic bag that contained a picture. He passed it to Ian. Ian pulled his glasses from the desk and set them on his nose for a closer look.

He frowned. "What's this?"

"It was taken the day of the bombing."

"Who took it?" Ian asked.

"A mother whose wee one was on the bus. She brought her daughter and took the picture, and then got in her car and drove off to head to work. She heard the explosion moments later, but didn't stop."

Aghast, Ian started. "Why not?"

"There was some construction going on across the street from the school. According to the report, when the Gardaí interviewed her, she said she thought the loud noise came from there. It was only when they showed up at her workplace that she learned the explosion was the bus her child was on."

Ian shuddered. "Poor woman." He knew exactly what she'd felt at that very moment. He shut his mind to the memory and focused on the innocent faces in the picture. He remembered quite a few of them. They'd been at the castle for Aileen's fifth birthday only a few weeks before they'd died.

"Do you notice anything interesting about the photo?"

Ian slowly realized what O'Brien was getting at. He removed his glasses with suddenly shaky fingers. "My Aileen's not in there. She's not in the photo."

"And neither is the nanny. If you'll turn the photo over, the mother had listed all of the names of the children. Then below, it says, 'Blessed to have escaped' and lists the four children who weren't there. Meself, Liam O'Reilly, Bailey Parker, and Aileen Burke."

Dizziness hit Ian and he leaned back to

shut his eyes for a brief moment.

"Are you all right?" O'Brien asked.

"I'm fine. Fine," Ian said. He turned his focus back on the officer.

O'Brien nodded. "I know 'tis a bit of a shock for you, but I think you're probably wondering the same thing I am."

Ian looked down at the picture once again. "Where were Aileen and her nanny?"

"Because it was impossible to identify every person, due to the fact that the bus and everyone on it was practically incinerated, it was assumed that Aileen and the nanny were there — especially when they were never seen again."

Ian nodded. "A reasonable assumption."

"But all indications point to the fact that they weren't there because they're not in the picture. So how did they manage to escape the explosion?"

Ian refused to allow himself to feel the hope that wanted to spring alive. He shook his head. "There has to be an explanation. Maybe they were late, maybe —"

"Sorry to interrupt, but they weren't late."

"All right. Can you possibly start at the beginning?"

O'Brien ran a hand through his hair. "I'm sorry. I'm not doing a very good job with this."

"You're fine. Just keep going. How did you get the picture?"

"The woman who took the picture had another daughter named Megan, who was ten at the time of the bus explosion. Fifteen years ago, the woman committed suicide."

"Suicide?"

He nodded. "Megan said her mam had been battling depression since the explosion —"

"Understandable," Ian muttered. He'd battled it himself. Some days he wasn't sure he'd won.

"Anyway, she left a note that said, 'I'm so sorry. I can't fight anymore. Please forgive me.' "

"Awful. So much pain, so much grief."

"To be sure. Megan's father died last month, and when she started cleaning out his house, she came across some pictures. The date on the back said they were developed about three weeks prior to her mother's death. Megan said something nagged at her. She thought Aileen had died in the bus explosion, so she wasn't sure why she wasn't in the picture, but thought it significant enough to bring it to me."

"As well she should."

"Megan feels like the pictures brought back all of the grief and her mother simply

19

couldn't fight it anymore — as she stated in her note. Now as you can imagine, the picture immediately caught her attention, it being her sister who was killed."

Ian drew in another breath. It seemed terribly hard for him to get the air he needed at the moment. Finally, he pulled a handkerchief from his pocket and swiped it across his eyes. He only just realized tears were leaking down his cheeks.

Hugh, who had been standing silently to the side, stepped forward. "Ian, let me —"

Ian waved him away and the man stopped, then stepped back. Ian turned his attention to the officer. "So they might not have been on the bus."

"I don't believe they were."

"You do realize that the day the bus exploded, most of my family members were killed in what I believe was a Mafia-related hit? My son and daughter-in-law, Aileen's two-year-old brother . . . all of them," he whispered. "All gone. Slaughtered like they were worthless." His heart thudded. "A two-year-old!"

The young officer swallowed and blinked. "I know. And I believe the two incidents are related."

Ian snorted. "We all believe that. The problem has been finding the people responsible." After all these years . . . "Wait a minute. Wouldn't the woman have heard about the attack on the castle and, as soon as she noted that Aileen wasn't in the photo, brought it to someone's attention?"

"You would think so. I asked the daughter that very question. She said she wasn't sure that her mother ever heard anything about the attack. She was too lost in her grief and too sedated to even be aware of her surroundings for a long time. And she never had the photos developed until shortly before her death. The headlines had long faded by then." He shook his head. "If she hadn't decided to develop that roll of film and then compare it against a class picture, we never would have known."

Ian swallowed and paused, gathering his thoughts and his strength. "I should have been here, you know."

"Why weren't you?"

"My wife was having chest pains. We'd left around four in the morning to drive to the hospital. It's the only reason we were spared."

He glanced at Hugh. "You drove yourself?"

"I did. Hugh wasn't living here at the time and I didn't want to wake anyone." He ran a shaky hand across his eyes. How he

21

wished he'd awakened someone. He drew in a deep breath. "All right, young man, if they weren't on the bus, then where were they?"

"That's what I was hoping to figure out."

Ian leaned back in his chair. "It's been so long. If she were still alive, don't you think she would have found a way to let me know?"

"I don't know, but she wasn't on that bus that day and neither was her nanny. Somehow she escaped the bus and I want to know if my friend is still alive."

"I want to know that too." He leaned forward and drew in a deep breath. "I've been hiding, so I have."

"What do you mean?"

"I mean I've been a hermit for the past twenty-five years. I don't go out and I have more security than the president of Ireland. I work from my office."

"I'd heard you'd yet to retire."

He huffed. "Retire? And do what? Twiddle my thumbs all day? No, working keeps me on my toes and makes the days not seem quite as long."

"I understand." Duncan paused. "The people who tried to kill you and yer family were never caught. You think they're still out there?"

"I don't know about that, but there's no doubt in my mind we were all supposed to die that day."

Duncan nodded. "Every last one o' you."

"Every last one."

Seven Months Later
Columbia, South Carolina
Saturday, 8:00 AM

Haley Callaghan woke slowly, the April sun filtering through the blinds she'd purposely left open last night. Saturday mornings were her favorites, mostly because she spent them at the teen center. She threw the covers off, hurried into the bathroom, took a quick shower, then pulled on her gym clothes.

Within minutes, she'd wolfed down a bagel with cream cheese, scarfed some almonds, poured her coffee into the travel mug, and was behind the wheel of her black Hummer. She glanced in the rearview mirror. No one behind her. At least no one who caused any internal alarms to go off. Yet.

Twenty minutes later, she wheeled into the parking lot of the Right Turn Teen Center. She loved the name and all it represented. Teens turning in the right direction and having fun while receiving guidance, unconditional love, and acceptance. And, Haley hoped, they were finding a healthy self-esteem, learning that they were uniquely and wonderfully made by a God who loved them unconditionally — something that was sadly lacking in most of their lives.

Stepping out of the Hummer, she slammed the door and turned. For a moment she stared at the building, satisfaction and peace flowing through her. Located in one of the poorest residential areas of Columbia off of Two Notch Road, the teen center was a bright spot, offering hope as a haven to those who needed it.

She took a step toward the entrance and stopped. The hair on the back of her neck tingled and she whipped around, scanning the parking lot.

And just like over the past week, she knew she was being watched. Last weekend, she'd been working outside with the horses on her property when a blue Toyota Camry had pulled up into her drive, then turned around and left. She'd thought nothing of it since her driveway was often mistaken for a side road. But since then, she'd spotted the car a number of other times. Sitting outside her office building, waiting outside the restaurant where she was eating. Parked across the street from church when she'd come out. Never too close, never invading her space — and she hadn't been able to snag a license plate.

She frowned and leaned against the car door, standing. Waiting. Watching.

And finally spotted it.

A blue Camry sat snugged up against the curb of the house across the street and two doors down. The empty house with the FOR SALE sign planted in the front yard.

Haley could make out someone in the driver's seat, but couldn't tell anything about the person. No one had followed her from her home. She'd made sure of that. So she was either paranoid or someone had learned her schedule and decided to come to the center because he knew she'd be there. Or it could be someone who had a score to settle with one of the kids. But she didn't think so. The person was following *her*. This was the third time she'd seen the car in the last couple days.

"That's it," she muttered.

Haley crossed her arms and wrapped her fingers around the butt of the weapon resting in the shoulder holster on her left side. She pushed away from the Hummer and started toward the Camry. She'd closed about half the distance when the driver backed along the curb to the driveway, executed a perfect three-point turn, and sped away going in the opposite direction.

And Haley couldn't see the plate.

She blew out a breath and released her weapon. He'd been watching her for weeks. She wondered how long he'd studied her before she'd finally noticed him. Probably not too long, but she couldn't seem to *catch* him. It might be time to start using her resources to figure out who he was. Like finding a way to justify getting some video footage off traffic cams.

Frowning, Haley walked through the glass doors and into the lobby area of the center. The indoor basketball courts were to her right. The dance studio was straight ahead and the art area to her left. Music blared from the sound system and laughter from the volunteers drifted toward her. The atmosphere loosened some of her tension.

Michelle Cox, nicknamed Cupcake, greeted her at the door. Short blonde hair framed her perpetually youthful face. In her midsixties, the years had added a few pounds, but she could still move with the best of them. A former professional dancer turned all-in grandma, she now poured her talent into the lives of the teens who frequented Right Turn.

"How's it going, Cupcake?" Haley asked.

"It's going and it's moving at the speed of light."

"What is?"

"Time, baby girl, time."

Haley laughed. "I know what you mean. How's the rehearsal for the talent competition coming along?"

"Donnalynn's got it covered. The woman is a dynamo." And the kids adored her. Donnalynn Davis, one of Michelle's best friends, was another lady Haley had learned she couldn't do without. The place would fall apart without the two of them. "She's got them registered and they'll be ready to roll next Saturday, perform on Sunday afternoon, and be home by Monday night," Michelle said. "Thank goodness for a teacher workday on Monday."

"Wow, it's so close. You're right about time flying." Haley rubbed her hands together and blew out a breath. "And they're really ready for this? A national audition?"

Michelle laughed. "Yes, darlin', they're ready. They've got the dance moves down and the choreography is mind-blowing. JC can do three flips in the air and land on his feet. These kids have been working every day for hours on end. They're good and they'll get through this first round. They're going to Vegas, you wait and see. Better start planning the fundraisers. You're still planning on going with us to the audition, right?"

"I wouldn't miss it for the world."

"Excellent."

"How excited is Donnalynn?"

"Beside herself. And everyone else too. She's already shown me the route four times, telling me where we'll stop for lunch, for restrooms, for a little bit of sightseeing, and for everything else in between. She's got it down to the minute, so we'd better leave on time."

"Did Donnalynn bring you some cupcakes this morning?" Haley asked.

"It's Saturday, isn't it?"

Haley smiled. "That it is." It was well known that Michelle was the cupcake queen. That woman loved cupcakes almost as much as she loved her grandchildren. "You've got a little something on your desk too."

Haley laughed. M&Ms, no doubt.

Donnalynn walked over, her short curls bobbing with each step. "You're talking about me, aren't you?"

"Michelle was just bragging about your organizational skills. I'm in awe."

The woman laughed, her dark eyes glistening with an inner joy that automatically attracted people to her.

The teens started filtering in. Michelle gave her a quick hug. "Now hush up and let's get busy. We've got work to do." The young men and women came from the neighborhood across the street, some from much farther. Those who were fortunate enough to have jobs and cars drove, the rest walked. It was hard to believe the first day they'd opened, they'd only had four kids show up. Now operating seven days a week at almost full capacity, they were going nonstop. She loved it.

"Haley, you made it this morning!" Fourteen-year-old Madison Tipton launched herself at Haley and she caught the girl in a hug. Baby lotion and teen perfume mingled together and Haley drew in the scent. Madison pulled away, her dark eyes gleaming with a gladness that tightened Haley's heart. "I love Saturdays, I love to dance. I love *you*!" Haley laughed and marveled at the girl's zest.

Madison had a rough history and a rougher home life and still she smiled. Haley hugged one teen after another — kids who didn't hug anyone, but hugged her.

Tears stung her eyes and she cleared her throat.

Once all of the kids were through the door, she shut it and locked it. If someone wanted in, the buzzer would alert her or someone in the office to check the door.

She peered back into the parking lot. The Camry was gone, but the creepy sensation of being watched still lingered, crawling up her spine in a way that made her want to rub it. She stared out at the street from behind the safety of the door, wondering what she was going to do, flipping through ways to figure out who the person was who kept following her. No one idea stood out to her. At least not a good idea.

But she *would* figure it out.

And soon.

"I think you should come home, Steven," his mother said. "Your father's not doing well. The pathology report came back and it's . . . not good. Naturally, we're going to fight it, but it's hard right now. I think your father needs you."

Detective Steven Rothwell hung up the phone and lowered his head into his hands.

He'd been expecting the call, he'd even been making arrangements for when it came.

31

So. This was it.

The job offer had come last week. All he had to do was accept it, pack up his belongings, and go home. His head pounded with the thought. With everything in him, he wanted to stay in his happy place of denial, but his dad needed him.

His mother needed him.

He'd be the dutiful son and do what he had to do. And truly, it wasn't duty that was sending him home. He loved his parents. His reluctance had nothing to do with them directly. It was *him.* He was the problem.

He prayed the memories didn't swoop in to haunt him, to steal what little peace he'd found by burying himself in work. Catch the bad guys, put them in jail, come home and eat a bit, sleep, then get up and do it all over again the next day. It had been very effective in allowing him to exist in a rather numbed state for the past few years. And numb was good. He'd searched for it long enough and had finally been successful in finding it.

But as soon as he went home, that would change.

He drew in a deep breath and let it out in one long, slow stream of air. "Okay, then," he said to his empty den. "Okay, then."

He picked up the phone and dialed the

number that would take him back to South Carolina. Back to his past and back to the place where his brother had been murdered.

[3]

County Mayo, Ireland
Wednesday, 1:00 PM

"We've found her."

The air in the large office vibrated with the announcement. Seated in the leather chair behind the desk, Ian slowly lifted his gray head and locked his eyes on Duncan O'Brien. The man stood in the doorway with Hugh right behind him. "I'll wet the tea, sir." Hugh closed the door behind Duncan.

"Where is she?" Ian asked. He almost didn't believe it.

"The United States."

"I've had a number of people looking for her. All failed. How can you be sure it's her?"

"The DNA test confirmed it."

"Do I even want to know how you got DNA from this woman without her being aware?"

The young man stepped farther into the office. " 'Twasn't hard." Respectfully, he waited until Ian gestured for him to take a seat. O'Brien chose the chair facing the desk. "What was hard — no, nearly *impossible* — was finding her. But we have."

"How?"

"We traced her through the nanny. I discovered the woman had diabetes and knew she'd need medical care. Her doctor here transferred a prescription to Belfast. From there, I found out she had a daughter the same age as Aileen."

"A daughter? She never had one. Not Aileen's age anyway."

"I know. I'm fairly certain the nanny, Iona, changed her name to Fiona Callaghan and declared Aileen as hers, changing her name to Haley Callaghan."

"I see." Ian felt old. And oddly young at the same time. His granddaughter might be alive. It seemed too much to hope for.

"Anyway, I contacted a cousin of mine who's a police officer in the States and had him run the name over there — and see if he could track her down."

Ian could barely stand the suspense. "And?"

"There was very little background information available. She went off the grid from about the age of twenty, then surfaced in Greece at a bodyguard school about five years ago. We were pretty sure it could be her. My cousin took a few weeks off and went down to South Carolina, found her, and simply followed her until she threw away a water bottle. Hence the easy-to-get DNA."

"Clever."

"Nothing one can't pick up watching crime shows."

"I don't watch crime shows." He looked away as he thought, trying to process this information. Aileen was alive! "And this man said nothing to her."

"As per our agreement, I instructed him to say nothing."

Ian nodded, steepled his fingers, and rested his chin on them. Then he stood and grabbed the cane that leaned against the desk. The cane was his one concession to old age. And he only allowed it because it could serve as a weapon too, should he need it. "When my wife died, she died a broken woman. The attack on our home left our only son, daughter-in-law, and grand-children dead. Now that you've brought me evidence that Aileen's alive, I need to plan accordingly."

"What do you mean?"

Ian drew in a deep breath. "I plan to restore her to her rightful place in this family. The business is now half hers and I need to make sure that she receives her share of the family legacy. It's the only thing I'm living for at this moment. Once she's back in County Mayo, then I can join my love in eternal rest."

"Are you ill?"

Ian chuckled. "I'm ninety years old, so I am. I don't need an illness to understand that eternity is looming in the near future for me." His mirth faded. "I have enemies, young man. I don't trust easily. But you . . . I find I want to trust you."

"Thank you for that. My sergeant told me you did your checking up on me."

"Of course."

"And you don't want anyone to know you're looking for Aileen . . . er . . . Haley."

"No." He drew in a breath and let it out slowly. "I must think before you do anything else." He paused. "Have you found the person responsible for the bus explosion that day?"

O'Brien's shoulders drooped. "Unfortunately, I'm still working on that one."

"Do you think Aileen would be in danger should I contact her?"

O'Brien shook his head. "I don't know

why she would be. Twenty-five years is a long time."

Hugh stepped forward. "Ian, that day was a terrible day. She's moved on, made a life for herself from what he says. If you share this news with her, you're going to radically alter her world as she knows it."

Ian turned his attention to his employee. "This is my granddaughter we're talking about, Hugh."

"Exactly. If 'tis indeed her, maybe you should leave her be. Where she's happy — and safe."

Ian winced. "You still think there's danger?"

"Of course I do. And you should too. They never caught the people responsible."

Ian rubbed a hand over his eyes. "The graffiti left on the walls of the castle led the Gardaí to believe it was a Mafia hit." He looked at O'Brien and pursed his lips.

"I know what the Gardaí think," the young officer said. "I've read the investigation report, so I know exactly what was done — and not done. Do you believe the attack was for a different reason?"

Ian leaned forward. "There's an old family feud with the O'Reillys that you'll know about if you've done your homework like you say you have."

"I have."

"But there's nothing that points to them or the IRA or anyone else as having anything to do with the attack, so the Gardaí chalked it up to the Sicilian Mafia. And if they're responsible, then they got away with it."

"Why would the mafia target you?"

"The Mafia does have some legitimate businesses in addition to their shadier practices."

"Of course."

Ian shrugged. "Twenty-five years ago, I was a lot more involved in Burke Shipping and Rail. I was getting close to announcing my retirement since my son, Charles, was quite comfortable at the helm. But there was one last deal to be made — and I outbid Shaughnessy Shipping in addition to O'Reillys."

"Ah, I see."

"You're familiar with them then? The Shaughnessys?"

"We arrest a lot of their workers on various charges. It's no secret they're mostly up to no good."

"That's the truth now, my boy."

"All right, so you made Lorcan Shaughnessy mad when you stole the bid from him."

"Oh, it made him mad, so it did. And he

didn't try to hide that fact either."

"So the attack well may have been a hit as revenge and moved on."

"Probably. Or it could have been the O'Reillys. Who knows?" Fatigue washed over him. "I must rest. And think. I'll be in touch about our next move."

Hugh stepped from the shadows to show O'Brien to the door.

When he returned, Ian blew out a slow breath. "What do you think about all this, Hugh?"

"I told you what I think."

Ian shook his head, disbelief and hope intermingled within him. " 'Tis a fret, isn't it?"

"A fret to be sure."

[4]

Columbia, South Carolina
Sunday, 8:30 PM

The spot between her shoulder blades had itched for the last three blocks. This was getting ridiculous.

She'd had a great morning at the center again yesterday. One week until the competition and the kids were looking like pros. Trent had behaved himself relatively well, she hadn't seen the mysterious Camry since it had pulled away from the curb yesterday, and all she wanted was a night to herself, tucked away in a dark movie theater. Just her and the story on the screen. And her large tub of popcorn and giant-sized M&Ms. And maybe a large Coke. And yes, she planned to eat it all.

So she'd set up the date with herself and had *planned* to see the eight-thirty showing but now found herself plotting the best way to end this silly cat-and-mouse game.

41

She was done with being followed.

The hair on the back of her neck spiked to attention; however, her stride never faltered as she strode down the sidewalk. Downtown Columbia rocked on this gorgeous Sunday night in April. The weather was about as perfect as one could ask for and the crowd was out. People scurried past her to get to the theater before the previews started.

The movie had moved down on her priority list. It was time to confront her shadow. Hovering on the fringes, never getting too close, but always there.

She shifted the thin strap of the small purse to her other shoulder. She didn't want it getting in the way if she had to reach across and pull her weapon.

Haley crossed the street and headed for the storefront that boasted plate glass windows. The person behind her kept pace. She got a glimpse of the figure as she passed the store and mentally took note of the dark hoodie with the hood pulled over his head, jeans, hands in the front pockets. He had to be roasting in that getup. She had on short sleeves, capri pants, and Converse tennis shoes, and she was warm.

He was about five feet ten inches tall. So he had three inches on her, but he was skinny. Wiry. He'd be strong. She reached across her chest and released the strap that held her Sig Sauer P245 in the shoulder holster. With a quick step, she turned the corner, stepped up onto the small concrete porch of the business behind her, and used her purse to break the naked bulb above. Glass littered the area around her feet and she let her purse fall to the ground. She blinked in the sudden darkness, waited for her eyes to adjust. He would have seen her turn the corner and heard the bulb break. He wouldn't be too far behind her. Haley shoved her back up against the wall, knowing she was almost invisible in the shadows of the small alley. The gun slid into her hand.

The man tracking her rounded the corner and came into view, his profile backlit by the streetlight. She knew he couldn't see her. His head swiveled, looking for her. When he took two more steps into the alley, she quickly moved behind him and held her weapon on him.

"Who are you and why are you following me?" She kept her voice low. Threatening. Laced with steely control.

He spun, then froze when he saw the weapon staring him in the eye. His hands shot into the air. "Yo, don't shoot, lady!"

The man was a kid. "Yo, you shouldn't try to mug someone who knows how to fight back." She paused and kept the gun steady. "Actually, you shouldn't try to mug anyone."

His breathing came in raspy pants. "I . . . I'm sorry. Look, I'll leave and we'll be square, right?"

"Why don't I call the cops and have yer sorry butt thrown in jail? Then we'll be square."

"P-please. Don't. I wasn't going to hurt you, I just wanted your purse."

"And I stepped off the stupid truck this morning."

"I-I got a little brother I'm taking care of." He stepped away from her and put more space between his head and the bullet end of her gun. "Okay?"

Keeping her weapon trained on him, she stepped toward him, reached up, and yanked the hood from his face. He had dark skin and darker eyes. Eyes that glinted desperation. While she kept the gun trained on him, she planted a hand in the middle of his chest and shoved him up onto the porch opposite the one where she'd hidden.

With her free hand she patted him down, shocked she didn't find any sort of weapon other than an old Swiss Army knife that was still nicely folded in his back pocket. She took it and stepped back. "Yer kidding, right? You were going to rob me, and now that yer backed into a corner, I should let you go?"

"No . . . I mean, yes. I mean . . . please?"

She snorted and kept her weapon aimed at him. She pulled her phone from her back pocket to dial 911. "Sorry, can't leave you on the street to find a less capable victim."

With a low groan, he dropped his head and shifted his feet.

Then pushed past her and bolted.

The brief second that surprise held her still gave him a bit of a head start. She wouldn't have thought he had it in him. Haley ran after him, tucking her weapon back into the holster as her feet pounded the pavement. She caught a brief glimpse of his back as he disappeared into a small café. She slid her phone back into her pocket without making the call.

Instead of heading into the café, she slipped down the alley next to it and around to the back.

The back door flew open and she stuck her foot out.

His right shin slammed into her leg and he went down with a cry. She dropped her knee into his back and pulled his hands behind him.

"I'm sorry, I'm sorry, I am. I mean it. Please let me go. I won't ever do anything like this again, I promise."

Sobs shook his thin frame and she almost couldn't make out the words. Haley didn't move, even though she had to admit she felt a tug of sympathy on her life-hardened heart. The boy continued to cry. Several people had come to investigate the chaos, including two café workers.

One pointed. "He ran right past me. Shoved me into the refrigerator. I'm going to sue!"

Haley ignored the woman and let her would-be mugger's hands go. She removed her knee, then bent down to grab the back of his shirt to flip him over. She saw the tears on his cheeks. He stopped fighting her, rolled to his side, and curled into a fetal position. When he covered his head with his arms, he had her heart. But he didn't need to know that yet.

Anger rose hot and swift. Not at the teen crying on the concrete, but at the person who'd beat him and taught him to assume that position out of reflex. She looked at the gawkers. "Show's over, folks." She pulled her mayor-authorized badge from the clip on her belt and showed it. She wasn't a cop,

46

but she had law enforcement authority. One by one the onlookers left until she was alone with the now-silent kid.

She dropped beside him. "What's yer name?"

He didn't move for a moment, so Haley stayed silent and waited.

Finally, he rolled to a sitting position and used the hem of his raggedy T-shirt to wipe his face. Then he pulled his knees to his chest and ducked his head. "Zeke," he mumbled.

"Zeke what?"

"Zeke Hampton."

"All right, Zeke Hampton. Why don't we go have a seat in the café and you try to convince me why I shouldn't arrest you."

"You a cop?"

"Something like that." She'd clarify later. She had the power to make an arrest, so she figured that was good enough.

He gave a low grunt and stood. "Figures."

"How old are you?"

"Eighteen."

"Try again."

A pause. "Sixteen. I'll be seventeen in three weeks."

"Now that you're being honest, come on and I'll buy you a sandwich."

He licked his lips. Then grimaced and

shook his head. "I . . . can't."

The kid was obviously hungry. "Why not?"

"I have to get home."

"Back to the little brother you're taking care of?"

"Yeah," he whispered.

"How old is he?"

"Twelve. His name's Micah." He glanced toward the street and Haley braced herself for another dash. But he didn't try it. Instead, he dropped his eyes to the ground. "I needed money to get his medicine. I didn't have enough this month."

"Not to sound like I'm judging you or anything, but . . . do you have government assistance?"

"Yeah, but that don't cover everything."

"Doesn't."

He let out a low laugh. "You sound like my granny."

"Is she with Micah?"

"No, she's with Jesus. According to her pastor anyway." He stood and shoved his hands in his pockets. "Look, I gotta split. If you're going to arrest me, then I guess you'd better do it." He pressed a hand to his temple. "My mama is going to kill me."

"Which pharmacy?"

"What?" His brow rose. "Why?"

"Because I asked. Take me there."

His eyes narrowed and for a moment she thought he was going to protest. Then he shrugged and turned to head for the street.

She grabbed his arm and he jerked away from her. She held up her hands. "Sorry. I need to get my purse." Assuming it was still there.

"Right."

She thought he might try to bolt again, but he led her back to the alley where they'd started the confrontation, and she breathed a sigh of relief to see her purse where she'd dropped it. She grabbed it. "All right. I'm right behind you."

Haley followed him, wondering what on earth she was doing. But he was a kid who needed help. She'd been there.

Four blocks away, he stopped and entered the Walgreens' front door. Haley followed him back to the pharmacy where he stopped at the register.

A clean-cut African-American woman with dark eyeliner and blue eye shadow stepped up to greet him. "Zee, how are you tonight?"

"I've been better, Ms. Amy."

"Sorry to hear that. Did Micah take a turn for the worse?"

He shook his head. "No, I did."

Haley heard the irony in his voice.

49

Amy frowned. "Zeke, honey, nothing's changed. I still don't have the green light from Medicaid for payment on the medication."

"Micah needs it, Ms. Amy, you know he does."

"I know." She bit her lip.

Haley stepped forward and handed the woman her card. "Here, put it on this."

"Don't you want to know how much it is first?" the woman asked.

"No, probably not." Haley wasn't wealthy, but she had a nice little nest egg. She'd get the money back once the pharmacy and Medicaid worked out the kink. In the meantime, she could tell this was the real deal and the kid needed his medicine.

Amy nodded, pulled a bag from the shelf, and set in on the counter to scan. She lifted a brow at Haley. "That'll be three hundred forty-three ninety-nine."

"Fine."

"All right then." She swiped the plastic and shot a glance at the boy beside Haley. "You going to introduce me to your new friend, Zee?"

Zeke looked at her and Haley realized she hadn't introduced herself. "I'm Haley Callaghan. *Zee* and I are recent acquaintances."

"Nice to meet you." She handed Haley

the receipt.

"You too." Haley provided the necessary signature and handed Zeke the bag. "Come on, kid, let's go check on Micah."

Haley's phone buzzed and she ignored it. She was supposed to be sitting in a movie theater all by herself and eating a gallon of popcorn. It was her day off. She wasn't answering.

Right. She pulled it from her pocket and glanced at the screen. Olivia.

"You gonna answer that?" Zeke asked.

"No." She texted Olivia.

> If it's not an emergency, I'll get back to you in about an hour. Or three.

Not an emergency

came the immediate response.

Have a new client for you. Will be in touch.

> Thanks. Let me know if you need anything.

"We're good," she said to Zeke. "I'm following you."

But still, frustration nagged at her. Zeke was not the person who'd been her shadow for the past three weeks. And the showdown she'd spotted, so he wasn't a pro. But he sure was good at avoiding confrontation.

And unfortunately, that someone was still out there. Possibly watching her even now.

But why?

[5]

Steven despised money. Correction, he was okay with money. He despised what the love of money could lead some people to do. He pulled on the blue gloves and stared down at the body in the trunk of the silver Jag. The man lay on his side, facing the front of the car. His hands were bound in front of him and his feet had been zip-tied together as well.

Steven guessed the poor guy had been dead for only a few hours at most since the pool of blood beneath his head was still wet. He shone his flashlight into the area and grimaced, doing his best to ignore the stench. He also guessed the bullet hole that had entered the back of the man's head and taken off the front of his face was the cause of death, but the ME would tell him more after the autopsy.

His partner of three days walked up to him. With gloved hands, Detective Quinn

Holcombe handed Steven a square piece of paper. "First officers on the scene said they found this on the ground by the trunk. It's the registration to the car. So far, we haven't found a wallet."

Steven looked at it. "Carter James. Lives on Edens Point Road." He blinked. "Whoa."

"What?" Quinn asked.

"I know that street."

"I do too. It's on Lake Murray. Lots of money out there."

"Yeah," Steven murmured. "Tell me about it."

Quinn raised a brow. "Something you need to share?"

"No." Not right now anyway. Steven rubbed his eyes with the back of his wrist. He turned to the nearest uniformed officer. "Any witnesses?"

The woman shook her head. "None that have come forward."

"Of course not."

She went back to talking to the man he assumed was her partner.

"What do you suppose Mr. James was doing around here?" Quinn asked. "Kind of out of his comfort zone, isn't he?"

Steven looked around. "Assuming it's Mr. James. Being on this part of Two Notch Road in Columbia, he was either looking for drugs or a prostitute."

Quinn's eyebrow rose. "How do you know Columbia so well? Thought you just moved here last week."

"I grew up in this city. I left shortly after graduation to head to Chicago so I could be a big-shot detective." He shot Quinn a wry sideways smile. "I'd heard Chicago was crime laden. I thought I could make a difference." And he was running away from memories, but no need to get into all that yet.

"There are a lot of crime-laden areas."

Steven's eyes touched on the buildings and the surrounding area. "That's for sure." He paused as his gaze landed on an unfamiliar landmark. "I don't remember that." He nodded to the building down and across the street on the corner. "Thought that was Pinehurst Park. What's that building back there? It looks new and seriously out of place." A metal roof jutted above the tree line one street over. A tall chain-link metal fence surrounded an outdoor basketball court.

"That's the Right Turn Teen Center. The park is still there, but Haley bought several acres next to it to put her center on."

"Haley?"

"A friend. You'll meet her." He moved and

shone his flashlight into the trunk, then swept it around to the side of the vehicle. "So did you make a difference?"

Steven opened the door to the Jag. "In some ways, I suppose." The numbness he'd obtained while in Chicago had disappeared the moment he'd walked into his parents' house. Just like it always did when he came for a visit. Unfortunately, he hadn't managed to get it back, but he was surprised that he was keeping his emotions under control. At least as far as his brother was concerned. Seeing his father weakening brought about a whole new level of grief.

He aimed the flashlight at the driver's seat, the driver's window, the steering wheel. Nothing out of the ordinary.

"What made you transfer to small-town Columbia?"

Steven paused, pain grabbing his heart. He cleared his throat. "Not so small. My dad was diagnosed with cancer six months ago. He's not doing well and Mom said it was time for me to come home." Steven kept his voice even, refused to give in to the urge to deny it was happening. "When the opening came available in your department and I was offered it, I took it."

"Aw, man, I'm sorry."

"Thanks." He shoved the personal

thoughts aside and focused back on the scene. "Wonder why they didn't steal his car?" He looked at the dash, the front seat, the floorboards. "Clean as a whistle, isn't it?"

"Yeah. Check for the keys."

Steven raised a brow and checked the ignition. "Nothing in here." Quinn pursed his lips and Steven scanned the rest of the car. "Nada. Did anyone find them?"

"Not if this is going the way I think it's going. But let me ask." Quinn walked over to the officers and Steven could hear him asking about the keys. His parents lived on the same street as Mr. James.

Steven hadn't grown up in the house his parents now lived in, and when he'd visited since moving to Chicago, he hadn't paid much attention to the neighbors other than to make sure there wasn't anyone suspicious loitering in the neighborhood. His mother had kept him updated when neighbors moved out and who moved in, but truly he had only half listened to that part of their conversations sometimes. He grimaced and felt ashamed of that fact for a brief moment.

He glanced at the poor man lying in the trunk and figured his mother probably knew him and, if he was married, his wife. Steven opened the glove compartment and pulled out the contents. Automobile guide, gas receipts, insurance card, valet key.

When Quinn returned, he shook his head. "No keys. This is just like the others. Kill the guy, dump him in the trunk, take the keys, and rob the house. And they don't care who's home. They've killed anyone who might stand in their way. Only homeowners not home at the time of the break-in, animals, and small children who can't identify them have escaped their wrath."

"How many deaths does this make?"

"Five in the last four months," Quinn said and rubbed his head. "The cases are on your desk to review. I was having them copied for you, so they didn't land there until this morning." He held up his phone. "I've got to get someone out to that address." Quinn dialed the number and ordered officers to the man's house, explaining that anyone at home could possibly be in danger. He hung up. "I pray we were fast enough this time."

"Yeah, me too." Steven thought about his parents. "I've got a phone call of my own to make. Excuse me a minute." He didn't wait for Quinn to respond, just stepped away, pulled his phone from the clip on his belt, and dialed his mother's cell number.

"Hello?"

"Mom?"

"Oh Steven, I'm glad you called. I was wondering when you'd be home."

"Might not be for a couple more hours. I'm working a case."

"Of course." Her voice held compassion. "Anyone I need to pray for?"

Steven drew in a deep breath. He should have known that would be the first thing she'd do. "Yes, you can pray, but I also need you to lock your doors and turn the alarm system on, okay?"

"What?" He started to repeat himself, but she interrupted him. "Never mind, I heard you." He heard the chirping of the alarm and then the dead bolt click into place. "Now what's going on?"

Bless her. Nothing much ruffled her, thanks to her law enforcement background. "Just stay inside."

"Does this have anything to do with the two police cruisers I just saw go past our house?"

"Yes, ma'am. Do you know Carter James?"

"Of course. He and his wife, Elaine, live a few houses down. She's part of my Thursday morning Bible study. Why are you asking?"

"I . . ."

"Steven, spill it, son. Is he hurt?"

"He's . . . well, it's possible he's dead, Mom."

Her quiet gasp reached him through the line and he closed his eyes for a brief moment.

"I'm assuming not from natural causes, since I can see the police cars at his house and I'm on the phone with you telling me to lock up. What happened?"

"We're not sure it's him yet, but a body was found in his car. He was shot through the back of the head and the bullet did serious damage to the man's face. The keys are missing, so sending the police to the house is just a precaution."

She went silent for a brief moment and he knew she was thinking. "Is this like the other deaths that have happened over the last several months?" she finally said.

He cleared his throat. "Yes. Just like them. Don't say anything to Dad unless he asks, okay?" His first instinct was to protect his mother, but when he called and warned her to keep the house locked and alarmed, he knew he'd have to be straight with her. She would find out eventually anyway, and she'd obviously seen the news detailing the rash of robberies and murders. She was a strong woman, she could handle the truth.

"I'll be praying."

"I know you will." He paused. "Love you, Mom."

"You too, son." She paused. "I'm glad you're home, hon."

"Thanks, Mom. I'm glad I'm here too."

He hung up, guilt eating at him. He needed to be a better son. Steven walked back to Quinn, who'd backed away from the body to let the medical examiner through.

"Robberies and murder," Steven said. "Could be a serial killer. Could just be someone who doesn't give a rat's behind about human life."

"That's the speculation. We're treating it as a serial killer. He has a signature."

"What's that?"

"At the homes he robs, he leaves behind a thank-you note."

"Sick son of a gun, isn't he?"

"We haven't released that bit to the media, so keep it under your hat."

"Sure. Have you brought in the FBI or SLED yet?"

"No, but I think the captain is ready to request their help." Quinn sighed. "We've been working this case day and night, pulling shifts and chasing leads. We can't find a good connection between the first four victims other than they're all rich guys who drive nice cars and live in expensive houses. There was alcohol in two of their systems, but not above the legal limit. One had cocaine in him and a history of drug abuse. If there's a connection other than being rich, we haven't come across it yet." He ran a hand through his hair. "The one thing that's got us stumped is this guy leaves a very expensive vehicle that's probably worth equal to what he steals from the houses. The only thing we can come up with is that he just doesn't have a way to hide or move the vehicle."

"Yeah. Hard to do either unless you're set up for it." Steven rubbed his chin, his mind spinning. "And all of the houses were entered?"

"Yep. It's usually a done deal by the time we find the body, but this guy hasn't been dead long. The blood is still wet." His lips thinned. "We may have caught our first break in this." His eyes roamed the area again. "This isn't a well-traveled road. He could have been out here a long time with no one finding him."

Steven pursed his lips. "Well, whatever Mr. James went looking for, he definitely found trouble."

"Amen to that."

■ ■ ■ ■

Haley didn't think Zeke would ever stop walking. She almost questioned if he was leading her on a wild-goose chase but kept her mouth shut and decided to see how this would play out. She continued to follow him until he finally turned off Two Notch Road onto School House Road. Not exactly the best part of Columbia. Someone was arrested in the area at least once a day. But it was an area she was intimately familiar with.

The teen center was just up the street. "You ever go to the Right Turn Teen Center?" She didn't remember him, but that didn't mean he didn't go. She was there mostly on the weekends, but the center was open after school too.

He shook his head. "No time for that. I go to school, work when I can pick up a job, and take care of Mom and Micah."

The kid needed some fun in his life. Something to keep him from thinking about mugging people — something to keep his mind off his worry for his little brother. "You should give it a try."

"What for?"

"Because it's fun? A way to meet new people? A way to stay out of trouble?" He shot her a dark look and she held up a hand. "I know. I was your first mugging."

"First *attempted* mugging," he muttered.

"Right. Sorry." Not. "Anyway, there are people there who you could turn to for help when you need it."

They walked in silence for another few minutes. "Any pretty girls go there?" he asked.

"A few."

"Might have to stop by then."

She gave a short huff of laughter. "Yes, you should do that." If the thought of pretty girls would get him there, then so be it. She could work with that.

He led her to an overgrown yard with a partial concrete driveway that had seen better days. The small blue house with chipping paint sat a few yards back at the top of the drive. To the side of the house, a rusty Ford pickup truck from the '80s looked old and tired. She wondered if that was the family vehicle. The rusted fence surrounding the property looked like it might fall down at any given moment, taking the well-used basketball goal with it.

Zeke went to the front door and twisted the knob. He gave a low curse, then glanced back at her. "I locked it when I left."

He stepped inside and Haley placed a

hand on her weapon, ready to pull it if necessary.

"Micah? Mom?"

"Back here, Zeke," a woman's voice called out.

Zeke strode through the small living area that contained a ratty couch, a recliner with a rip on the left arm, and a small TV straight from the 1960s. Three medical textbooks sat on the coffee table next to an old computer that had seen better days. The computer still worked, though, and a website for a nursing school was open. "Who's studying nursing? Your mom?"

Zeke stopped. "Yeah. She's trying to, anyway. It's hard for her to keep up, with Micah being so sick and all, but she's determined."

Haley followed Zeke into the hall and into the nearest bedroom. A young boy who had to be Micah lay in a bed near the window. Her heart clenched as she took in the scene. He had an oxygen tube in his nose and an IV hooked to his left arm. A heart monitor blipped off to the side.

"Mama, why was the door unlocked?" Zeke asked.

"Your father came by."

"He's not my father."

"The closest one you got."

"Better off without one then. Mama, you know Richie's only using you. A blind person could see it. When you gonna wise up?"

Haley had a feeling it was an old argument. Was the father she mentioned the one who had beaten the teen? The woman sitting next to the boy on the bed set the book she'd been reading aside and drew in a deep breath. "He takes care of me, Zeke. Takes care of us. He loves us and I need him to —" She looked up and finally noticed Haley. She blanched. "Who are you?"

"She paid for Micah's medicine." Zeke tossed the bag onto the bed. "Something Richie ain't never done, so don't try to tell me how that dude loves us."

"I'm Haley." Haley stepped a little closer. She guessed the woman to be in her midthirties with a young face and weary eyes. Haley moved her gaze to Micah. "What's wrong with him?" she asked softly.

"He needs a heart transplant," Zeke said. "He's on the waiting list."

"Been on it," Micah rasped. "I'll get one soon, though, I will." He breathed deep and closed his eyes.

Zeke blinked and Haley caught the sheen of tears in his eyes. He moved next to the bed and ruffled his younger brother's dark hair. " 'Course you will, buddy."

"Why'd you pay for it?" the woman asked.

Haley lifted a brow. "Because Zeke didn't have the money."

Zeke's mother looked at her son. "You said you did."

"I lied." He didn't sound very repentant about it.

"But then how were you going to get the medicine?"

Zeke shifted and his hard-nosed attitude dissolved. He shot a desperate look at Haley and she bit her lip on the words she'd been about to say.

At her son's silence, the woman's thin shoulders slumped, her defeat like a heavy mantle around her. She looked at Haley. "I don't have the money to repay you."

"I know," Haley said. "Don't worry about it." Micah didn't look like he had a lot of time left before he would die, and Haley's heart went out to them. She didn't agree with Zeke's actions but could understand them. Even more so now that she'd seen the little family. She looked at Zeke's mother, who resembled her oldest son. "Why isn't he in a hospital?"

" 'Cuz hospitals cost money." She shrugged. "They said he would be okay for a while here at home. There's a nurse who comes by every other day to check on him."

Haley frowned. "What's your name?"

"Belinda." Small and thin in stature, she lifted her chin and narrowed her eyes. "And I don't accept charity."

"It's not charity. Zeke's going to be doing some work for me."

Zeke blinked. "I am?"

"He is?" his mother said.

"What am I going to be doing?" Zeke finally sputtered.

"Working off your debt. You play basketball?"

"Yes."

"Then I have a job for you."

"I already got a job. Sort of. I cut grass."

"Then we'll work around your schedule, which sounds pretty flexible."

He opened his mouth to respond.

The sound of rapid gunfire and breaking glass interrupted him. Zeke dove to cover his little brother. Belinda threw herself over both of her sons, and Haley palmed her weapon even while she raced for the front door. "Call 911," she yelled over her shoulder. She hoped one of them had a phone.

The bullets hadn't come close to the bedroom where they'd all been gathered, but they'd done some serious damage in the living area. The couch was shredded.

She stepped up beside the front door and held her gun ready. Then pushed the door open and peered out into the darkness. A sedan sat on the curb under the streetlight directly across from the front door of Zeke's home. Haley noted the make and color of the car. A noise behind her sent her to her knees. She pivoted and raised the weapon.

Zeke's hands flew into the air. "Whoa, it's just me."

"Get down! You want to get shot?"

He dropped to the floor. Squealing tires on asphalt jerked her back to the vehicle. As another round of bullets pelted the house, Haley slammed the door shut with her foot and rolled up against the inside wall.

"Zeke? You okay?"

"Yes!"

"Stay down."

"Don't worry. I'm staying down."

"Did you call 911?"

"That's what I came to tell you. The phone's in the kitchen."

Haley pulled her phone from the clip on her belt and dialed 911.

[6]

Steven paused and lifted his head. He looked at Quinn, who was studying the ground underneath the trunk of the Jag. "Did you hear that?"

"No." Quinn removed his Bluetooth device from his ear. "Hear what?"

"A bunch of pops. Sounded like gunfire. That was the second time I heard it."

"From where?"

"Don't know."

"Detective?" They both turned and saw a crime scene unit member waving at them.

"I got this," Quinn said. He trotted over to the woman.

Steven's phone vibrated on his hip and he snagged it. They were almost finished with the scene. CSU had arrived and had taken over. He was ready to call it a day. A night. Whatever. He'd been at it since five this morning, and his stomach was protesting its emptiness while the rest of his body wanted his bed. He held the device to his ear. "Yeah?"

"Shots fired on School House Road," the dispatcher told him. "Officers are on the way. Is Quinn with you?"

"Yeah, why?" So he *had* heard something.

"He's not answering his phone. Tell him Haley called it in."

Steven ran over to Quinn. "Hey."

The man looked up. "Yeah?"

"You got your phone on? Someone named Haley called 911 with a shots fired report. Dispatch wanted to let you know."

His partner grabbed his phone from the clip on his belt and looked at it. He frowned and slid the button up on the side. "Forgot to turn it back on." They headed toward their black sedan. He pulled the keys from his pocket as he jogged. "Where?"

Steven gave him the address.

"That's about a minute from here. Tell dispatch we're on the way."

Steven climbed into the sedan. He hit the lights and siren as Quinn expertly wheeled the vehicle from the scene and onto the street.

"You mentioned a Haley earlier. Who's that?"

"My wife's best friend. Or one of them."

Wife? He hadn't realized Quinn was married. "She's a cop? The best friend?"

"No, she's a bodyguard, but she carries a badge, thanks to a special mandate from the mayor. She's former law enforcement but now works for the Elite Guardians agency — as does my wife."

"What's the Elite Guardians agency?"

"I'll have to explain later, but if you hang around us long enough, you'll soon learn everything there is to know about it." He pulled to the curb of the run-down home. They'd beat the uniformed officers, but Steven heard the approaching sirens. He glanced around and saw nothing to indicate the shooter was still around. Quinn pointed to a woman standing in the front yard, weapon at her side. "That's Haley."

She turned to look in his direction. Strands of red hair blew around her face. The rest she had pulled back into a messy ponytail. Even with the distance between them, no matter that he was unable to distinguish the color of her eyes, he still felt the power in her gaze. "Wow."

"Yeah, a lot of people have that reaction when they meet her."

And he hadn't even met her yet. Quinn left the lights flashing and climbed from the car. Steven did the same.

She turned her attention to Quinn. "What

took you so long?"

They'd arrived less than two minutes after her call. Steven snorted back a chuckle. He didn't figure it would make a good first impression to arrive at a drive-by and start laughing. But secretly he decided he liked her spirit.

"We were about a block over investigating a homicide. Where's the shooter?"

"Drove away about three minutes ago. I called in a BOLO."

"I'll go after him," Quinn said.

"Don't bother. He's been gone too long. You won't find him. This area is a maze. He could be anywhere by now. Let the officers on the streets do their job."

Quinn nodded to Steven. "This is my new partner. Haley, meet Steven Rothwell."

She moved closer and held out a hand. He shook it. "Welcome to the fun," she said.

Steven scanned the home front that now resembled blue Swiss cheese. "Thanks."

She eyed Quinn. "You didn't say anything about getting a new partner. Where's Bree?"

"Her sister was involved in a car accident three days ago. They're not sure she's going to make it. She'd already put in the request for a leave of absence to deal with family stuff, so when Steven applied and accepted the offer of a job here, they stuck him with me."

Haley winced and looked Steven in the eye. "Poor guy. You have my sympathy. I have the number for a good psychiatrist when you're ready." Steven smothered a chuckle and Quinn rolled his eyes. She sobered. "I'll call her later."

Steven gestured to the house. "Anyone hurt?"

"No, but it was only because none of us were in the front room at the time the bullets started flying. I stayed down mostly, but managed to get a glimpse of the vehicle. Dark sedan. Maybe a Buick. No plates. And that's about it."

"Not much to go on," Steven murmured. He looked around. "I'm guessing there won't be any security cameras in this neighborhood."

"I wouldn't think so. Not this area." She shook her head. "So many good people suffer because of the actions of a few. They're trapped in this neighborhood, longing for a better life —" she thought about the textbooks on the table in the house — "*working* for a better life, and this is what they have to put up with."

"Yeah." Steven was surprised she'd voiced the thoughts. She didn't come across to him as someone who shared easily.

Three more police cruisers pulled up, lights flashing. As the officers piled out of their vehicles, Quinn flashed his badge and started barking orders. "Canvass the neighborhood, see if anyone saw anything."

The officers fanned out and Steven saw movement at the front door. His hand went to his weapon and paused. A young man stepped out. "Haley?"

Haley turned and walked over to the teen. "Zeke. Are your mom and Micah all right?"

"Yeah, just scared." He shoved his hands into the front pockets of his jeans and eyed the police officers surrounding his home. "They going to catch who did this?"

"I can't promise they will, of course, but I *can* promise they'll do their best."

Haley pulled the teen aside and looked into his angry brown eyes.

"They could have killed my mom or Micah!" He slapped a fist into his other palm. "I find out who did this, I'm gonna pop 'em. I'm going to find a way to get them back."

"No you're not," Haley said. He stared at her, defiance rolling off of him in waves. "But I can sure understand why you'd want to. If I were in your shoes, I'd feel the same way. Angry and wanting revenge." Flashes blipped across her mind. The sound of gunfire echoed in her ears. Different gunfire than what she'd just heard. She shook her head and focused back on the teen. "But it doesn't fix anything, Zeke, okay? Don't let the hate take root."

His brow rose and he looked at her like she'd grown another head. "You sound like my grandma's preacherman."

She gave a light laugh. "I'm no preacher. I've just been there and it didn't do much for me."

Some of the anger faded from his face and surprise took its place. "Who'd you hate?"

"Someone who betrayed me and took joy in doing it."

He blinked and crossed his arms. "That's just not right."

"No, it wasn't." She cleared her throat and forced the memories away. "Now," she said. "Can you tell me who might want you dead? Someone you tried to mug? A gang member?"

He frowned. "I ain't in no gang." He looked down at his feet. Haley noticed his tone, his use of the English language changed from when she'd collared him as well as when they were in the pharmacy. "And I done told you that I ain't tried to

76

mug nobody. Ever." His eyes lifted briefly to meet hers. "Until you anyways. And I'm real sorry about that."

"Good, you should be." He ducked his head. She softened her voice. "But thanks for apologizing." He regretted his actions, but the fact that he even attempted to rob her raised all kinds of red flags for her. Intervention needed to happen now or Zeke would wind up just another statistic with a rap sheet. Right now, he was still a good kid in a bad situation. "I like your heart. It's in the right place."

He stilled and then nodded without looking at her. She turned to find Zeke's mother in the doorway. She had her arms crossed in front of her and her freckles stood out on her light brown cheeks.

Haley walked over to her. "How's Micah?"

She shuddered. "He wanted to know about the loud noise. I told him it was a couple of cars backfiring."

"He bought that?"

"No, but he's too weak to care about it much right now. He went back to sleep after I gave him his medicine and assured him that everything was all right."

Haley looked at the bullet-riddled house. "Do you have a place you can go, a friend or a relative you can stay with?"

Belinda frowned. "Why? You think they'll be back?"

"I certainly wouldn't rule it out."

The young mother shook her head. "No." She tugged on a stray strand of hair and glanced at Zeke. "I mean, I guess we could go stay with Richie —"

"No way," Zeke said. "I'll take my chance getting shot up before I'll stay with that —"

His mother shushed him. "You know I don't approve of that kind of language. I've already called him. He'll be here in a few minutes."

Zeke flushed, his anger burning in his dark eyes. Haley caught his gaze but he looked away, jaw tight, fists clenched.

His mother turned to Haley. "If we had some other place to go, we wouldn't be here."

Haley had been afraid of that. "What about a shelter?"

She held up a hand. "I'm not leaving my house."

"Even if it means protecting your kids?"

She winced. "We have too much medical equipment. I'm not like other people. I can't pick up and move without risking my child's life."

She had a point.

"Richie will make sure we're protected,"

Belinda said. "He'll find out who did this."

Zeke huffed a short laugh of disbelief.

Haley glanced at him, then back at Belinda. "Any idea why someone would want to do this to you?"

"No. I don't."

"Are you sure? Your kids could have been killed tonight."

"I know," she whispered. Tears filled her eyes and her lower lip trembled. "You think I don't know that?"

"If you know anything, tell me and I'll help you."

Belinda blinked the tears away. "But I don't know anything. I don't know why someone would do this. And why do you care anyway?"

Haley lightly touched her shoulder and looked into her eyes. "Because that's what I do."

He hid behind the large shrub and used the high-powered binoculars to watch the excitement playing out in the yard of the ugly blue house across the street. With the rental car parked out of sight behind a business closed for the evening, he had no real concern of being caught. As the scene unfolded, he growled, a low sound that threatened to rupture into a full-throated scream of rage and frustration. He'd had an assignment, a target, and he'd failed to take out that target. His employer would not be happy. But no matter. He hefted the automatic weapon. A simple reload and he'd be back in business.

[7]

Steven couldn't tear his gaze away from Haley while she offered comfort to the mother and the teen she'd called Zeke.

The mother was obviously shaken, unsure of what to do next — and he didn't blame her.

He knew she was scared the shooters might return, scared she wouldn't be able to protect her kids, scared about everything right now. He'd spent enough time talking to psychiatrists to have the checklist in his head. He stepped closer. Haley was frowning. She started to say something, but the woman held up her hand to stop the flow of words, turned, and went back inside.

Haley looked at Zeke. "Is Richie the one who beat you?" she asked softly.

Zeke's eyes held a chill that could have frozen Lake Murray over in the middle of a summertime heat wave. "Don't know what you're talking about. And if you call Social

Services and say he is, you'll sign our death warrant, you understand?"

Steven's gut clenched. Right. He could see Haley's skepticism as well.

A car engine roared behind him and he turned to see a black Mustang pull to a stop behind the cruisers. He heard Zeke curse beneath his breath. The driver got out of the car and Steven noted he was bald, at least six feet four inches tall. He wore a muscle shirt that proudly exposed his tattoo artwork. He stood next to his car for a moment, taking in the scene around him. A small smirk curved his lips and Steven raised his guard a bit higher. The police presence didn't seem to faze the large man. Good. Maybe that meant he hadn't done anything wrong.

"Richie?" Haley whispered to Zeke.

"Yeah." The teen's low voice vibrated with fear — and hate. Then again, Steven thought, maybe Richie just hadn't been caught yet.

Steven stayed near in case he was needed.

Richie took one look at the house and let out a low whistle. "What you done got yourself into, boy?"

"None of your business, Richie, so you can leave. No one wants you here anyway."

Richie's dark eyes blackened even further

and a shudder swept through the teen. "Now that's just not true," Richie said. "Getting a little big for your britches, aren't you?"

Zeke stepped back even as his eyes flashed his defiance.

Richie's feral smile faded. "I'm here to see your mama. She called me."

"She's inside."

"Guess that's where you'd better be too, then." He reached out with his large hand and caught Zeke around the upper arm. "Don't want to get in the way of the po-po here."

Zeke tried to jerk away, but Richie held firm.

Haley stepped forward. "Let him go."

Richie stopped, then met her gaze. "You got nothing to do with him. You don't get a say in how I handle my son."

"I'm not your son," Zeke spat. "Get your hand off me."

Richie simply tightened his grip and glared at the teen. "You sure are brave all of a sudden. Why's that?"

Steven stepped toward them, but Haley beat him to it. She slipped up and rested a hand on Zeke's shoulder. "Let go of him or I'll arrest you for assault and child endangerment and anything else I can think of."

Richie didn't move at first, then slowly released Zeke's arm. His eyes were cold, hard chips of ice, but his reptilian smile returned. "Of course, little lady. Just trying to make sure he's not in the way here."

"He's not."

Richie scowled, turned on his heel, and walked inside the house without a backward glance.

Zeke's breath whooshed out. "You just made yourself an enemy," he said. "He won't forget that." He lifted a hand as though to touch her shoulder, then dropped it back to his side. "I'm sorry."

"Don't worry about it, Zeke. I'm not a cop, I'm a bodyguard. I can take care of myself. He called you 'son.' Is he your biological dad or not?"

"No way. If I had that man's blood in my veins, I'd drain it." He shook his head and walked into the house.

Steven watched him go. "You think Richie will wait until we're gone to start beating on him?"

She scowled. "If he's using Zeke as a punching bag, he'll make him pay for his defiance and our intrusion. Mostly for me making Richie back down."

"I'm guessing they have no place to go?"

"Nope. I offered to take her to a shelter,

but she wouldn't hear of it — and I understand why, for the most part. But she said some gang members have been harassing Zeke about joining them. She wonders if it was some of them who decided to make a point tonight."

"Either join up or die?"

"Yes."

"So, we leave and the shooters come back and finish the job, or we leave and Richie uses his fists on Zeke."

"Either way, we can't leave." Haley's eyes narrowed and her jaw tightened. "Nobody's touching that kid if I can help it."

"We need to report it."

"We should, shouldn't we?"

"But you're not going to."

"I'm not a cop, per se. I don't have an obligation to report it."

He cut her a sideways glance. "That's debatable."

"Probably, but you know as well as I do, if Richie's arrested, he's just going to be out on the streets within a few hours. He has plenty of dirty money and probably a host of lawyers on his payroll."

"Aren't you making some snap judgments?"

"More like experienced, well-educated judgments." She shook her head. "If this were just any domestic dispute, I wouldn't hesitate, but my gut is screaming at me about this situation."

"So what are you going to do?"

"What I'm good at. My job." Haley pulled her phone out and tapped the screen. "Olivia's off today and tomorrow. I hate to bother her." She used a finger to scroll and read. "Maddy's working, Katie's just getting back in town in about an hour, Lizzie's covering for Katie, and Charlie is filling in for Olivia." She tucked the phone away. "And tonight's my night off. I'm actually the only one without a case right now. Supposed to get a new client tomorrow — only someone else is going to have to take that one." She nodded in Zeke's direction. "I just got my new client."

"Some night off."

"Yeah." She looked at the house. "Guess God had other plans."

"He has a way of doing that sometimes, doesn't he?" he murmured. He wasn't so happy with God right now but wasn't going to get into that with her. He looked at his phone. He needed to check in with his mother. He hadn't heard anything come across the wire on any activity in their neighborhood, but the night wasn't over yet.

"All right, while these guys are still here, I

86

need to get my car." She glanced over at Quinn, who was back on his phone. "I walked home with Zeke and left my car near the AMC theater on Bush River Road. Didn't realize I was going to hike for miles when I left home this evening. I'm not interested in walking back."

"You need a ride?"

Her brow lifted. "Yes."

"Come on, I'll take you. Looks like you and Quinn work together quite a bit. I need to catch up." He'd just met her and he liked her. He definitely wanted to get to know her better.

She tilted her head and studied him, then her shoulder lifted in a small shrug. "Didn't you and Quinn ride together?"

Steven knew he flushed, he was just glad the porch light was dim and she probably couldn't see it. "Yes, but he still looks busy. I can come back and get him."

"I'll ask him to keep an eye on the house until I get back. I don't trust that Richie guy not to start throwing punches."

"We really should report this."

"Not only do I not trust Richie, I don't trust that Social Services will be able to do anything about the situation without some-one getting hurt."

"It's not your call to make," he murmured.

"Then you call them. You're the cop."

He groaned and dropped his head. He was obligated, mandated by the state of South Carolina to report a domestic violence situation. The fact that Richie didn't live there didn't matter. He suspected a minor was in danger. He'd call, but he'd speak to the social worker of his choice. Just as soon as he talked to Quinn about who that choice might be. He texted him the question.

Haley walked over to his partner and placed a hand on his shoulder. Quinn turned. She said something to him and Quinn's gaze lifted to connect with Steven's. Steven kept his face blank, aiming for bored. Quinn's brow rose and his lips tilted upward. Then he looked back at Haley and nodded. Said something. She punched him in the arm, and he winced, then handed her the keys to the vehicle.

Steven couldn't stop his lips from turning up. When Haley turned to head back his way, he quickly removed the smile and crossed his arms. "Quinn's okay with the plan?"

"Of course," she said with so much sweetness he was surprised she didn't gag. "You can drive." She held the keys out to him and he took them.

"I can," he murmured. They climbed into

the department-issued Chevy Impala and Steven clicked his seat belt into place. Haley did the same and he pulled from the home. "How did you happen to be here tonight? I don't think you said."

"You could say I met Zeke in a dark alley and then I followed him home."

He pulled his gaze from the road for a split second to blink at her before turning his attention back to driving. "I'll let you explain that."

She let out a chuckle that, as far as he could tell, didn't have much humor in it. "Zeke has a little brother who's sick and needs medication. Apparently, something happened with the claim and Medicaid denied it. They'll work it out, but Micah doesn't have the time to wait on them."

Steven shook his head. "Red tape. I hate it."

"I agree with you on that one. Anyway, Zeke decided he'd mug me and steal my purse."

"I'm guessing you changed his mind?"

"I did."

Steven wished he could have seen that go down. "Did he have a weapon on him?"

"Other than an old pocketknife, nothing. He didn't want to hurt me, just wanted to get his kid brother his medicine. And besides, he said he never tried to mug anyone before. I was his first attempt."

"You believe him?"

She pursed her lips and narrowed her eyes. "I don't know why, but I do."

"How much was the medicine?"

"About three fifty."

He jerked. "Three hundred and fifty bucks?"

"Yeah."

"Unbelievable. What a ripoff. You paid for it, didn't you?"

She shrugged. "Three fifty isn't that much. Some medicine is in the thousands. I was skeptical at first, but when I walked into the pharmacy, Zeke and the pharmacist were on a first-name basis. He's in there getting medicine for his brother all the time. It was legit."

"A classic case of being stuck between a rock and a hard place. What do you do? Let someone you love die —"

"Or be driven to steal the money — something you know is wrong and wouldn't ordinarily do — in order to save that someone you love."

"Yeah."

She fell silent for the next several minutes.

"Where are you from?" he asked. "I hear the accent."

"Belfast, Ireland."

"You're a long way from home."

"I am a long way from Ireland. This country is now my home."

He had a feeling there was a story there. She didn't say much of anything else other than to give him the directions on how to find her car.

He stopped perpendicular to the vehicle she pointed to, then slid a glance in her direction. "You're kidding me."

She lifted a brow. "What?"

"A Hummer?"

One side of her mouth curved upward. "Yeah. It's nice, isn't it?"

"I think I need to get into the personal protection business."

"I didn't pay for it. It was a gift."

He grimaced. "Oh. Sorry. I made a snap judgment, didn't I?"

"Kind of." She waved a hand in dismissal. "But it's understandable. A lot of people do."

"Dare I ask who gave it to you?"

"A former client. Her name was Helen Young. She had a stalker."

"Uh-oh."

"It's not what you think. He didn't kill her. In fact, my former client is still healthy and loving life. Helen's in her late sixties and very wealthy. She'd been married to the love of her life, Ivan, for fifty years before he passed away of pancreatic cancer three years ago. She mourned the fact that they'd never been able to have any children, but finally accepted it wasn't meant to be, and she and Ivan made it their mission to use their money to help others — especially teens. A year and a half ago, she met Frank, who was a widower and in his seventies. Apparently, he could be quite the charmer, and Helen admitted she liked him a lot and may have eventually married him. But then Helen found out that Frank simply wanted her money and had even promised her fortune to *his* children and grandchildren. Of course she dropped him like a hot potato."

"And he didn't like that?"

"Actually Frank didn't seem to be terribly upset about it, but one of his sons didn't like it at all. He sent threatening letters, showed up at her house several times, and tried to bully her into marrying his father. Things like that."

Steven shook his head. "What was he thinking?"

She frowned. "That older women make easy marks. Anyway, she hired our agency, and Helen and I grew particularly close in the six months I was with her. She's lived an amazing life and I never tired of hearing her stories. One night while I was on duty, Frank's son tried to kill her. I stopped him."

"Stopped him how?"

"I . . . shot him."

"Is he dead?"

"Yes."

"I'm sorry."

"I am too. I'm sorry he chose to behave the way he did. I'm sorry he's dead. I'm not sorry I stopped him from killing Helen." She cleared her throat and looked away. Then pulled in a deep breath. "Anyway, to make a long story short, the Hummer had been her husband's baby. It was his last purchase before he took a turn for the worse. My car was an old clunker on its last legs and it finally died while I was working with her. Later, when the dust settled and all was said and done, I was at her house one afternoon and she excused herself. When she came back, she handed me the keys and said she'd be honored if I'd be the one to drive Ivan's Hummer."

"She liked you a lot."

Her eyes warmed. "Still does. We try to have a meal together at least once a month."

They fell silent. She didn't move to get out of the car. Instead, she kept her hand on the door handle.

"Have you noticed the car parked across the street?" he asked.

"The blue Toyota Camry?"

His respect for her shot up another level. "Yes."

"I noticed it. I think it's the same guy who's been following me for a while now."

"The guy in the driver's side who hasn't taken his eyes off of us since we pulled up?"

"Yep."

"Want to ask him what he wants?"

"I'd love to." She released the strap that held the weapon in her shoulder holster. "I've got your back."

"And I've got yours."

Haley exited the vehicle. It had to be the same guy who'd been following her. Didn't it? She honestly wasn't sure, as he obviously didn't feel the need to hide — or run — from her this time. Whoever had been in the car before hadn't wanted her to approach him. Which made her suspicious that he'd sit still now and let her do so.

But that was exactly what he was doing. As she and Steven got closer, the man placed both hands on the steering wheel. "Very considerate of him to keep his hands in view, isn't it?" Steven asked.

"Very. Guess he doesn't want us to shoot him."

The man had his window down and simply continued to watch them until they drew within speaking distance. "I see yer hands on your weapons," he said. "I mean you no harm. I'm not even carrying a weapon. Do you mind if I open the door an' step out?"

Haley blinked at his heavy Irish brogue. "That's fine."

He did, then leaned against the door, hands away from his sides.

"Did you need something?" Steven asked.

"I've been looking for Haley Callaghan."

Haley relaxed a fraction. "You've found her. Who are you?"

"My name is Duncan O'Brien. I'm a member of the Gardaí in the Republic of Ireland."

Her heart skipped a beat, but she simply raised a brow. "Why would a member of the Irish police be looking for me?"

"Call me Duncan, please." He glanced around. "Is there someplace else we could talk? Someplace not so open and a wee bit more private?"

Haley paused, then had to admit she was curious. "There's an all-night internet café about two blocks from here. Care for a walk?"

"Grand." He locked his vehicle and motioned for them to lead the way.

Haley hesitated and glanced at Steven. "I don't want to hold you up. You'd better get back to Quinn."

Steven frowned. "Quinn will make sure Zeke and his mom are protected, then he can catch a ride with one of the other officers." He pulled her aside and lowered his voice. "Let me stay with you until we know for sure this dude isn't up to anything he shouldn't be."

Haley didn't think he was — however, she couldn't deny it might be smart to keep Steven with her. Not that she didn't feel confident in her ability to take care of herself, but for some strange reason, she didn't want Steven to leave yet. "All right, come on then, both of you."

Once inside the café, with their coffees and pastries in front of them, Haley was impatient to get to the point. Fatigue gripped her and she wanted her bed. But curiosity held her rooted to her chair.

O'Brien sat across from her and Steven next to her. Haley took a sip of her strong black coffee and didn't care that it burned on the way down. Next, she took a bite of the cinnamon roll and sat back. She waited for O'Brien to look up. "Why have you been following me?"

"Not me. That was another man I hired to find you. I only arrived here in the States a couple of days ago."

"I see. Why?"

"Does the name Aileen Burke mean anything to you?"

A shiver raced up her spine. She stared. "I used to dream about that name." Haley leaned forward. "Why do you ask me about it? How do you know it?"

Duncan shifted. " 'Tis very hard to know how to deliver this kind of news, so I'm just goin' to spit it out."

"Aw, sure look it." Haley bit her lip. Bring an Irish accent around and she was right back into it as well, the accent and the sayings. "I mean, yes, tell me, please."

A faint smile curved his lips, as though pleased at her Irish response. Then he frowned. "When you were five years old, your home was raided in a Mafia hit. Almost your entire family was wiped out except for your grandparents and your nanny."

"Nanny Iona." The name slipped from her.

His eyes lightened. "You remember her?"

She shook her head. Where had that come from? "I don't know why I said that." She heard the thickening of her accent as some unknown emotion clogged her throat.

"Because you're Aileen Burke and — we believe now — that your Nanny Iona saved you from death somehow and disappeared with you."

Haley sat still, her coffee and pastry forgotten. Flashes — memories? — blipped across her mind. Snatches of a time and place with people she didn't know why she thought about. "Explain, please."

He nodded. "I'm with the cold case department in the Republic of Ireland, County Mayo area. I grew up wanting to be a member of the Guard so that I could work cold cases. I finally got to do that. About seven months ago, I started working on yours."

"I'm not a cold case. I grew up in Belfast."

"Right. I know that now. But originally, you were born in County Mayo, Ireland, and for the first five years of your life, were the princess of the castle Rock Moran."

"This is crazy, you realize that, right?" Haley glanced at Steven. He'd remained silent during the entire thing.

"Do you remember anything about the day the castle was attacked?" Duncan asked. "Where you were? Where your nanny was?"

Haley shook her head. "I don't." But the flashes continued. Nanny holding her tight.

No, not Nanny. She wasn't nanny, she was her mam. Mam held her. "Don't look, don't look," she whispered.

"What?"

"She told me not to look, but I did."

He leaned forward. "What did you see?"

"My dad, on the floor with a big red stain on his chest." She looked up and met the guard's eyes. "I used to have nightmares about it, but that's all it was, she told me. Just dreams. Bad dreams and I needed to forget them."

"Who told you that?"

"Me mam." The accent she'd worked so hard to get rid of spilled from her lips as naturally as if she'd never stopped using it.

"Aileen." She blinked at him and he held up a hand. "Sorry, *Haley,* your mam died that day in the attack on the castle. If you saw your dad on the floor with a bloodstain on his chest, you had to be there. Are you saying you were? That you remember?"

She rubbed a hand over her face and drew in a breath. "I don't know what I'm saying." Another flash. She was in bed and had a cold cloth on her forehead. "I was sick. I had a fever."

"I was sick that day too," he whispered.

Haley pressed a hand to her temple. "They were dreams, something I saw on television when I should have been in bed. I've long forgotten about them." She stared at him. "Why are you telling me all this?"

"Your grandfather wants you to come home."

[8]

Haley laughed, a sound that held no humor, and stared at the man. "My grandfather wants me to come home? Hmm. Well, first of all, I'm not convinced he's truly my grandfather."

"And second?"

"America has been my home for quite a few years now." She cleared her throat. "I've also got a good job that I love, good friends — and kids who depend on me. There is no more Ireland for me." She didn't have many good memories of the place. Just hardship, struggle, betrayal.

And death.

"What about family?" Duncan asked. "Don't you want to know your family? Or what's left of it. You've got a few cousins, not first cousins, but still blood relatives." He paused. "I researched you as I was searching for you, to be sure, but may have missed a few things. I didn't see that you were married. Do you have family here?"

"I'm not married. I've no family here in America. And I've no family in Ireland. Me mam died when I was fifteen." She fell back into her natural speaking voice. "I lived on the streets and managed to finish high school and then some college." She heard Steven's indrawn breath and gave an inward grimace. She didn't tell people that fact unless she had to.

"You disappeared from the time you were twenty until the age of twenty-five, when you showed up in Athens, Greece, at the bodyguard academy," Duncan said. "Where were you for those five years in between?"

She kept her gaze steady on his. "It doesn't matter."

He hesitated, then nodded. His eyes went to the windows, then to the patrons in the restaurant, then back to her. "All right, I won't push that, but will you please reconsider and come back to County Mayo? Yer grandfather is an old man and gettin' older by the minute. He wants to see you."

"I don't believe you." But she almost did.

"What can I do to convince you?"

"Nothing. It's preposterous. What is it you're really after?"

Duncan narrowed his eyes, leaned forward, and pointed at her. "You were supposed to die that day too, you know."

She pursed her lips and glanced at Steven, who'd remained silent and — stoic. Haley turned back to Duncan. "Isn't that a bit of a stretch?"

"They blew up yer bus."

The words were like a punch to her midsection. "What do you mean? What bus?"

"There was a field trip that day. Twenty-one children — all the children in our class — were killed, along with six adults. You and I and two others were the only ones who weren't there. But the attack on the castle and the attack on the bus were the same day, minutes apart. It's not a coincidence. You and yer family were targets." He rummaged through his bag and pulled out a small section of newspaper.

Haley stared at him, sickness rolling in the pit of her belly. "The zoo." She took the old, yellowed paper from him, and the headline glared back at her. BURKE FAMILY ATTACKED, ELEMENTARY SCHOOL BUS BOMBED. ARE THEY RELATED?

"The zoo," he said.

She barely had time to process the article when he pulled a picture from his breast pocket and passed it to her.

She stared at it and memories assaulted her. Memories she'd thought were dreams.

Like blips in a movie trailer, the images came to her. "The school was red, was it not?"

"It was."

"There was a playground outside the classroom."

"We had some good times there."

"We were classmates, then?"

"We were." He offered her a slight smile that disappeared fast. "Do you understand what I mean by saying you were supposed to die that day?"

"I think I'm beginning to. I mean, I believe this all happened, I do. I'm just not sure it happened to *me*. That I'm Aileen Burke." She shook her head. "I can't wrap my brain around it." Even though the memories were starting to tumble over themselves . . . like the sound of a little one crying in the middle of the night. She'd wanted to help him, so she'd crawled into the crib with him and soothed him back to sleep. Then there were the friends from the little red school, racing from one end of the playground to the other.

But how could it be? Just . . . how? She thought those memories were simply dreams. Figments of an overactive imagination.

"I know it's hard," Duncan said, "but it

doesn't change the facts."

She didn't say anything for several seconds, then narrowed her eyes. "There was a baby . . . a toddler . . ." His sweet grin and green eyes swam in her memory.

"Yer brother, John. They killed him too."

She flinched. So the little one had been her brother. If she were to believe this crazy story. But she couldn't deny the flashes of memory. Or whatever they were. "How do you know you've found the right person?"

He flushed but didn't look away from her. "I got yer DNA and had it tested." At her shock, he held up a hand. "It was simply a water bottle you threw away, I didn't break into yer house or anything."

Haley rubbed a hand over her ponytail. "It's not even believable."

Duncan reached into his bag and pulled out a small photo album. "Yer grandfather gave me this to show you." He handed it to her.

She took it and opened it. A young couple stared back at her. "Daddy," she whispered. "Mam." She looked at the baby on her mother's hip. The one she'd heard crying in the night? "John." Duncan stayed silent, so she flipped the page. And stared at a younger version of herself.

"That was taken two weeks before the attack."

She flipped a few more pages and came across an older man and woman. "Grandparents?"

"Yer grandmother died a few years ago, but like I said, yer *daideo* is anxious to see you."

"What about my . . . mam's . . . parents?"

"They died in a car accident shortly after yer parents were married."

Haley rubbed her forehead. "I can't deny the memories or the fact that the people in the pictures are familiar." She paused. "All right, say I believe that I'm Aileen Burke. I was supposed to die but didn't, obviously."

"No, you disappeared."

"Yes, you mentioned that," Haley said. "My question is, why? Why the attack on my family, why kill all those children just to get at me?"

"The motive for the attack was never discerned. At least not a motive that was clear-cut. There was speculation, but nothing ever proven. Everyone at first thought it had to do with yer grandfather's money."

"An understandable thought."

"To be sure. His will stipulated that should he die, yer great-uncle Niall and your father would inherit. At the time he made out the will, they were the two who were running the company. Should yer father die before you reached legal age, yer mother inherited along with Niall. Should both of your parents die at the same time, Niall would continue running the company, and you and your brother's share of the fortune would be held in trust until you reached legal age. Then half would revert to you and half to John when he came of age."

"Sounds to me like that gives Niall some serious motive to get rid of my family," Haley murmured.

"The Gardaí thought so, too, and did a full investigation, but came up with nothing that pointed to him. No ties to the Mafia, no large sums of money that couldn't be traced or explained. Nothing. Should the company go to you, he's still well provided for by yer grandfather. Niall appeared to be devastated at the loss and fully cooperated with the investigation."

"Doesn't mean he wasn't behind it."

"True, but nothing panned out when it came to proving anything. If he was involved, he knew how to cover his tracks."

"He's not running the company now, is he?"

"No, his son, Kane, is. Along with Lachlan, Niall's grandson, and Maeve, Lachlan's wife. They've pretty much taken it over — under the supervision of yer grandfather."

"He still has his finger in the pie?"

"He does."

"Niall retired about a year ago when he started having health problems. Now Kane, Lachlan, and Maeve are the top dogs there."

She chewed her bottom lip while she thought. "And nothing else happened after the attack on the family?"

"Well, actually, there was an attempt on yer grandfather's life shortly after the attack on the castle and the bus explosion. But after that, he surrounded himself with security and rarely left his home. Said he couldn't leave his wife a widow with no one to take care of her. When she died, he still remained pretty secluded, giving the explanation that he didn't want to give anyone a target."

"I see." She digested the news.

"I know yer daideo wants to see you, and he won't be happy with me for saying this, but — if you come back to Ireland, you could be a target again once it's known yer still alive."

"But why?"

He shrugged. "Memories can be long. If the people who perpetrated the attacks are still around, they may want to finish the job." Again his gaze flicked to the windows. "I've felt like I was being watched since arriving here, but I don't ever see anyone, so I'm not sure."

"And you approached Haley?" Steven suddenly spoke, a frown on his face.

Duncan sighed. "I did. I couldn't keep playing the cat-and-mouse game with her." He smiled. "She would have caught me eventually." His lips tightened. "But now I'm worried."

"Why?" Steven asked.

"Why would someone be watching me? Follow me all the way to the States? Like I said, it worries me." He ran a hand through his hair. "I almost didn't let you approach me. But if there's someone following me, then they know where you are anyway and I needed to give you a warning, at least."

Skepticism flowed through her, but she kept it to herself. "Who knows you're here?"

"Yer grandfather, Ian Burke, my superior who allowed me to come, and the man I hired to find you. As far as I know, that's the sum of it." He cleared his throat and turned his gaze back to hers. "So, how about it? Will you be comin' home?"

Steven listened to the conversation play out between the two. He felt like he'd been dropped into another universe — or like he should be looking for the movie cameras. And if he felt like that, he couldn't imagine what was going on inside the woman he'd just met. A woman he found intriguing and wanted to get to know better. A woman who obviously had quite a story.

One, he admitted to himself, that he very much wanted to hear. And he also had to admit he wanted to know where she'd been those five years she hadn't wanted to talk about. He frowned. It wasn't like him to be so curious about someone else. He had enough on his plate for now, with his father's illness and a desk piled high with inherited cases that needed his attention, even though it was only his third day on the job. His phone buzzed. Quinn answering his text about the social worker.

Quinn
Ask for Lydia Smith.

Thanks.

He tucked his phone back onto his clip and tuned back in to the conversation. "I can't give you an answer right this moment," Haley was saying. "How long are you here for?"

"I'm to return Monday morning," Duncan said.

"Today is Sunday. You mean Monday as in tomorrow?"

"It didn't take me as long to track you down as I'd thought it might. The man I hired sent me the information he'd gathered on you, and I was able to locate you easily. I can always change the ticket if need be."

"No need," she said. "So the man you hired is the one who's been following me?"

"He was, and he grabbed yer DNA as soon as he had the chance. Sorry about all the secrecy, but I didn't want to bother you if you weren't the right one. I had instructed my man not to have any contact with you."

"Was he driving the same car you have?"

"He was. He left the car for me at the airport. I simply picked it up when I landed."

"Well, at least it's starting to make sense to me. And I now know who was following me. That's a bit of a relief," Haley said.

"He said you tried to approach him, that he could tell you planned to confront him."

"So he ran."

"So he did." Duncan let out a low laugh. "As soon as we knew you were the one, your grandfather wanted to meet you and sent me after you."

"What were my parents' names?"

"Charles and Irene Burke."

She whispered the names under her breath. "They sound familiar. It all sounds familiar, but . . ." She spread her hands and sat back in the chair. "It's just so far-fetched I can't wrap my mind around it."

Steven could understand that.

Duncan stood. "Take a couple of days to think about it."

Haley stood as well. "I will." She turned to Steven, who also rose to his feet. "I need to get back to Zeke's place."

Steven looked at his phone. "Quinn's been texting me. They're finished at the scene, but he wanted you to know he's keeping an eye on the house and the family until we get back."

"That's good."

"But this isn't. He said Zeke came out right after Richie stormed off and was pretty shaken up. Zeke said Richie is fired up about you getting into their business and disrespecting him." His eyes snagged hers. "He said he was going to kill you, and Zeke wants you to know Richie could make it happen."

Haley frowned. "I don't like that."

"I don't either."

She sighed. "All right, I'll keep an eye on

my back. As for Zeke, ask Quinn if he has a cell phone he can leave with him. I don't want him to be without one."

"I'll get him to take care of it."

They walked toward the door while Steven sent the request to Quinn. Once outside, Steven drew in a lungful of the night air. Slightly humid, but not too bad yet. He enjoyed it while he could. During the summer months, he knew he would feel like he was drowning. Duncan walked on the sidewalk nearest the road while Haley walked beside him as they headed back toward the cars. Steven brought up the rear in case the two of them had more to say to each other. But they'd fallen quiet. Others passed them, the streets busy this time of night. His phone vibrated and he looked at it. "Quinn said he's taken care of the phone. He's having one of the officers run up to the convenience store to get one."

"Good. I'll pay him back."

She'd heard him and responded appropriately, but Steven could tell she was distracted. Duncan had his hands shoved into his pockets, yet held himself alert, rigid almost. Cars whipped by them, people on their way to wherever it was they were headed. Haley stopped abruptly, nearly causing Steven to run into her.

"All right," she said to Duncan, "I'll go."

"What?" Duncan had taken three more steps. He spun to face her.

"I'll go. If this is all true, I want to meet him."

"Just like that?" Steven asked.

"Well, sort of just like that. I can't leave until after the kids' performance. I promised I'd go with them and I meant it. I can't let anything get in the way of that. Not even something as crazy as this."

"What kids?" Duncan asked.

"I run a center for teens. They're auditioning for a national talent show and I promised to go with them this weekend. I can't back out now."

"When is the earliest you can leave then?"

She tapped her lip. "A week from Saturday."

"He'll be glad to hear it."

She stayed still and studied Duncan, her mind working. "And they never found who blew up the bus?"

"They never did, I'm sorry to say."

A light breeze ruffled her hair. She looked at Steven, then back to Duncan. "I think I remember them."

"Who?"

"The children in the picture. I remember playing with them. Once we were in Belfast,

114

I used to talk to them when I was lonely and scared, especially at night when we were sleeping under a bridge or in an abandoned warehouse. They were my playmates, my imaginary friends." Steven reached out and gripped her upper arm in a supporting gesture. She rubbed her eyes. "But you're saying they were real."

"Very real."

"Then I want to know who killed them."

Haley started to add that she intended to find out, but the sound of a roaring engine caught her attention. Senses still on alert from the previous adrenaline rush, she spun to see a black coupe coming straight for them. Hard hands on her shoulder threw her off balance and she stumbled back. Screams echoed around her and her back slammed into the storefront.

A thud echoed.

Gunshots sounded.

Pain exploded in her left side.

Her legs went weak and she collapsed onto the sidewalk. Time slowed. She registered people screaming, running, and mass chaos. Terror pulsed around her. More shots, this time from Steven, who'd moved in front of her to return fire.

Her focus narrowed, she shoved aside the

pulsing pain and stumbled to her feet. Warmth and wetness coated the area just under her rib cage. The world spun and fire licked along her nerve endings even as she reached for her weapon.

The coupe screeched away and she was having a hard time staying on her feet. Then Steven was there in front of her, his hands on her shoulders. "Call an ambulance!" Who was he talking to?

He pressed and her legs gave out. Gently, he lowered her back to the ground. Anger ignited. She'd worked hard to get up and now he was making her sit back down.

"You've been shot, Haley," he said, "so stop being stubborn and sit. I need to look at the wound."

Shot? "Is that why my side feels like it has a hot poker in it?"

"Definitely."

"Oh. Great." Yes, the feeling was familiar. She'd healed from one gunshot wound, now she had another? Lovely. She licked her lips and looked past him. "Looked like a different car."

"Huh?" He wasn't looking at her. He was too busy lifting the edge of her tattered shirt to look at her side. He gave a low whistle. "Yep, that's gotta sting."

She gave a shaky laugh. "A little bit." Then

she groaned. Weakness invaded her and she decided she wasn't mad at him anymore for making her sit. "Where's my gun? I dropped it."

"Here." He slid it over to her.

Haley wrapped her fingers around it and stayed still while, through waves of pain, she let her gaze probe the chaos. The car with the shooter was gone, the screams of the people had morphed into wails from the approaching sirens. Police cruisers squealed to a stop at the curb, and officers with their weapons drawn hovered behind their open doors, scoping the area before moving into the possible line of fire.

"Go after him!" Steven pointed in the direction the car had disappeared. "A black Buick coupe. License plate has JZ in it."

"And a five," Haley whispered.

Steven relayed the message.

"There weren't any plates on the car outside Zeke's house," she said. "At least none that I could see. I'm pretty sure it's a different car anyway."

Officers piled back into their cruisers and two peeled away in pursuit.

Haley's eyes landed on the man to her right. "Duncan!" He didn't move. She shoved Steven aside and pushed to her feet. She swayed, then caught her balance and stumbled over to the fallen officer now surrounded by helping hands. Blood covered his chest and she froze. *"Don't look. Don't look."* The words echoed in her head. And like a snapshot, a picture frozen in time, she saw her father on the ground, the red stain spreading. "Don't let him die," she whispered. "You can't let him die."

Then more hands were pulling her away and guiding her toward the waiting ambulance. "You need to get to the hospital," Steven said. "Let's go before you bleed out."

Bleed out? Surely it wasn't that bad. The sticky wetness coated her fingers. Or maybe it was? "I don't want a hospital."

"Too bad, you're getting one," Steven said.

She craned her neck to look back at Duncan. "Is he alive? He needs to go first."

"As of right now. And he'll be on the next one as soon as they stabilize him. Anyone you want me to call?"

"Olivia," she said and gave up the struggle. Steven actually lifted her off her feet and set her on the gurney. She gaped at him, the pain in her side almost fading with her shocked surprise. Almost.

"Sorry, who?"

"Never mind. Call Quinn and tell him. And tell him to keep someone on Zeke's house." The pain sent waves of nausea through her. She laid back on the gurney, the pillow cushioning her head. There were a number of ambulances in the vicinity and she knew Duncan would be next. *Please, Lord, don't let him die.* Her mind spun and she fought the desire to sink into darkness. She couldn't pass out now. Had Richie managed to act that fast? Apparently so.

The pinch in her arm told her she had an IV. She saw the young paramedic pulling medication from a bottle. "No narcotics," she gasped.

He paused. "Ma'am —"

She narrowed her eyes. "You give me narcotics and I'll . . . I'll . . . do you severe bodily damage. You understand?"

He narrowed his right back at her. "No narcotics. Got it. We'll go with Toradol. It won't make you sleepy but it'll take the edge off, okay?"

"Yes, that'd be great." She grimaced. The threat to hurt him might have been a bit harsh. Haley cleared her throat. "Sorry. I really wouldn't hurt you."

He glanced up at her from where he was adjusting the IV. "Appreciate that."

She could tell he didn't consider her a real danger. "I just can't be groggy right now."

"I understand. It's not the worst anyone has said to me. Don't worry about it."

But she *was* worried. Not about the exchange with the paramedic, but the fact that it appeared she'd made an enemy tonight. Someone had just tried to kill her. And poor Duncan. Was he the one who'd shoved her out of the path of the car? Out of the way of the bullets? She touched her side. Or at least most of them. *God, please don't let Duncan die. Not because of me, please, not because of me. I can't live with his death too.*

She let out a pain-filled breath and closed her eyes. She wondered what Richie's last name was, because she had a few words to say to him when she found him — and a pair of cuffs with his name on them.

[9]

Steven pulled into the hospital parking lot. He didn't know why he felt compelled to follow Haley's ambulance, but he did. In the few hours they'd spent together, she'd fascinated him, made him want to know her better. And now he was worried about her and wanted to know she was going to be all right.

He also remembered her saying it had been a different car. Richie's car? No, Richie had driven a two-door black Mustang, not a Buick. The same car as the first drive-by? Close, but she'd thought that one was a sedan, not a coupe.

He'd put out a BOLO on it, then called his mother on the way over and told her he wasn't sure when he'd be home.

She'd assured him she understood, that his father was sleeping, and while there were still two police cruisers within sight of the house, the neighborhood was quiet. He was relieved and promised to text her updates as to when he thought he might get home. It probably wouldn't be anytime soon. He glanced at the clock. At just a little past midnight, he thought it felt more like three in the morning. His phone rang as he walked into the hospital. He stopped just outside the revolving door and grabbed the phone from the clip on his belt. "Hello?"

"His name is Richie Derrick," Quinn said. "A lowlife with a rap sheet a mile long. Armed robbery, assault, possession of weapons, parole violations. Even arrested on a murder charge, but got off."

"Why is this guy even out of prison?"

"Money talks. He's allegedly put contracts out on gang members, but no one's been able to prove his involvement. He doesn't usually get his hands dirty unless he's got a good reason, and he's got ties to organized crime."

"Any gang affiliations?"

"Yeah."

"Which one?"

"Looks like the Gangster Disciples are trying to make a comeback. They've also got some mafia connections."

"And Haley not only made good old Richie back down, but she's sticking her nose into that family's business. That definitely doesn't sit well with him." Steven sighed. "He probably put out a contract on her as soon as he left the house."

"And maybe the kid too. He really stood up to Richie and it was obvious Richie didn't like it. We're going to have to find a way to protect him as well," Quinn said.

"Haley's already got that bee in her bonnet. So what do you want to do?"

"I can make sure there's a higher police presence in the area, but short of assigning him a bodyguard . . ."

"Right." He had a feeling Haley would want to take care of that one. She was drawn to the teen. He wondered if it was due to her own poor background. She'd said she'd grown up on the streets of Belfast. How had she managed to get to where she was in life? He looked forward to finding out the answers to those questions. "Haley was going to stay there tonight."

Quinn fell silent. "Let me see if I can find someone to cover the house tonight."

"All right. I'm headed into the hospital to see how she's doing."

"Olivia, Katie, and Maddy will probably be there shortly."

"Maddy's your wife. Olivia is another friend. Who's Katie?"

"The other member of the bodyguard

123

agency. They're partners and best friends. When one gets hurt, they all hurt." He paused. "Actually, I guess you could say *we* all hurt."

A pang of something that he thought might be envy hit him. Hard. Even though there'd been a six-year age gap between them, he'd had a closeness like that with his brother. Until he'd been snatched away from him at the age of twelve. The same age as Zeke's little brother, Micah. After his brother's death, he'd had a hard time opening his heart to love. He pushed aside the memories, wishing he could push aside the hate that went with them. "I understand. Talk to you soon."

"I'll let you know when we have Richie in custody."

"I'll be waiting." Steven hung up.

Uncertainty hit him as soon as he entered the hospital's Emergency Department. What was he doing? He didn't even know this woman. She had plenty of friends who would circle around her and make sure she was all right, that she had everything she needed. And yet . . .

He stopped at the desk and flashed his badge. "Haley Callaghan."

The woman consulted her computer, then pointed to the double doors leading to the back. "Right through there. Stop at the desk and ask for her. They'll let you know if you can see her or not." She pressed a button and he made his way to the desk she'd indicated. Again, he flashed his badge and asked for Haley.

"Relationship?" she asked.

"I was there when she was shot. I need to ask her a few questions."

"Let me check." She turned and disappeared down the hall. Within two minutes she was back. "She's awake and said you could come in. Room 314."

"Thanks." He hesitated, then turned back. "Do you know anything about a Duncan O'Brien? He was in bad shape when he was brought in."

The nurse checked the computer. "He's in surgery."

"Great. Thanks. And Haley will probably have several friends show up. Let me know when they get here and I'll try to wrap things up."

She nodded.

Steven found room 314. An officer stood next to the door. The man looked up from his phone when Steven approached. "ID please."

Steven showed it, then knocked before he opened the door. He peered around to find

Haley propped up on the gurney. Her pale face was the only outward sign that she was in pain. No one else was in the room. "Hey," he said.

Surprise brightened her features. "Hey. What are you doing here?"

"I was in the neighborhood. Thought I'd check on you."

"I'm fabulous." She shifted and her jaw tightened. "Do you know anything about Duncan? No one seems to be able to find out if he's still alive."

"I asked when I came in. He's in surgery."

She breathed a relieved sigh. "Then he's still alive."

"As of right now."

"Good."

"I guess your wound isn't life threatening."

She grimaced. "No. They checked me out and said it was just a graze." She narrowed her eyes. "Hardly about to bleed out."

"Sorry, it looked like a lot of blood at the time. I was worried."

"Right." She let it go. "They'll be back in a minute to stitch it, dress it, and give me some antibiotics. Then I'm out of here."

"Let the doc make that call."

"Right."

Steven moved closer to the bed. "Quinn's

tracking Richie down."

Haley scowled. "Hope he saves a piece of his hide for me."

"Yeah." He paused. "You think it was Richie?"

She blinked. "Who else could it be?"

"Whoever was following Duncan?"

"*If* someone was following him. I'm not convinced."

A knock on the door pulled his attention from her, and he turned to see the doctor enter, followed by a man and a woman he assumed were nurses, but he stopped them anyway. "May I see some ID?"

They both presented what appeared to be legitimate identification. Steven moved aside. He caught Haley's amused look and shrugged. She smiled.

The male nurse pushed a cart with supplies up to the side of her bed. "We're going to stitch you up."

Steven backed toward the door. "I'll just be outside."

"Thanks, Steven," Haley said. "I appreciate you being here."

Her soft gratitude flowed over him and made him glad he'd followed his instincts. He stepped out of the room and turned to see three concerned faces.

He blinked. "Let me guess. Olivia, Katie,

and Maddy?"

"Who are you?" the dark-haired, dark-eyed one asked.

"Steven?" This from the dark-haired, blue-eyed, very pretty lady on his far right.

"Yes. Are you Maddy? Quinn's wife?"

Her eyes lit with an inner glow at the mention of her husband's name. "I am."

"Quinn described you perfectly." Would any woman ever look like that at the mere mention of his name? He gave a mental snort. Not if he didn't start dating.

She let out a low laugh. "And you."

"I'm Olivia," the blonde said. She reached out to shake his hand. "And this is Katie."

Katie nodded. "How's Haley?"

"She's going to be fine. It was just a graze."

"She really needs to learn how to stay out of the path of bullets," Maddy muttered.

Steven raised a brow.

"She was shot about a year and a half ago," Katie said.

He frowned. "Wow."

Olivia gave a low chuckle. "Haley's resilient. She's been through worse."

Worse than getting shot? Twice? He really had to know more about her. In time. "I'll leave you ladies for now. It was a pleasure to meet you."

Maddy held up her phone. "Quinn said to pick him up. He's got a lead on Richie."

"Thanks." He headed out of the hospital in spite of the desire to linger at the door and listen in on the conversation that would soon be taking place in Haley's room. He grimaced. What was he thinking? That wasn't his style. But still . . .

Haley welcomed the ladies into the room. She needed information and a ride back to her car. ASAP. The nurse had finished stitching her up with orders to be careful, not tear open her side, and to take her antibiotic. Yeah, yeah. She'd been this route eighteen months ago. Thank goodness *this* wound hadn't required surgery. And right now, she wasn't hurting much. The numbing medicine was doing the job. Which meant she needed to move while she could. Once the medicine wore off, pain would be her friend for a while.

"You guys didn't have to come out here," she said. "It's getting close to one o'clock."

"Are you kidding?" Olivia asked. "If it was one of us, you'd be right where we are."

True enough. "Can you check and see if a Duncan O'Brien is out of surgery yet?"

"Sure."

Olivia left the room and Haley found

Katie and Maddy studying her. "I'm fine, I promise."

"Right." Maddy stepped forward and dropped a bag at the foot of the bed. "I didn't have time to go by your house, but I brought you some clothes from my closet. A pair of capris and a short-sleeved T-shirt. I figured they would do since we're probably around the same size."

"Thanks."

"And I prefer them returned without bullet holes if you think you can manage that."

Katie snickered. Haley scowled. Maddy slid up beside the bed and grasped her hand. "I hear you need a bodyguard. It's a good thing I've got connections."

Haley laughed, then winced as pain shot through her side. "Cute, but I don't think so."

"Well, at least watch your back until this Richie Derrick guy is in custody," Maddy said.

"That I can do. How did you hear about all this?"

Katie shrugged. "Quinn told Maddy what happened."

"And I passed the word," Maddy said.

Haley's gaze bounced between her friends. "So if you guys are here, who's got eyes on the clients?"

"Charlie and Lizzie and the two new bodyguard academy graduates I think Olivia's going to hire full time, Christina and Laila," Maddy said.

"So the all-girls club grows bigger, huh? Discounting Charlie, of course."

Maddy shook her head. "Charlie doesn't count. He's Olivia's brother. And you know business is booming and Olivia only hires the best." She glanced at her watch. "I'm going to have to get going. I've been up since this time last night. I'm getting punchy."

"Go," Haley said. "Thanks for coming."

"Thanks for getting shot on your day off. At least no one has to cover for you until tomorrow."

"Actually, I just finished a job, remember? I don't have any clients right now." Well, discounting Zeke and his little family.

"Oh right," Maddy said. "Nice. Couldn't ask for better timing if you had to get shot. Good job."

Haley gave a pained laugh. "Sure. It was the least I could do." She sobered. "Truth is, I actually do have a new client and I'm going to need your help with him."

"Who?"

She explained about Zeke and his brother and mother. "Will you try to be available if

131

I need help?"

"You have to ask?" Katie crossed her arms and frowned.

Haley grimaced and rolled her eyes. "Consider it a courtesy."

"Oh, well, thank you, but you know we're here for you and your clients."

"Perfect. I'll fill you in when I know more." She eyed them and said a silent prayer of thanks for them. "Olivia said she had another client for me, though. You think she'll be able to make other arrangements?"

Maddy nodded. "You know Olivia. She'll work with you."

Yes, she would. "You guys be careful," Haley said. "People are crazy." Olivia stepped back into the room and Haley tensed. "Duncan?"

"He made it through surgery," Olivia said. "He's still unconscious, but hanging in there."

Relief swept her. If he'd died because of her, she honestly didn't know how she'd live with that. "Thanks."

"Do you need a ride to your car?"

Haley thought about it, then shook her head. "I don't know how much longer they're going to keep me here, and I want to see Duncan before I leave. You guys go on and I'll manage."

Olivia frowned. "If you're sure."

"I'm sure. I can always call a cab."

"A cab?" Olivia lifted a brow. "I don't think so. According to Quinn, this guy could still be after you." She sat in the chair. "I'll just stay here until you're done, then give you a ride home."

"Liv, I'm fine. Get out of here and go home to your husband. All of you. Scram. There's a cop on my door. If I need a ride, he can give me one."

The three of them exchanged concerned looks, and while Haley appreciated it, she wanted to physically push them out the door. She didn't need them going without sleep and getting hurt on the job.

At least Maddy had some common sense and motioned to the door. "You'll call us if you need anything?"

"You know I will."

Finally, when they realized she wasn't backing down, they left and Haley texted Quinn.

> I'm getting out of here
> shortly. I hope. What's the
> word on Richie? Is someone
> on Zeke's house?

She waited and got no response. Antsiness

133

ate at her.

Hello?

When she still didn't hear back from him, she dialed his number. Voice mail. She hung up and dialed Steven's. Same thing. So she tried a group text between the three of them and hoped one of them would answer her soon.

She thought about Zeke. Was he all right? And what was up with Quinn and Steven? Why weren't they answering? Quinn had assured her he'd keep eyes on Zeke's house, so she wasn't *terribly* worried. But what if Richie had come back and she just hadn't heard yet?

She waited another thirty minutes, then gave a groan. That was it. Haley pulled the IV from her arm, then held a paper towel over the area until it stopped bleeding. She slipped out of bed to — very carefully — pull on the clothes Maddy had so thoughtfully brought her. The wound, the pain dulled by the Toradol and the numbing meds, still had her moving slowly, but she finally managed. She was tired from everything, but she'd had a three-hour nap before she'd awakened to head to the theater, so she wasn't exhausted. Which was a good thing, because she wasn't sure when she'd get the chance to sleep again.

Steven had stepped into his parents' home in time to help his father into the bathroom, then back to bed. They'd gotten Richie and processed him. Since he was in the system now, there was no need to call Social Services. Relief hit him as well as fatigue. It was time to crash for a few hours now that Haley was out of danger. When Steven returned to the kitchen, his mother was nursing a cup of hot tea. "You should be in bed."

"I know." She blew across the top of the steaming brew, then took a cautious sip. "I'm having a hard time sleeping these days."

He took a seat in the chair opposite her.

She reached over and covered his hand. "It was a hard night for you?"

"Yes."

"You don't want to talk about it?"

He shook his head. "I don't know, Mom. Even after all these years of being in police work, it's still heartbreaking to see what humans can do to one another — and that wasn't even the worst I've seen."

"As long as it still bothers you, you're okay. Does this have anything to do with

Carter's death?"

"They stuffed him into the trunk of his car and then shot him. At least he didn't see it coming. Whoever he is. We're pretty sure it's Carter, but waiting for tests to confirm it. His face was blown off, so . . ."

She grimaced. Not at the visual, but because she understood. Before she'd met and married his very wealthy father, she'd been a police officer. One of the few women cops in her day. She'd turned in her resignation the day she found out she was pregnant, but Steven knew she missed it occasionally. She was partly the reason he'd become a cop. His brother was the other reason. He cleared his throat and rubbed his eyes. His phone had been buzzing for the last hour and he hadn't had time to answer Haley's texts, thanks to dealing with Richie and his vociferous protests of innocence. He started to type in a response, but noticed Quinn had already done so.

"Why don't you go on to bed, son? I'm going to sit here a while longer."

Steven hesitated, then stood. "I'll see you in the morning. Try to sleep, Mom."

Tears sprang to her eyes. "I'm worried about him," she whispered.

"I know." He had to swallow twice to get

rid of the sudden lump in his throat. "I know."

"What am I going to do if he doesn't beat this? First Michael and now Hank." She shook her head. "I don't know if I'll survive it."

Steven froze for a brief moment at the mention of his brother, but then he pulled her into a hug. "When the time comes, we'll have to be strong for each other, all right? But he's not in the grave yet. He's still got some good days left and only God knows how many. Let's enjoy them with him. And we can pray for healing."

She squeezed him and sniffed. "Right. Of course. Sorry to get so maudlin."

"Not maudlin, Mom. I understand. Time will go quickly and it won't be enough. It'll never be enough." He gave her another hug. "Even if I had another hundred years with both of you, it wouldn't be long enough." He pinched the bridge of his nose, then dropped his hand to his side. "I'm sorry for wasting time and not being around like I should have been for the past several years."

She swiped the tears from her cheeks. "I understand, Steven. I'm just grateful for the knowledge of eternity in heaven."

"Yeah," he whispered, "me too."

"Oh," she said, "I meant to tell you that

your aunt is coming over tomorrow. I have some errands to run and she's going to sit with your father."

"What? I thought that's what I was here for."

"Having you here is a blessing, Steven, but you have a job and you need to work it while you can. I'll need your help soon enough." She patted his arm. "Go on, get some rest."

He smiled. "With both of us ordering each other to bed, don't you think we should take our own advice?"

Her chuckle gratified him. She set her teacup in the sink, bussed his cheek with a dry kiss, then left the room. Her bowed shoulders attested to the weight on them and he wondered if it was time to hire outside help. But while his father was weak, he wasn't bedridden. Steven glanced at the clock on the stove. Just past two in the morning. His thoughts went to Haley and he pulled his phone from his pocket to read the texts from her, wanting to know if anyone was on Zeke's home. He shot her an answering text, assuring her that all was well on that end. He scrolled to the next text from Quinn.

Maddy texted. Haley's fine and being

He wondered how she would get her car. Probably one of the ladies she worked with would take her. He rose and headed for bed, his mind refusing to let go of the attractive bodyguard. She'd just had her life turned upside down and he knew how that felt. Maybe that's why he was so drawn to her.

Or maybe it was something else.

All he knew was that she intrigued him and that probably wasn't a good thing. He closed his eyes and immediately saw her face. In his mind's eye, he pictured the different expressions he'd seen on her beautiful features in the short time he'd known her. As he drifted, her face stayed with him — and he momentarily forgot why being attracted to her wasn't smart.

He rolled to his side and punched the pillow. He'd worry about it tomorrow.

At two forty-five in the morning, downtown Columbia wasn't exactly a hotbed of activity, but there were still some folks at the all-night internet café. And the movie theater she'd planned to lose herself in a few hours ago was just letting out of the 12:30 showing.

Haley stepped carefully out of the police

139

cruiser, her hand pressed to her side as though that would keep her stitches more secure. Just before leaving the hospital, she'd gotten Quinn's text to let her know that Zeke's house was quiet, and Richie was in custody and they would question him first thing in the morning. Grabbing Richie had been the reason for his delay in responding to her. He'd also let her know that the officer on Zeke's home would be leaving at three. Other officers would drive by occasionally, but no one was available to sit on his house. "But," Quinn had told her, "odds are they won't be back tonight."

Haley wasn't so confident. She waved her thanks to the officer, Lucas Tagg, who'd been a reluctant participant in her escape from the hospital. "Appreciate it."

He frowned. "Are you sure about this? I really don't think this is a great idea. And if something happens to you, Quinn will kill me."

Haley crossed her arms. Then winced at the pull on her side. "I'll be fine. Richie's in custody, but the people who shot up Zeke's house aren't. If they come back, Zeke's going to need protection."

He scowled. "I don't like it."

She gave him a small salute. "See you later, Lucas. Thanks for the ride."

Haley shut the door on his continued protests and climbed into her Hummer. Then sat and caught her breath. She wasn't feeling quite as good as she'd pretended. All she really wanted to do was go home and slip beneath the covers of her bed.

But concern for Zeke overruled her protesting body. Within minutes, she was back at his house sitting on the curb with her window down and the engine off. All was quiet, and within thirty minutes, she was fighting to stay awake. Another half hour passed. She closed her eyes for a brief moment.

Until she heard the low hum of an approaching vehicle.

Her adrenaline spiked and her fatigue dissipated. She sat up and felt the pull of her stitches. Ignoring the pain, she squinted through the darkness. The streetlamp hampered her vision rather than enhancing it. She couldn't make out the type of car, but her pulse quickened as the vehicle slowed. Haley reached for the weapon she'd placed in the center console and held it ready to lift and shoot if she needed to.

The dark vehicle drove under the light and she breathed a little easier. The black truck wasn't the vehicle she was looking for. But it slowed and she tensed again. When it stopped in front of her, she waited. The driver turned the engine off and opened his door.

The interior light came on and she blinked. Steven? She placed her weapon back in the console and waited for him to walk over. "What are you doing here?"

"My phone woke me up."

She motioned to the passenger seat. "Hop in."

Once he was in with the door shut, he turned to her. "How are you feeling?"

"Like I've been shot." She paused. "But I guess that's better than feeling dead."

"Absolutely."

She saw his eyes rove over her. Not in an insulting way, but more like he was assuring himself that she really was still in one piece. She cleared her throat. "What's keeping you awake other than your phone?"

"What makes you think something other than my phone is keeping me awake?"

"Am I wrong?"

"No."

"So?"

He let out a low chuckle that didn't hold much humor. "A lot of things."

"Such as?"

"Such as the fact that two drive-bys in the same night is a bit much to take in."

She touched her side. "You're telling me."

"Quinn texted. They had to let Richie go."

"What? Why?" She grabbed her phone and stared at the missed text messages. And four missed calls. She checked the button on the side and slid the volume up. She'd turned it off in the hospital and forgotten to turn it back on when she'd left. "Great."

"Quinn figured you'd be here. The plate on Richie's car is different than the one we got off the car at the drive-by shooting scene."

"He switched it."

"It's possible."

"But you don't think so?"

"Not entirely. And there's no way to really connect Richie to the shooting. He drives a black Mustang, not a Buick."

"Any security video?"

"Nothing that's turned up yet."

"And if it does, it probably won't show anything that would prove he's the shooter."

"You never know." A comfortable silence fell between them. He finally decided to break it. "Something's been nagging at me."

"What's that?"

"Did you really grow up on the streets in Belfast?"

She let out a low laugh. "That's been nagging at you?"

"Yes."

"Oh, okay then." She gave a short nod. "I really did."

"So how did you get to where you are now? What pushed you?"

Haley paused, then turned in the seat a bit to look at him. The moonlight fell across his face, highlighting his features in a subtle way. He really was very attractive. "Where'd you get that scar on the edge of your chin?" She reached out to touch it and his warmth seeped into her finger and shot up her arm. Interesting. His eyes narrowed and heat rushed into her cheeks. Grateful for the darkness, she dropped her hand.

"Got it when I jumped out of the window of my treehouse trying to play Tarzan with a tree limb that was rotten."

"Ouch."

"Yep. Are you avoiding my question?"

"No, I'm just not sure how to answer it." She fell silent, then said, "I'm very observant. I watched my mother fight and scrape for every penny we had. I learned from the people on the street how to survive, but in some ways, how to live. Or not live. The street people helped me graduate from high school."

"How's that?"

"My mother died when I was fifteen. One

of my friends simply took over the role and another posed as my father when I needed a parent to show up. They signed all the papers that needed signing and banded together to make sure I had what I needed." A sad smile crossed her lips. "They were my family."

"Where are they now?"

"Some are still on the streets." Another light shrug. "They have their life, it's what they know. Some I send money to occasionally. Those people have steady jobs and a flat now, they just need a little extra every so often." She cut him a look. "Those are the two who impersonated my parents. They're actually married now and have opened a shelter for the homeless." Satisfaction gleamed in her eyes — as well as love for the people she considered family. "They're doing well and we talk every so often."

"That's amazing."

"Yes. Not every teen on the street has my story, as I'm sure you know. I had it easy compared to some. I was protected, sheltered from some of the harsher elements of the homeless life."

"Your past is why you built the center."

"Hmm. Yes, for the most part." Haley covered her mouth and yawned. "Sorry."

"You should be sleeping."

She looked toward the house. "Yes, but I can't take a chance on them coming back to finish the job. And now that I know Richie is out, I'm going to be doubly alert."

"You think they were trying to kill Zeke or just scare him?"

"If he'd been in the front room, he'd be dead. Along with anyone else."

"Yeah."

Another yawn took over and she shook her head. "Sorry. Again."

"Stop apologizing. I'm not sleepy. Catch a few z's if you want."

She chuckled. Low and without humor. "I wish I could. I'm sleepy, but my brain won't shut off."

"Thinking about Duncan?"

"Yes. And all he had to say. And about Zeke and little Micah who needs a heart and what I can do to help them."

"Sometimes you can't."

"Can't help?"

"Yeah."

"I know." She looked at the house again. "But sometimes you can."

[10]

Steven watched Haley blink as the sun rose. She rubbed a hand down her face and fastened her gaze on his. Awareness hit her and she blushed, then cleared her throat. "Okay. So . . . I guess I slept more than a few minutes?"

"You needed it."

"And you didn't?"

"I'll go home and grab a few hours, then help Quinn keep an eye on Richie. I'm curious as to what his next move will be." He paused. "I called Social Services as soon as I heard of Richie's release."

She stilled. "And?"

"I told them we had the suspected abuser under surveillance and there was no immediate danger to the family. I also told them to make sure when they came by the house, there wasn't a black Mustang out front, and if there was, as long as there was

147

no violence going on, they needed to wait until it left. I did my best to make sure they understood that if they showed up when he was at the house, things could get violent for everyone." He paused. "I also told her whoever went to the house would need to take an officer with them just to be on the safe side."

"I understand. You didn't have a choice. You're a mandatory reporter. I would have done the same thing, truthfully." She frowned. "I'm sorry you felt like you had to stay here all night."

"Wasn't all night, just a couple of hours."

"What time is it?"

"Almost 7:10. It's been quiet. A couple of cars drove past, but nothing suspicious."

The front door opened and Steven saw Zeke step out with a backpack slung over his shoulder. The teen came to an abrupt stop when he saw them. Haley waved at him and he walked toward them. Steven didn't note any bruises on the young man's face, but that didn't mean there weren't some hidden on other parts of his wiry body.

"Sweet ride," Zeke said and let out a low whistle. "I might have to major in body-guarding if this is in the budget."

"It's not unless it's a gift from a client," Haley said.

"A rich client."

"Definitely."

Zeke ran a finger along the side of the door just below the window as though he'd never touch a Hummer again. "You been sitting out here all night?" he asked.

"Yes," Haley said. "Or for the last few hours anyway. Someone else was watching until I could get back."

He frowned, his eyes going back and forth between her and Steven. "But . . . why?"

"Because I didn't want to take a chance on anyone coming back." Haley glanced at the door, then back at him. "How's Micah?"

"He's all right." Zeke shrugged. "As all right as he can be, anyway. Mom's getting ready to take him to the doctor's office, so I'm catching the bus to school."

Steven thought the boy looked tired and figured he probably hadn't slept much. He leaned forward. "Zeke, are you sure you're telling us everything you can about the shooting last night?"

Zeke huffed. "I'm telling you, man, I don't know who those dudes were. I didn't even recognize the car. It's not like anything anyone drives around here. Too fancy. Except the guys on the upper tiers of the drugs and the gangs."

Steven backed off. Zeke didn't know him

149

and had no reason to trust him. But he seemed to like Haley. Maybe he'd talk to her at some point. "Okay then," Steven said. "You need a ride to school?"

His eyes lit up and some of his fatigue faded. "A ride in this? Hoo . . . yeah!" Almost before Steven could blink, the kid was in the back seat. "Dreher High School, please," he said in a haughty — and bad — British accent.

Steven caught Haley's raised brow. "It's not but a couple of miles. You can bring me back to get my car. Do you mind?"

She narrowed her eyes. "You just want to ride in my Hummer too."

"Guilty."

She rolled her eyes, but he caught the amusement on her pretty features. "Boys," he heard her mutter. "Sure. I can do that." She started the car and pulled away from the curb. "How was Richie last night, Zeke? He throw those fists around any?"

"Aw, Richie's a punk. And no, he kept his fists to himself. He wasn't about to do anything with all the police still around."

"What about later?" Steven asked. He could see Zeke in the rearview mirror and saw the kid lift a shoulder.

"He left not too long after he got there," Zeke said.

"Want to press charges?"

Zeke met his gaze. "For what?"

He wasn't going to admit to anything. "You think Richie had anything to do with that drive-by last night?" Steven asked.

Zeke blinked. Then frowned. "No. Why would he do that?"

Steven had to admit the perplexed expression didn't appear to be feigned. "You never know with some people."

"Well, that's true, but Richie doesn't drive that kind of car. And doesn't have a reason to shoot up my house. He's not going to mess up a source of income."

"Source of income?" Haley asked.

Zeke's face went blank. "Never mind."

Haley started to say something else, then snapped her lips shut. She fought the morning traffic in silence and Steven knew she was thinking about how to respond.

"You can let me out at the convenience store across the street, okay?" Zeke said.

"I don't mind taking you to the door."

"Uh, no thanks. I don't need anyone asking a bunch of questions about who my new friends are with the sweet ride."

"Right." She pulled into the parking lot and stopped.

Zeke paused on his way out of the vehicle and turned back to Haley. "So what's this job you're wanting me to do for you? To pay off my debt."

"We'll talk about it later, but it means showing up at the Teen Center around 4:00 today. Will that work with your schedule?"

"Uh . . . yeah. Sure. Okay then. See you at 4:00." Zeke hopped out, threw them a wave, and darted toward the crosswalk at the corner.

"Hey, Zeke, wait!" Steven called.

He stopped and jogged back to the car. "Yeah?"

"Does Richie ever hit or threaten to hit Micah?"

Zeke's eyes frosted over. "Never. He wouldn't dare."

"Why not?"

"Because he knows I'd kill him — one way or another I'd kill him. See ya." And then he was gone.

Steven let out a low breath. "He's serious."

"Dead serious. We need to make sure he doesn't have a reason to act on that threat."

"Well, at least the three of them are safe for now."

"For now. I'll let the school's resource officer know to keep a close eye on him." She continued to stare after Zeke.

He raised a brow. "What are you thinking?"

"I don't like that comment about them being Richie's source of income."

"What do you think it means?"

She pursed her lips and shook her head. "I don't know."

"He could be Belinda's pimp."

"Could be, but I don't see how that's possible when she has to be with Micah pretty much 24/7."

He glanced at her.

"What?" she said.

"You're going to figure it out, aren't you?"

She shot him a tight smile. "I don't have time to do the digging, but I'll ask Maddy or Olivia to see if they can do it." She pulled out her phone and tapped the screen. When she was finished, she put her phone away. "All taken care of. Now, I've got to think about possibly getting a ticket to Ireland."

"You're still going?"

"Yes. However, I need to do some research first. I want to find out everything I can about that day — and all of my supposed family members — so I know what I'm walking into."

"I thought your grandfather was going to send his plane if you decided to go."

She grimaced. "Yeah, I'm not so sure

153

about that."

"Why not?"

"I don't know, I'm just . . ."

"Adjusting?"

"Yes."

"That's understandable." He paused. "Want some help?"

"Don't you have cases to work on?"

"Hmm . . . yeah, but those cases aren't going anywhere." He frowned. "And besides, I'm still thinking about the shooting."

"Which one?"

"Both."

8:00 AM

Haley pulled to a stop next to Steven's vehicle and tried to ignore the fresh waves of fatigue washing over her. And the pain throbbing in her side. She really shouldn't be tired, though. She'd certainly slept hard in the car for the few hours she'd gotten. She felt her face heat once more at the memory of waking up and seeing him looking down at her with that amused look in his eyes. Ugh. How embarrassing. At least he hadn't kidded her about it.

She grabbed her phone. "Let me just bring Olivia up to date on where I am." She shot a text to Olivia to do just that, but also added the request for help in lining up a schedule of protection for Zeke and his little family. Olivia texted back that she would see what she could do. Haley had complete confidence that the situation would be taken care of and she could go home and rest. She shot a look at the man next to her. A very interesting, good-looking man. "So, you think Richie will come back?"

"He was pretty steamed with your interference."

"I know, but he'd have to be crazy to come after me now. He knows we're on to him. I mean, even if he managed to kill me, he'd still get caught and wind up in prison."

Steven pursed his lips. "You know as well as I do he may not care about that."

She grimaced. "And I suppose he could always hire someone to do his dirty work for him. I'm mostly worried about Zeke and his family paying the price for me ticking off his mom's boyfriend."

"I have another theory for you."

"What's that?"

"What if that drive-by has something to do with what you learned last night?"

"What? About what Duncan told me about my supposed past?" She frowned at him. "That doesn't even make sense. I hadn't even talked to him before the first drive-by."

"And maybe that's why the first drive-by happened when it did. So you wouldn't get the chance to talk to him. After all, he said he thought someone was following him."

Haley processed that idea and shook her head slowly. Then stopped. Someone *had* been following her. But that someone had turned out to be Duncan and the man he'd hired. "Following him to get to me? I don't think it's likely."

"Well, how about this then? You got some pretty life-rocking news. News that you don't really seem to have reacted to at all. What's really going on behind those beautiful green eyes?"

Beautiful? She blinked and looked away. Then let out a shuddering breath. "I've been so distracted, I haven't really had time to think about it."

He looked out the window toward his car. "All right. So what are you going to do now?"

He turned from the window and she met his gaze. "I'm going to go home and think about it. Think about everything. Including your crazy theory that the shootings had nothing to do with a gang-involved, former-probably-still felon and something to do with my past."

"That's a good idea. And get some rest

156

while you're at it."

"Right."

"I'll follow you home."

She frowned. "I don't need you to do that. I'm fine. Quinn's got people keeping an eye on Richie, remember? I'll know if he gets anywhere near me." But his words played in her mind. Was it possible that the shooting had something to do with Duncan's news? "Duncan's just found me — or the guy he hired did. If what you think is fact — that the shooter was after me, not Zeke or his family — then this guy has just been biding his time, waiting for Duncan to be confident that he's found the right person. And tonight, he decided, was the time to act on that. In public, parked right out on the street waiting for me to come out of a busy café, with plenty of other people around."

"It does sound kind of crazy when you put it like that."

"That's because it *is* crazy. It's too big of a stretch."

"I don't know. I mean someone tried to kill you twenty-five years ago, right? That someone thought he'd been successful. If that person got word you were still alive, he might not be happy about it."

She shook her head. "I guess anything is possible."

"Just think about it."

"All right, I'll do that. But I'm skeptical."

"No kidding."

Steven got out of the Hummer and jogged to his vehicle. He drove off with a wave and Haley sat looking at the sad little blue house. The old Ford truck was gone and she figured Zeke's mother had taken Micah to the doctor. She said a quick prayer for them all and started to drive off when she caught sight of a police cruiser in her rearview mirror. She pulled to a stop and climbed out. The cruiser stayed behind her, but the officer rolled down his window. She recognized him. Brad Hudson, a twenty-year veteran of the force who loved being a cop and did his job well. She'd had the pleasure of working with him several times over the past few years. "What are you doing here?"

"Quinn asked me to keep an eye on you," he said.

She huffed and barely resisted the urge to stamp her foot. "Why does everyone think I need eyes on me?"

He held up his hands as though to defend himself. "Don't get testy with me. Take it up with Quinn."

"I'm not being testy."

"If you say so."

"I say so!"

"Fine."

"Fine," she said. She wanted to scream. Okay, so maybe she was being a bit testy. "Sorry."

"We're good."

"I'm going home."

"Awesome. I'll get to see where you live." He sounded thrilled. Not.

Out of energy and willing to admit defeat when she had to, she carefully climbed back into the Hummer, mindful not to pull her stitches, and headed toward home.

When she arrived, she parked in her garage while Brad planted himself at the top of her circular driveway. She shook her head and clipped her phone to the case on her belt as she entered her home through the door that led from the garage into the kitchen.

Once inside, she dropped her purse and her weapon on the kitchen counter and went straight to her favorite recliner. She supposed she should go upstairs, take a shower, and get in the bed, but first she wanted to check on Duncan.

While she waited for the hospital to pick up, she realized she'd never gotten her grandfather's number or any way to contact him. But she could find him. And probably with very little effort.

She focused on the person who answered. "I'd like to find out about Duncan O'Brien's condition, please."

"I'll transfer you."

The recliner felt good. Very good. The thought of climbing the stairs to her bedroom sapped the rest of her strength. She might just take a nap first.

"May I help you?"

"Yes." She repeated her request.

"I can only say that for the moment, he's stable."

"Please, can you tell me anything else? He took that bullet for me."

"I'm sorry, ma'am. I really can't. Not unless you're family."

Haley grimaced. "I'm not. Thank you." She hung up. Stable was okay. Stable was one step better than critical. He was still alive and that meant there was hope. She could cling to that for now. And as soon as she woke up, she'd work on that research she needed to do. And she might even call Steven and ask if he wanted to help her. There was just something about him . . .

He parked his car on the side of the road after following Haley and her watchdog to her house. He'd walked the perimeter of the home earlier and learned as much as he could about it before he mapped out the plan to kill her.

She'd pulled into the garage a few minutes ago and lowered the door, so he figured she was now in the house. The light in the kitchen came on, confirming his suspicion. He glanced at his watch, then back at the cruiser sitting at the top of her circular drive.

Dumb.

The guy was just sitting there. Just one cop against him? He smothered his chuckle. He might not even have to kill the guy. Which was good. He had only been paid for one death, although if he had to kill another to complete his assignment, he wouldn't hesitate.

He pulled away, drove to the street behind Haley's property, and parked on an old two-track access road not far from her pasture. A quick search on the internet brought up the listing of the home, and he scrolled through the description of the house to learn that the master bedroom was at the top of the deck's stairs. The killer checked his weapon, screwed the suppressor on the end, and made his way to the back of the house. He pulled his phone from the pocket of the lightweight black jacket he'd donned just for this job. The black cargo pants held

161

any tools he might need to gain access to the house, such as the radio frequency blocker for the home alarm system he noted. Sweat rolled off him in buckets, but for now he would have to be hot. From the bottom of the deck's steps, he studied the back of the house.

Excellent. He could enter the French doors, kill her, and leave the way he came in.

Plans made, he crept back around to the front of the house to check on the police officer. Still sitting there. He shook his head. Fine. He could sit there until someone discovered her cold, dead body. The killer made his way back to his vehicle. He'd be back when darkness fell.

[11]

Monday, 1:00 PM

Five hours of sleep was enough to revive him. Before Steven headed out the door, he checked on his father, who slept in front of the television, and kissed his mother. His aunt Sadie was on her way in. She hugged him in the middle of the driveway. "I'm so glad you're home."

"Me too." He kissed her cheek. "Dad's sleeping. Mom just finished a bowl of ice cream, but if you don't tell her you know she already had one, I'm sure she'd be willing to eat another on your behalf." His aunt, along with his mother, was an ice cream fanatic and never turned down a bowl of the sweet stuff.

"I'll be sure to keep my lips sealed. Where are you off to?"

"To check on a friend."

She squeezed his arm. "You're a good boy."

He laughed. In her eyes he probably was still a boy. "See you later."

She walked through the garage, heading for the door that would lead into the kitchen, and Steven climbed into his truck.

He marveled that he still had Haley on his mind. She'd really made an impression on him. His desire to see her puzzled him. And amused him. He didn't have any business being interested in her. Not at this point in his life when he was so unsettled about what his future held. Investigating an attraction with Haley wasn't smart.

And yet he found himself driving toward her home anyway.

His phone rang. Quinn. He hit the Bluetooth button. "What's up?"

"I've been talking to the dead guy's widow."

"Elaine."

Quinn went silent. "Yes. Elaine James. No disrespect meant."

"None taken. And he might not be the dead guy. Have they ID'd him yet?"

"Not yet. His prints weren't in the system, so they're having to go another route. His wife is providing a toothbrush and has allowed evidence techs access to his office to gather prints. Should have something soon."

"Are you there now?"

"Yeah."

Steven did a U-turn. "Hold on. I'm two minutes away."

"What are you doing out here?"

He sighed. Might as well get it out in the open. "I'm staying with my parents for the moment. And they live just down the street from Carter and Elaine James."

More silence. "Oh. Okay. See you in a few minutes." He hung up.

Steven grimaced. He wasn't ashamed of his parents, but he'd learned early to hide — or at least play down — the fact that he was from a wealthy family when it came to those he worked with. Most of the guys on the force struggled paycheck to paycheck, and they didn't always look favorably on those who were on a higher economic level.

Within the promised two minutes, he'd pulled in front of the James house. Quinn and Mrs. James were seated on the front porch in matching white wicker rockers. Steven got out of his truck and walked up to join them. After a short introduction, Steven asked, "Mrs. James, have you heard from your husband?"

"No. I was just telling Detective Holcombe here that Carter isn't answering his cell phone and he hasn't called." She wrung her hands together, then grabbed another tissue from the box near her elbow. "But when he's out of town, he calls sporadically, so I haven't been overly concerned about not hearing from him. Do you really think the man in the trunk is my Carter?" Tears filled her eyes and she blinked.

"We don't know, but I'd say you need to prepare yourself for the possibility."

She sniffed. "Thank you." She studied him. "You're Gabriella's son."

"Yes, ma'am."

"She stopped by earlier this morning. Brought me some coffee and a cinnamon roll and let me cry on her shoulder."

It didn't surprise him. "Sounds like something she'd do. Would Carter have loaned the car to anyone while he was out of town?"

"No. He didn't like to fly. He always drove. And that was the car he used, so . . . no."

"All right, then why was Carter in that part of town?"

She shook her head. "I don't know. He wasn't even supposed to be in town. He called me around noon yesterday to tell me that he was heading to the conference and would call me today. When I didn't hear from him, I figured he just got busy and would call when he could."

Quinn rubbed his chin. "I hate to tell you

166

this, but we checked with the conference. He never checked in."

She gaped. "What? And no one called to tell me this?"

"We've got officers trying to locate him." Steven scratched his chin. "What exactly was he doing out of town?"

"He was teaching at a seminar for CPAs. It's an annual two-day thing. I was supposed to go with him but wasn't feeling well, so I stayed home. And now I find out he's in town. And . . . possibly dead?" A sob slipped out on the last word and Steven rested a hand on her thin shoulder. "It doesn't make sense. None of this makes sense."

"It sure doesn't and I'm sorry." Steven waited a moment to allow her to gather herself. "Do you know what he was wearing when he left?"

"A white shirt and black slacks, I think."

Steven paused. The guy in the trunk had been wearing khakis and a blue shirt. "Does he have any specific birthmarks, tattoos, or scars?"

"Um. Yes, he has a scar on his chin from when he fell off his motorcycle. And a large scar on his right leg from the same accident. It's faint, but it's there."

"All right, we'll check into this. Do you

have anyone coming to stay with you?"

She drew in a shuddering breath. "My daughter and two sons. I've called them and they're all on their way. It will take a while for them to get here since they all live several hours away."

"Do you want me to get Mom to come sit with you?"

"No." She patted his arm. "But thank you. She has enough on her plate with your father. I'll . . . manage." She twisted the tissue clutched in her fingers. "I called the morgue and asked to see him, but the woman I talked with said he was . . . she said his face was . . . that I wouldn't be able to . . ."

Steven placed a hand over hers. Tears tracked her cheeks and she closed her eyes for a moment to gather her composure.

"I want to wait for my daughter to be with me," she finally whispered.

"Of course you do. It's okay to wait until she gets here." Steven frowned. "Someone stole his keys."

"I know. That's what the officer told me last night." She swiped the tears from her cheeks and sniffed. "I've already arranged for the locks to be changed later this afternoon."

"That was quick."

She sighed. "I don't know what else to do. Making arrangements, taking care of details, those are things that I'm good at. It helps me not think so much."

"Sure. I understand."

She paused. "Did you take any pictures? You take pictures of crime scenes, don't you?"

"Yes, of course."

"Was the man in the trunk wearing a wedding ring?"

Steven frowned. "Yes. That's how we knew he was married."

"If I could see it, I'd know if it was his or not."

Steven cleared his throat. "His hands were covered in blood. I'm not sure you'd be able to tell anything looking at the pictures."

Her lower lip quivered again and she pressed a hand to her mouth.

Steven shoved his hands into his front pockets. "What about his office? Does he keep anything there that someone might need a key for?"

Quinn stayed silent, seeming content to let Steven do the talking.

Mrs. James shook her head. "I don't know. Nothing that I can think of. I mean, he has all of his work there. Truly, I don't know what he keeps there. He's an accountant —

it's not like he was working on state secrets or anything."

Steven shot a glance at Quinn and knew his partner was thinking the same thing he was.

Was Mr. James doing some accounting on the side for someone who didn't like the numbers? That was his first thought. "All right. Thanks, Mrs. James. I'll get Mom to check on you in a while."

She patted his hand again and rose. "I need to call Selma, Carter's secretary. This is going to hit her hard."

"Let's wait until we know for sure that it's Carter," Steven said. "We should hear something soon."

She went inside and Steven saw two cars pull in the drive. There were three ladies per car and when they got out, each held a covered dish. He figured Mrs. James would be all right for now. But he'd still tell his mom to check on her. It would be hard when she was all alone again. If the man was Carter. If it wasn't, then . . . where was he?

"What's next, partner? You taking the rest of the day off?"

Quinn shrugged. "Naw. Maddy's working so I might as well do the same. Want to go see what Richie's up to?"

"Sounds good to me. Heard anything from Haley?"

"Nope. And I haven't heard anything from the cop on her house, so hopefully that means all is well." He paused and Steven caught the sideways glance Quinn shot him. He braced himself.

"So, rich boy, you want to follow me so I don't have to come back this way?" Quinn didn't disappoint.

Steven rolled his eyes. "Sure."

"Maybe we can do dinner later. You can buy."

"Shut up." He hurried to his truck before Quinn could say anything else about his parents' money. He didn't mind the man knowing, he just wasn't in the mood to be hounded about it. Then he smiled and shook his head. The fact that Quinn felt like he could needle him about it said a lot, though. He'd seen the spark of amusement in his partner's eyes and knew Quinn wasn't being snide or pushing his buttons.

He was treating him like a partner he'd known for longer than three days. And Steven had to admit, he appreciated that.

He dialed Haley's number and got her voice mail. The fact that she didn't answer didn't bother him. He knew there was an officer on her house. He hoped the fact that she didn't answer her phone was a sign that she was resting.

Haley woke with a gasp, the ache in her side intensifying with each passing moment. Nightmares had intruded, forcing her to relive the shootings. Shootings that had blended into each other, overlapping the details, morphing into something that never was. She saw Duncan taking bullets in front of Zeke's house and Steven carrying Micah while bullets riddled their bodies. Then she'd dreamed she was racing from a shower of bullets only to finally figure out she was hit. Then her legs had quit working and she'd been paralyzed, unable to run, to escape. To breathe. Shivers raced through her.

Was that why she'd awakened? Because of the pain in the dreams or the pain from her wound? Probably both. Before she'd fallen asleep, she'd texted Zeke and told him to be at the center at 4:00, even though she was unable to make it. Michelle had promised to put him to work coaching some of the younger kids in basketball.

She glanced at the clock. 9:07. Morning or night? The darkness outside her window said night. Which meant she'd dozed most of the day away. The nightmares lingered.

She tried to blink the images away and forced her thoughts to happier things. Like the fact that she had amazing friends and coworkers.

Katie and Maddy had come by around five with food. She'd eaten, then plopped herself back into the recliner two hours later, full and sleepy once more. They'd left with promises to check on her again later and she'd drifted back into a healing sleep. At least until the latest nightmare had awakened her.

Haley glanced at her cell phone. Three missed calls and four texts. One from Michelle.

Michelle
Zeke did an amazing job with the boys. Where did you find him?

Then another text thirty minutes after that, also from Michelle.

We're ready for this competition. We've got the bus lined up and our entry paid for. The kids are so excited.

She shot back an answer.

Sorry. Fell asleep. Found
him in a dark alley. I'll
explain when I see you.
Glad to hear he did well.
Looking forward to cheering
the kids on in the audition.

A restlessness stirred inside her and she pressed a hand to the wound as she stood. Ibuprofen would be a good thing. Or she could take one of the Toradol pills the doctor had sent home with her. She slid her phone back into its clip and moved gently, trying to remember where she'd tossed her purse. The kitchen counter? On the way to retrieve it, she stopped to look out the front window. A police cruiser still sat there and she could see the shadow of the officer's outline, thanks to the partial moon.

A low creak from overhead made her pause. When the sound came again, her heart picked up speed. She lived in an older farmhouse in the Blythewood area just outside Columbia. She'd fallen in love with the place the moment she'd seen it, and the fact that it was a short sale hadn't fazed her. After eight long months of patience, she'd finally signed the papers and now it was hers. Well, hers and the bank's.

And now her upstairs floors were creaking.

But that was impossible, because the only thing that would make them creak would be someone walking on them.

And no one was up there. Right?

Being shot at twice in the last twelve hours had made her a tad antsy. She had her phone still in the clip on her belt and she palmed it. She shot a quick group text to Quinn, Steven, and the girls.

> Think someone is in my house. Maybe. Could simply be paranoia. Stand by for confirmation. Might need backup. Don't answer this text.

She silenced her ringer. No sense in having the phone give her away. She moved to the counter and snagged her weapon, the pain in her side suddenly rating low on her priority list. Gun in her right hand, phone in her left, Haley made her way to the stairs.

How would someone get in? And why? Could it be Richie — or one of his minions — had tracked her down?

She stepped lightly, moving up, effectively trapped between the wall and the banister.

She paused. Maybe she should just wait downstairs and let him come to her. If there was a him.

Had she locked the door from the balcony to her bedroom? She couldn't remember. She had an alarm system and used it most of the time, but knew they weren't infallible. Even a high-grade, expensive one like hers.

Haley made her way to the top of the stairs. Her bedroom was to the left and part of the reason she'd chosen the house. She could sit out on the deck overlooking the pasture, where she kept three horses. But the deck had stairs. Someone could have come up the back way. But probably not. She was being paranoid, right? And who could blame her? The sound was . . . what?

She couldn't come up with what it could be. Other than a person who shouldn't be there.

Her heart pounded in time with the pain in her side. She moved on silent feet to the entrance of her bedroom. The door stood open and she easily spotted the figure beside her bed, thanks to the sliver of moonlight filtering through her blinds.

Haley sucked in a silent breath.

He raised a hand, pointed his weapon, complete with suppressor, and fired three quick shots into the lump that could have passed for her lying in the middle of the bed. She debated the wisdom of taking the guy down by herself. Physically, there was no way she could overpower him. She could simply shoot him. He'd just sent three bullets into her bedding, thinking it was her. She'd be completely justified in putting three in him from where she stood.

But she didn't want him dead. Shoot to wound? Not in her condition. If she didn't put him down, he could come after her and finish the job. She'd be better off staying out of sight and calling for backup. Only if she used her phone, the light might draw his attention. Then again, she'd sent the text. She had a feeling no one was going to wait for her to confirm she needed backup. Her friends were on the way. The thoughts flipped through her in a matter of seconds.

She finally settled on waiting to see what he'd do next.

Would he realize she wasn't in the bed? That her blood wasn't soaking through the sheets and heavy comforter?

Why was he just standing there?

Finally he moved.

He reached for that comforter and her heart stilled even as she lifted the weapon to shoot him when he'd realize she wasn't there. If he came her way, he was dead.

Her front doorbell rang. Haley jerked and sucked in a quiet breath while she held her gun steady.

Her would-be killer spun on his heel and slipped out of her room as quietly as he'd entered.

[12]

Steven had waved to the officer watching the house and approached the front door. He lifted a finger to punch the bell again when the door opened, revealing Haley's tight face and flashing green eyes.

He snapped to attention. "What is it?"

"Go around back," Haley said. "Someone just killed my bed and ran down the steps."

Steven pulled his weapon, hollered to the other officer, and took off around the side of her house. The fence to the pasture slowed him a bit, but he caught a glimpse of the dark-clad figure. "Police! Stop!"

The person ignored him and, instead, grabbed ahold of the mane of the nearest horse and vaulted onto his back. Steven raised his gun, but he couldn't shoot a fleeing suspect in the back, and he hadn't seen a weapon, even though Haley had indicated he had one. Steven ran after him, even thought about mimicking the guy's movements and hauling himself onto the horse not three feet away.

But he didn't ride. He pulled to a stop and watched as the figure got farther and farther away. Frustration nipped at him.

"Did you see him?" Haley's breathless question spun him around. She stood slightly bent at the waist, her hand pressed against her wounded side.

"I saw him. Where will he jump off?"

"Probably the road. The fence ends about four feet from the two-lane road straight ahead. He can jump the fence and be gone in under a minute."

Too fast for him to run to the car and drive around there. Steven pulled his phone and punched in his direct access to dispatch. When the woman answered, he gave her his location. "Got a possible suspect on horseback headed to Conrad Hills Road. He's probably got a vehicle waiting and he's armed and dangerous."

He hung up after hearing her assurances that she had units on the way. When he looked back at Haley, her pale, tense features stood out in the darkness. Her home was located far enough way from the road that no streetlights touched the area.

The officer who'd been watching the

house approached. "I didn't see him. I'm sorry."

Haley shook her head, her hand still pressed to her side. "He came in on foot through the pasture. Some periodic perimeter checks would have been appropriate, but he would have been watching for you and would have timed his attack accordingly. Or just killed you if you got in the way. Don't blame yourself. It's not your fault."

"Feels like it." He turned and trudged back the way he came.

Haley placed her fingers in her mouth and let out an ear-piercing whistle. The horse that had carried the intruder to the road came back through the trees at a gallop. The other two trotted over and nudged her. She looked at Steven. "I usually have treats when I whistle." She patted their necks, then turned to look up in the direction of her bedroom. "Should we take a look?"

"Ready when you are."

"Is she dead?"

The hired assassin shifted the phone to his other ear and watched the police cruisers pull into her driveway. "Yes. I put three bullets into her while she slept." At least he thought he had. He hadn't had time to check before the doorbell rang. "Someone

181

came to the door and I had to run, but the target has been terminated." He felt a vague dissatisfaction with himself that he hadn't pulled the blankets back before running. But he'd watched her enter the house —

And now she was walking toward the cops who'd arrived. He swore and knew he had to get going. They were already starting to canvass the neighborhood and would be questioning any potential witnesses.

"What is it?"

He'd never had this much trouble taking out a target. "She's not dead." How was it possible?

"Thought you said you put three bullets in her." His employer's frustration came through the line.

He wanted to hit something. "I thought I did. Obviously not."

"Then make sure. No one crosses me. Take care of her once and for all."

"You hired me to do a job. I'm doing it."

"Well, no, actually you're not. She's still alive."

The assassin drew in a deep breath and knew who his next target might just be. The idiot he was on the phone with had been a huge headache to work for and he was just about done with the whole assignment. "She won't be alive for long. Be prepared to

182

transfer the rest of the money."

After sending the text to Quinn and the others letting them know she was all right and they didn't need to rush to her aid, Haley studied her bed. The three bullets had ruined her covers, sheets, favorite pillow, and mattress. She crossed her arms and frowned at the feelings roiling inside her. She didn't like it when her emotions wanted to take over. She'd worked hard at remaining aloof in times of high stress, especially when she had clients who depended on her to keep a cool head.

But this . . .

Quinn, who'd ignored the second text and had bolted to her home as soon as he'd gotten the first, walked into the room, took one look, and shook his head. "Wow. You're batting a thousand in the enemy department, aren't you?"

"Apparently."

"Maddy, Katie, and Olivia were heading this way as well. I managed to convince them that I had you covered and would keep them updated."

"Thanks." She ran a hand through her hair. "So it wasn't Richie?"

"Nope. I had my eyes on him when the

183

call came in on this."

"One of his goons?"

"That's what I'm thinking. I mean, he has to know we're watching him. He probably just put the word out and told someone to get it done."

Haley nodded even as she frowned. "I don't know."

"What don't you know?"

"The guy in my bedroom was so . . . professional. He didn't come across to me as a simple gang member. Not that gang members can't be professional . . ." She paused. She wasn't making any sense. "This guy . . ." She shook her head. "This *feels* different. Like he's done this before many times."

"Like an assassin?" Steven asked.

She flashed again to the moment she'd watched him pull the trigger, heard the slap of the bullets hitting her bed. "Yes. Exactly like that."

"It's possible. Richie definitely has the resources to hire an assassin that fast," Quinn said.

Haley pursed her lips. "Can you get a look at his financials? See if any money has left his accounts in the last few hours?"

Quinn nodded. "Let me check with someone in gangs. I'll see what I can do."

She turned toward Steven. "How's Duncan? Have you gotten an update on him?"

"The docs seem to think he's going to pull through. He's not conscious yet, though."

"I want to talk to him when he wakes up."

"Why?"

"Because if it's not Richie trying to kill me, then I'm willing to concede that you could have a valid point. The attempts could be related to Duncan and my newly discovered family, and I want to know if there's more to the story."

The crime scene unit moved in sync around her bedroom. Her French doors boasted print powder, as did her bedside table, even though she didn't think he'd touched it. She flashed back to the moment he'd fired and, in her mind's eye, saw the black gloves on his hands. There wouldn't be any prints.

"How'd your intruder bypass your alarm system?" Steven asked.

She blew out a breath. "I don't think I armed it when I got home, but he probably jammed it the same way that guy did Maddy's." At his quizzical expression, she waved a hand. "Quinn's wife, Maddy, was attacked and kidnapped from her home a little over a year ago. From what we could tell, the kidnapper had disabled the alarm by jamming the radio frequency. It's so easy it's scary, as long as one has the right equipment and the know-how. Which this guy did." She nodded toward the French door. "*My* guy probably did the same thing, then simply cut a hole in the glass, flipped the lock off, and let himself right in." She shivered. She hadn't heard a thing. She'd never felt vulnerable in her house before. Sure, she knew it wasn't impenetrable, but it had always been her safe haven, her escape from life and the real world.

This guy had ruined that for her. Anger licked at her in a sudden surge, hot and fiery, and she knew if she could get her hands on him right now, she'd probably do something she'd regret later.

Or not.

She'd have to get rid of the French doors and put a —

No. She wouldn't. She liked her French doors and she was keeping them — after the crime scene officers removed the pane that had been cut. They'd check for tool marks . . .

She drew in a deep breath. Tonight was not the night for decision making.

"Is there someone who can come stay with you for the rest of the night?" Steven asked.

She shook her head. "I'm not going to be

sleeping anyway."

"You need to."

"I just woke up. Besides, I slept all day. I'm good for a while." Especially with the rush of adrenaline still pumping through her veins.

"How's the wound?"

"Painful. But not unbearable." So Richie had an alibi. That didn't mean anything. He could have sent someone to kill her. And yet . . . someone had blown up the bus she was supposed to be on twenty-five years ago and now someone had tried to kill her again. Because Duncan had found her and it was discovered that she was alive? She still thought that was a bit of a stretch. But she wouldn't discount it. "I'm guessing this was all Richie's doing and nothing more."

"Maybe."

"You don't think so?"

Before he could say anything else, an officer popped his head in the door. "Haley Callaghan?"

She looked at him. "I'm Haley."

"There's a man here who says he's your grandfather and he needs to talk to you."

She blinked. "I don't have a grandfather." At least not one in the United States.

"He says he just landed a couple of hours ago. He came from Ireland? And he's driving a sweet Rolls Royce. Well, he and another guy who looks to be almost as old as he is. The other guy was driving."

"Oh." Okay then. She ran a hand over her hair and fought to process this new development. "All right. Tell him to wait in the den. I'll be there shortly."

"We checked him out. He's clean."

"Good," Haley said even as she tried to push the shock away. "Good. Thank you."

A hand fell on her shoulder and she turned to see Steven looking at her with concern. "Are you okay?"

"I really have no idea."

[13]

Steven wondered what it would take to make her snap. He had a feeling he might not be far from finding out. The shoulder under his palm was certainly tense enough. Although he had to admit, all he had to go on was that *feeling.* So far all he'd seen was a backbone made out of steel. From what little he'd learned of her past and the way she grew up, her desire to keep Zeke and his family safe was more than just duty, it was personal. And now she had to deal with all of the emotions rolling around inside of her due to Duncan's soul-rocking news — and the arrival of a grandfather she'd known nothing about just a few hours earlier.

But he knew what it was like for work to become personal. He was well acquainted with that roller-coaster ride. "Where will you stay tonight?"

She shrugged and he dropped his hand. "I'll figure that out later," she said. "Right now, I'm going to meet my . . . uh . . . grandfather."

"All right. I'll just stay here and —"

"No," she said, a slight note of panic in her voice. She grabbed his hand. "Come with me."

He paused. "Are you sure?"

She let out a short breathy laugh. "It's silly, isn't it? He's just a man and I'm nervous." She let go of his hand and ran her palms down her jeans. "And I'm clinging to a stranger. I obviously need therapy."

He blinked. She'd take down a potential mugger and stand up to a thug gang member who was twice her size, spend the night outside a kid's house with a bullet wound in her side, but was anxious about facing a ninety-year-old man by herself. "It's not silly and I'm not a *total* stranger." He affected a wounded look and she gave him a smile. At least he thought it was supposed to be one. It looked more like a grimace. Her nervousness was actually kind of endearing. And she'd reached out to him, stranger that he was. But he didn't want to be a stranger. "Come on. You can do this."

Haley blew out a quick breath. "Right. You're right. I can do this." She paused. "But it's still silly." She walked toward the door, then stepped into the hallway. Steven

190

followed her down the stairs into the foyer. She stopped at the entrance to the den and her shoulders lifted then fell as she drew in a deep breath and let it out slowly. And that was it. She approached the two men in her den. One was seated on the end of her large L-shaped couch. The other stood by the mantel looking at the three pictures she had there.

"Hello. I'm Haley. Which one of you is my . . . um . . . grandfather?"

"I am." The gentleman on the couch stood with the help of his cane. Haley moved toward him and stopped in front of him, leaving about a foot between them. Steven sensed she might have restrained herself from reaching out and hugging the man.

For ninety years old, he looked good, his back as straight as if he had a steel rod running from the base of his spine to his neck. Steven guessed him to be about six feet two inches or so, since he towered over Haley by about six inches. Ian Burke still had a head full of hair, white as snow.

He wore a short-sleeved collared shirt, dark trousers, and black loafers. He looked casual and comfortable, and if Steven hadn't known he was as rich as Midas, he sure wouldn't have suspected it. The man's eyes hadn't moved from the woman in front of him. He lifted a hand to touch her hair and she let him wrap a curl around a finger. "Aileen," he whispered. Tears welled in his green eyes and he drew in a shuddering breath. He cleared his throat and dropped his hand back to his side. "I mean, Haley."

"I was Aileen to you," Haley said in a soft voice.

"Aileen. That you were. Are. Could I . . . hug you?"

Haley stepped forward and wrapped her arms around the man's waist.

Haley stood still, feeling this man's arms around her and wondering what had happened to her life. She had twenty-five years to catch up on. Maybe.

"I'm sorry to be intruding so late, but I couldn't wait another minute to see you."

A tremor went through him and she stepped back. He let her go, but she sensed he didn't want to. A flash of a younger Ian Burke blipped across her mind. He held her in front of him on a horse and she heard her laughter as they trotted through a green field. "You're the reason I love horses," she blurted.

Tears filled his eyes and he blinked them away. "You wanted to be on the back of a horse from the moment you knew what the animal was."

"I remember that. I think."

"To be sure you do."

Did she? Or did she just desperately want to? Uncertainty flooded her. She glanced at Steven, who stood silent in the doorway and briefly wondered why his presence calmed her. She'd have to think about that later.

Haley turned back to the man she believed was her grandfather. She hadn't had the time to do the kind of research she'd wanted to do before meeting him. But maybe that was a good thing.

"Please. Sit. I'll get you some tea."

"We can forgo the tea just now, if that's all right with ye?"

"It's all right." She focused her attention on his companion, who was still standing near her mantel. He'd stayed silent thus far. Her grandfather sat and she motioned the other man to the wingback chair. He hesitated, glanced at her grandfather, then seated himself on the edge, back ramrod straight.

Her grandfather nodded to his friend. "This is Hugh McCort. He's been in my employ in some shape or form for the past forty years. He's a faithful employee and" — he cleared his throat — "a good friend."

Hugh started, then looked down. "Thank

193

you, Ian." He spoke to the floor, but his gruff voice carried.

"Of course." Her grandfather looked back at her. "You've lost your accent."

Haley smiled. "I haven't lost it, it's just been . . . diluted, I guess. It still comes out occasionally."

A police officer poked his head in the door. "Is it all right if I go up?"

"Of course," Haley said.

Her grandfather frowned. "What's going on? All the Gardaí — I mean, police. What are they doing here?"

"Someone broke into my home tonight. They'll be leaving soon."

"Broke into your home? Are you all right?"

"Quite, thank you." She didn't want to get into it right now. "Please, tell me what you're doing here."

"I got impatient. O'Brien hadn't called and wasn't answering his phone. I have a private plane and decided to put it to good use."

"Where's your pilot?"

"Hugh has been flying since he could walk. One of the reasons I hired him long ago. Anyway, we snuck away from the castle under cover of darkness and took off." He ran a hand through his white hair and she had another glimpse of what he'd looked like as a younger man — a powerful businessman. "I haven't flown since before you disappeared. It was . . . invigorating. I feel twenty years younger already."

"Duncan said you shut yourself away for a long time," she said.

He sighed and his thin chin quivered. "I did. I fell into a deep depression. The only thing that kept me going was your grandmam and, eventually, work. And then another attempt was made on my life and I realized that if I died, they would win."

" 'They' being whoever killed the rest of the family."

"Exactly."

"So you fought back."

"The only way I knew how. By becoming a recluse and staying alive." He closed his eyes and inhaled. When he opened them, they held intense grief before he blinked it away. "Now, it sounds as if O'Brien made contact with you. Did he?"

"He did."

"Then do you know where he is? I'm quite worried about the lad."

She reached out and grasped his fingers. "He was shot last night. But he's in the hospital and expected to recover."

Her grandfather paled and Hugh gave a low gasp. "Shot?"

195

"It was an ambush as we were coming out of a restaurant last night. Duncan took the worst of it."

"Oh my, oh my, that's terrible." He rubbed a hand across his forehead.

"I know, but he should be all right."

"Who did this? Who would shoot Duncan?"

"I . . . I'm not sure." Indecision raced through her. Did she tell him that she was the target and Duncan the poor collateral damage? Yes. She wouldn't start their relationship — or whatever — with secrets. "I don't think he was the intended target. But we'll check on Duncan in a bit. Right now, I want to ask about the day the castle was attacked."

A light shudder shook him. "That was a day I'll never forget and try not to remember."

"I understand."

"Go ahead. Ask your questions."

She rubbed her palms together. "You have no idea who was behind the attacks?"

He paused, then shook his head. "I can't say that I do. Oh, I've had my theories and I've even hired investigators over the years to look into it, but I have no idea. It comes back to a particular mafia family that was prevalent twenty-five years ago. And I suppose it very well could have been them."

"But . . . ?"

"But I'm not so sure."

"Did they have a reason to target you?"

"Indeed. Back in the 1800s my father was very active in bringing the railroad to County Mayo. That's how we amassed a great deal of our family fortune. Then later, in the 1920s, he saw that the government wasn't utilizing the sea to its advantage. B&I was the great shipping company and my father wanted to throw a bit of competition their way. If you know your Irish history, you know that even after Ireland won her independence from Britain, Britain still had control of our shipping. And even though many Irish lads were employed by the British, my father wanted more. He wanted Ireland to be fully free of Britain's hold on the shipping industry."

"So he built his own shipping company."

"That he did, me dad. He was a clever fellow with a keen instinct for business."

"Looks like he passed that on to you."

"He did." Her grandfather breathed in. "But there were some who were none too happy about all of that. There was a feud between our family and the O'Reillys, another shipping company. But that went way back. And truth is, it was initially investigated, but nothing turned up."

Haley made a note to do her own investigation. She studied him. Took in every detail about him. "I want to know them."

"Who?"

"My family. I want to know who they were. Who they loved, what they hated, their favorite foods . . . everything. Do I have cousins? Aunts or uncles?"

His eyes reddened and he swiped a shaky hand over them. "You have three cousins removed but no first cousins. Your father was my only child and we were surprised to get him. Your dear grandmam and I had been married twelve years before he came along. I was closing in on forty and she was thirty-seven when he was born. I have a brother and a sister. They're quite a bit younger than I." He nodded toward Hugh. "But you were great friends with Hugh's niece, Siobhan. She was just a couple of years older than you. You were more like sisters than friends."

"She talks about you to this day," Hugh said.

Haley shook her head. "I don't remember her." Did she? Siobhan. The name triggered something deep within. Laughter, giggles, merry-go-rounds, swinging so high she could touch the sky . . . She turned back to

198

her grandfather. "What did I call you?" she whispered.

"Grand," he said. His Adam's apple bobbed. "I was *Daideo* to you and wee John."

She swallowed the lump in her own throat and realized she was coming to accept this whole crazy story. *"Daideo."* Yes, she remembered that. But still . . . "I don't mean to hurt you, but I want another DNA test as well."

He simply nodded and she realized he'd expected her to ask. For some reason the thought comforted her.

"Where are you staying?" she asked.

He shot a glance at the man who'd remained mostly silent. "What was the name of the hotel?"

"The Marriott."

"That's it."

Haley hesitated, thought about what she was about to say and whether or not she wanted to. And whether or not it would be safe, but . . . "Would you want to stay here? I have plenty of room. I . . . I mean, if you think you'd be comfortable. If you'd prefer your own space, I certainly under—"

"We'd be honored," her grandfather said softly. "We'd love to stay here, but I don't want to impose."

Haley shook her head. "Not at all. I keep the rooms ready just in case someone needs them. And each room has its own bathroom so that should help. But —" What if they shouldn't? What if Richie sent the killer back?

"But?"

"It might not be safe. No, never mind, that's probably not a good idea." She couldn't put them in danger.

"Not safe? Does that have to do with this break-in that happened tonight?"

"I think so. I seem to have made a rather dangerous man angry when I intervened in a domestic violence situation."

"Then we should definitely stay."

Haley shook her head. "You should definitely go."

"No," Steven said. "They should stay."

"What? Why?" Haley stared at him.

"Safety in numbers?"

"Tell that to Duncan."

He winced.

"No," she said, "there's a good chance Richie — or one of his goons — could try to strike again. I don't want anyone else getting hurt because someone is after me."

Her grandfather rose, steadied himself with his cane, and stepped over to her. He took her hand. "I want to stay. Please. You're

200

a bodyguard. You keep people safe, do you not?"

"Well, yes, but I'm not usually the target." Her phone buzzed and she read the text.

Zeke

I need u. Richie's here n I think he's going 2 kill us all this time. Help us.

14

Steven blinked when Haley shot to her feet. "What are you doing?"

"Going to help Zeke. Richie's there." She raced out the door after yelling for Steven and Quinn to follow her and the others to stay with her grandfather and his friend.

Steven was already on the phone requesting officers be routed to Zeke's residence. "Haley, you should stay here," Steven shouted at her. "There are still too many questions — who is the shooter? Who was in your bedroom?"

She climbed into the driver's seat and slammed the door. He opened the passenger side. "You should stay here," he repeated.

"Not a chance," she said. "And besides, Richie's at Zeke's house. He's not planning his next move on how to send me on to eternity."

"But —"

"He's terrorizing a family with a sick kid,

Steven. I hate bullying and that's all he is — a bully."

"I agree, but he's a possibly deadly one."

"That *I* made angry."

She shot him a pleading glance and he knew he might as well give in. She was going. "Then get in my car," he said. "I've got the lights."

Haley jumped out of her Hummer with a gasp of pain, but didn't let that slow her as she raced to the passenger side of his truck. Quinn was waiting on them in his own vehicle when Steven climbed in, hit the lights, and squealed away from the curb. Quinn fell in behind them. She went silent and he could almost see her brain working. He glanced back at the road. He needed to focus on his driving, not her. "What are you thinking?" he asked.

"Second-guessing myself."

"Why?"

"Duncan was watching me before everything went down with Richie."

"Yes."

"I've also thought about what you said. What if the attack really wasn't related to Richie? I just can't get the guy that broke into my house out of my head. He's done this before. He skirted the officer on duty and he came with murder as his intent. He was prepared, efficient, and deadly. If I had been in my bed, I wouldn't have known what hit me."

He glanced in the rearview mirror. Quinn was right on his tail. "Then someone else wants you dead."

"But who? Why?"

"Someone from your past? Someone who knows you're still alive and doesn't like the fact?"

"But how would they know?"

She grabbed the door handle as he took a particularly sharp turn. "Could be Duncan was right and someone followed him right to you," he said.

"Right."

He flew through the streets and cut the time in half that it would normally take to reach Zeke's house from hers. To him, it felt like it took a year. Domestic violence situations always got to him. Finally, he pulled to a stop at the edge of the drive. Other officers were there, cruiser doors open. Two officers stood talking. Steven relaxed a fraction and climbed from the vehicle, making sure his badge was visible on his belt. "What's the situation?"

The two officers turned. One a pretty blonde, the other an older man with graying hair and hard blue eyes. "Got a domestic violence call. When we got here the guy was gone and nobody's talking. It was all a misunderstanding." He rolled his eyes.

Haley stepped up beside Steven. "I'm going to check on Zeke."

She walked toward the front door and halted when it flew open. Steven turned from the officers to see Zeke's frantic face.

"He's not breathing!" Zeke shouted. "I think he's dead. Someone help him."

Haley pushed past him and raced into the house. Steven bolted after them.

Haley rounded the doorway and into Micah's room, where she found his mother crying and attempting to do CPR at the same time. She looked up at Haley's entrance. "Call 911! His heart's stopped." She continued to do compressions.

Haley pulled her phone from the clip on her belt.

"I've got it," Steven said from behind her. "Do you want to wait for the ambulance or put him in the car?"

"I've got an AED, but I've never used it before. His heart's never stopped before," Belinda said through her tears. "Grab it, please. There. On the desk. I read the instructions, but I —"

Haley found it and rushed to the bedside.

The woman already had her son's shirt open, his chest exposed. She felt for a pulse and couldn't find one.

"Do something!" Zeke cried. "He's dying!"

"You know how to work it?" Belinda gasped.

"Yes. Do you know how to do mouth-to-mouth?"

Belinda nodded.

"Breathe when I tell you to breathe. Move when I tell you to move, got it?"

"Yes, yes, just help him."

Haley grabbed the sticky pads and placed them on his chest. "Breathe."

Belinda blew a breath into her son's lungs.

"Now don't touch him." Haley then hit the analyze button. The machine ordered her to deliver a shock. "Stand clear."

Zeke and his mother moved back and she pressed the shock button.

Micah jerked and Haley placed her fingers on his pulse — or where he should have a pulse. "Breathe again, Belinda."

She did.

"Come on, come on," she heard Zeke mutter. "Please, Micah."

Haley waited. Praying to feel something. Anything. But got nothing. "Clear again." She went through the cycle once again and was ordered to give him another shock. She did. He jerked.

"Ambulance is almost here," Steven said.

Haley felt for his pulse while her own thundered in her ears. "Come on, kid," she whispered. And then she felt it. A flutter under her fingertips. Then another and another. "Got it! I got a pulse." She kept her fingers there while she checked his breathing. He wasn't. She placed her mouth over his and blew while feeling his weak pulse beating beneath her fingers.

After several seconds Micah sucked in his own breath. She strapped the oxygen mask on him and turned up the flow.

Steven placed a hand on her shoulder. "Paramedics are here."

She stumbled back, her heart racing, side hurting. She pressed a hand to it and took a deep breath.

"You saved him."

She looked up to find Zeke standing in front of her, tears tracking his dark cheeks.

"You saved him, Haley. Thank you." He wrapped his arms around her and cried into her shoulder.

Her gaze met Steven's and she thought she might have seen a sheen of tears in his dark eyes.

"It's okay, Zeke," she whispered to the

trembling teen. "It's okay."

And then the paramedics rushed Micah out the door and into the back of the ambulance. Belinda followed, her purse thrown over her shoulder, her hair wild and face tear-streaked.

Zeke pulled away from her and swiped a hand across his eyes. "I want to go too."

"We'll take you." She looked at Steven. "That okay?"

"Sure."

Steven sat across from Haley in the all-night cafeteria in the basement of the hospital. She'd eaten exactly two bites of her chicken salad and scarfed about a gallon of coffee while her eyes continued to dance from her food to the clock on the wall to him.

"Who takes care of your horses when you're working?" he asked.

"A neighbor friend has a sixteen-year-old son who's a horse nut. Nathan comes over just about every day to clean the stalls and fill the water trough. I pay him a little something even though he insists he would do it for free."

"That's nice."

"Yeah." She pushed a piece of chicken to the side.

"You need to eat more," he said.

208

She took another bite. Then swigged the coffee. "All right. I have to admit, I might not be thinking very clearly right now. The last two days have been rather intense."

"Intense?"

"For lack of a better word."

"No, it's a good word. An accurate word." She glanced at the clock on the wall again.

"Where were you those five years?" he asked. "The five years Duncan couldn't find any information on?"

She paused for a split second, then grabbed her coffee and took another sip. "Why?"

"Because I'm nosy." He leaned back and crossed his arms while he studied her. "You intrigue me. I find myself thinking about you. A lot."

A laugh slipped from her, but her cheeks reddened. "At least you're honest about it."

"So? Will you tell me? Why were you so completely off the grid that even Duncan, a man with amazing resources at his fingertips, couldn't find you?"

She stole another look at the clock.

He figured thirty seconds had passed since her last glance. "Belinda said she'd text you."

This time her eyes went to the phone sitting face up on the table. "I was working."

"Where?"

"Ireland."

He groaned. "Come on, Haley." What had made her so tight-lipped? "I saved your life."

"You did not. Duncan did."

"I'm sure he wouldn't mind if I took the credit."

She huffed a short, tired laugh. "We need to check on him."

"Fine. We can go by his room before we leave."

"Yes, let's do that."

They fell quiet. She finished her chicken salad and he figured it was a stalling tactic. But at least she was eating. When she swallowed the last bite, he raised a brow. "So?"

Another sigh followed by a sip of coffee. "It's more *who* I worked for, than *where* I worked."

He stayed silent. She'd either tell him or not.

"Quinn likes you," she said.

"We think alike. That helps us get along."

"Probably. Quinn also thinks he's right about everything. And that he has to know everything."

True. Steven had figured that out within five minutes of meeting the man.

"Another thing you two have in common."

He laughed.

She looked him in the eye. "G2," she finally said.

His eyes widened and his brows shot upward. "Whoa. Didn't see that one coming."

"So you're familiar with it?"

"Of course. Irish Intelligence. The equivalent of our CIA."

"Indeed."

"How did you get involved with G2?"

She hesitated, then shrugged. "I grew up on the streets of Belfast mostly. But when I was ten, my mam . . . or nanny . . ." She rubbed her eyes. "I'll just call her my mam. She managed to get a job at a grocery store as a cashier. Eventually, she saved up enough to put a down payment on a small flat and we moved in — along with four others that we considered our family. We looked after one another and were very tight."

"What about school?"

Haley's eyes darkened and he figured she was remembering, seeing the images of her mother in her mind. "She taught me. We spent a lot of hours in the library, not just for the books and videos, but for the bathrooms as well. I've washed my hair in many a library sink." She shook her head. "I'm not exactly sure how she did it, but she kept me on grade level until she died." Sorrow flashed in her eyes.

"I'm sorry," he said.

"I am too."

"You were fifteen?"

She nodded. "It wasn't long after that, that we lost the flat and had to move back to the street. I knew my only way to better myself was to finish school, so with a little help from the street people, I managed to get some identification, get enrolled, and finish high school."

"Where did you live? Still on the street?"

"Under a bridge mostly. It was pretty close to the school, so that's where I stayed. Sometimes I wound up sleeping in back alleys with the others, scrounging for food when I could, stealing what I needed."

His heart hurt for her. "It was a hard life."

"It was. But one of the friends who lived with us was from the Middle East. He spoke Arabic. For some reason he was determined that I learn his language and he tutored me every day. He made me speak it, write it, memorize it. Anyway, it was while I was living on the streets that I overheard a conversation about a terror plot — in Arabic — to blow up a cathedral. I walked into the nearest Gardaí house and reported it. They stopped the terrorists and I graduated high school. The day after I got my diploma, someone from G2 approached me and asked me if I'd consider working for them. They needed people who were fluent in Arabic. I said I would."

"So why did you leave?"

"For a number of reasons." She shook her head. "But mostly because my handler betrayed me."

"And that sounds like a story in itself. Will you tell me?"

She glanced at her watch and stood. "Maybe. One day. I want to check on Duncan."

They dumped their trash and he followed her to the elevator. His phone buzzed and he pulled it from the clip to look at it. "That's Quinn calling." He held the device to his ear. "Hello?"

"Richie says he wasn't anywhere near the house, didn't lay a hand on anyone, and was on his way to the hospital to support his girlfriend while she cares for her sick son."

"I hope you informed him of his new destination."

"Absolutely. He's back in custody and none too happy about it. He's made a physical threat to Zeke. Said it wouldn't surprise him if the kid met an accident due to his being clumsy and all."

"Whoa."

"Yeah."

"Keep me updated. And we'll keep an eye on Zeke. I'll also let his mother know about the threat."

Steven recounted the conversation between Quinn and Richie to Haley. Her mouth tightened and her eyes narrowed, but she said nothing. He stepped off the elevator and followed Haley to Duncan O'Brien's room. A nurse stood at the station just outside the door typing on her laptop.

"Is he awake?" Haley asked.

"He was a few minutes ago."

"Great." Haley tapped on the door, pushed it open, and stepped inside.

Steven shut it behind him.

"Duncan?" She walked over next to the bed and looked down. Steven could see the tension in her shoulders, the worry on her face. "Duncan?"

Steven moved so he could see the man. The color in his face rivaled that of the sheets he lay on. Pale, almost gray, he looked bad. But his eyes fluttered open. "Aileen?" he croaked.

She took his hand in hers. "Yes."

"Oh, Haley, I mean. Sorry." His voice sounded stronger this time.

"It's all right."

"You're okay then? You weren't hurt."

Her hand went to her side. "A bit of a scratch, but I'm fine, thanks to you."

"They know," he whispered. "Somehow they know."

"Who knows what?"

"They know I'm here and that I've found you."

She looked up at Steven and he moved so Duncan could see them both. "We believe the shooter was a man who's a part of a gang. He and Haley had a confrontation Sunday night and he wasn't real happy about it. We believe he came after her and you just got caught in the middle."

Duncan shook his head. "No. They didn't want me in contact with you." He raised shaky hands and pressed his fingers to his eyes. "I'm so sorry. I shouldn't have taken the chance and talked to you."

15

But who was "they"?

"It's okay," Haley soothed. "Don't stress yourself. You did the right thing. You needed to talk to me, to let me know that someone might now know that I'm alive and where I am — and not be happy about it."

"I don't know. I do know I need to contact your grandfather and tell him where I am."

"He knows."

Duncan stilled. "But how?"

"He showed up on my doorstep earlier. He's at my house."

"What?" He gaped at her.

"Yes, that was pretty much my reaction too, but he and his friend, Hugh McCort, flew in today on his private jet."

"Oh no, that's not good."

"Why?"

"Your grandfather has enemies. Very powerful, far-reaching enemies that he has no way of protecting himself from because he doesn't know who they are. He should have stayed in Ireland, where he had security and protection. As long as he stayed at the castle, he was relatively safe. This could end very badly for him — and you."

He shifted, his fingers worrying the sheets. Haley covered his hand with hers. "I'll make sure he's all right. He's got police protection on him as we speak."

Her words seemed to soothe him somewhat.

Haley needed to check in on Micah and Zeke, and then she needed to get with Olivia to plot a schedule for the two new clients she was determined to take on — her grandfather and the Hampton family. She patted Duncan's hand. "I'll look in on you later. Get some rest."

His eyes drifted shut. She followed Steven out of the room and they paused just outside the door.

Haley rubbed her eyes. "All right. I need to make a list."

"Of what?"

"Of my thoughts. Of all the crazy stuff going on that I can't keep track of." She groaned. "And I need to go home and make sure my g-grandfather — and Hugh — are settled in. And I probably need to stop at the grocery store." She started to pace. "I'm not prepared for guests. I mean, am I supposed to get up and cook breakfast in the morning? Or . . . or . . . what? What am I supposed to do?" She spun and waved her hands. "What. Am. I. Supposed. To. Do?"

Steven grasped her upper arms, and even in her close-to-panic state, she could tell he was careful not to jar her wounded side. "Haley. Chill. Stop. It's going to be all right."

She drew in a deep breath. "Right. Sorry. I didn't mean to dump this on you." What was she doing? She didn't have panic attacks. She was calm. Cool. Nothing bothered her or rocked her off her axis.

Except someone shooting at her twice — no, make that three times — not to mention wounding her. And the whole issue of learning that her entire past had been a lie and that someone had killed most of her family. And then there was the small matter that her mother wasn't her mother . . . She pressed her hands to her eyes and tried to still her mind.

"It's fine to dump on me. I don't mind."

"Thank you, but I do." He wasn't Olivia or Katie or Maddy. What was she doing? Another cleansing breath. "No. It's okay. A momentary little breakdown there, but I'm fine." Or would be.

"You're entitled."

"Maybe so, but now it's time to think. I need to get coverage for Zeke and his family. We need to get a picture of Richie and any of his known associates to the nurses and other staff."

And she needed to formulate a plan on how she was going to investigate her own twenty-five-year-old cold case while a continent away.

Because it was past time justice was served for those who'd been killed, and she was ready to do the serving.

Tuesday Morning

Steven hung up his phone and pushed through the glass doors of the precinct. He made his way to his desk to find Quinn already there, seated at the one opposite him. The sounds of the department echoed in the large room. Phones rang, voices blended.

Some better than others.

"I said I'd take care of it!" Quinn bellowed into the phone crammed against his ear. "Call me again and I'm going to send an inspector over there and shut you down, understand me?" He slammed his cell phone on the desk and glowered at it.

"Do I want to know?"

Quinn transferred the glare to Steven. Steven simply grinned. Quinn's laser-like stare faded into one of frustration. "Someone hacked my bank account. A check I wrote bounced and the guy wants his money. I've already straightened everything out at the bank and Maddy's going to take the money by later today, but that's the fourth time he's called in so many hours." He paused. "I only yelled that one time."

"Wow, from what I understand you've shown admirable restraint."

"Tell me about it. Restraint." He clicked his tongue. "That's my middle name today."

"You still write checks? I thought only old people did that these days."

Quinn narrowed his eyes. "Was that a crack about my age?"

Steven put on his best innocent face. "Not at all."

"Liar. And yes, I occasionally still write checks." He looked down and then back up. "You do realize we're about the same age, right?"

Steven spread his hands, palms up. "Age is just a number. It's all about how you feel — and act."

"So you're saying I act old?"

"You write checks."

"Shut up and sit down."

Steven smothered a grin, took his seat, and found three messages for return call requests.

"How's the kid?" Quinn asked.

"Micah?"

"Right. Micah. And Zeke."

"They're hanging in there. Zeke and his mother are staying at the hospital right now with Micah, so they're pretty safe. I've alerted security to be on the lookout for anyone suspicious hanging around Micah's room."

"Good." Quinn's phone rang and he grabbed it with a growl. Then the frown faded. "It's the morgue." He pressed the device to his ear. "Hello? Yeah, Francisco, what do you have?"

Quinn listened and Steven wished he could hear the conversation. Francisco, he'd learned his first day on the job, was one of the medical examiners. The one Quinn seemed to prefer to work with.

"Uh-huh. Okay, so who is he?" More listening. "All right. Well, when you figure it out, let me know, will you? Right. Thanks." He hung up.

Steven booted up his laptop. "What was that all about?"

"Our guy in the trunk? Mr. James?"

"Yeah?"

"He's not Mr. James."

Steven paused, then realized he wasn't surprised. "All right. Then who is it and where's Mr. James?"

"Two questions that have the same answer — I don't know."

Steven rubbed a hand across his eyes. "That's good news — and bad news. We need to find Carter James."

"If he hasn't turned up by now, it's not looking good for him."

"I know." So they were looking at one murder, possibly two. "Any John Does in the hospital or the morgue?"

"I'll find out." Quinn picked his phone back up.

Steven looked up to see a rookie he'd met yesterday walk past him. "Hey, Garrison."

"Yeah?"

The kid looked like he was about twelve years old. "Do you write checks?"

"Checks? What kind of checks?"

"You know. *Checks.* Those little rectangular pieces of paper you can use to pay for stuff?"

"I know what checks are." He frowned. "No. Can't think of the last time I wrote one. Why?"

Quinn looked up from his phone, his glare more ferocious than when he'd been on the

222

phone with the irate merchant. Steven burst out laughing. Garrison looked confused, then rolled his eyes and walked off.

Steven had a hard time wiping the grin off his face. Score one for the new guy. Quinn would get him back and he didn't even care. He turned back to his laptop while Quinn moved all the way across the room to make his calls.

Steven read the next email in the lineup and all sense of fun left him. Richie was still in his holding cell, but his lawyer would have him out before lunch.

Haley walked down the stairs and into her kitchen to find her grandfather seated at the table sipping a cup of coffee. His friend was nowhere to be seen. "Good morning." She aimed herself at the Keurig. She set her weapon on the counter as she fixed her drink.

"Good morning, Haley." He pressed a hand against the side of his head and winced.

She paused. "Are you all right?"

"Just a wee bit of a headache. Would you have something I could take for it?"

"Of course." She reached into the cabinet where she kept a bottle of ibuprofen and handed him two. He took them with a coffee chaser.

"Did you sleep well?" she asked.

"Oh, to be sure. The time difference might take its toll on me in a few hours and I'll need a nap, but for now, I'm content."

She paused at the word. Content. Had she ever been truly content? Maybe in the last few years since she'd been with the agency. At least more so than she could ever remember. She'd found God in Greece at the bodyguard school and had discovered a new sense of peace and acceptance. Acceptance in the sense that she could use her past to help those in the present. She studied the man at her table. "I'm really your granddaughter, aren't I?"

He sipped his coffee, then set his mug down and looked her in the eyes. "You are."

The doorbell rang and she held up a finger. "Hold that thought." She grabbed her gun from the counter and held it behind her back while she approached the door. She glanced out the window and saw a man standing on her porch with a clipboard. A large moving truck sat idling behind him.

Haley opened the door cautiously, yet curious.

"Hi, are you Haley Callaghan?"

"I am."

"I have a delivery here for you."

Tension swept through her. She relaxed her grip on the weapon. "I didn't order anything."

He consulted his clipboard. "Steven Rothwell did and said to deliver it to this address."

"Hold on one second." She shut the door, flipped the safety back on, and pulled her cell phone from the back pocket of her jeans. And saw she had one text waiting. It had come in just a few minutes ago. She opened the app and read,

Steven
Expect a delivery sometime
this morning. Happy Birthday.

Haley shook her head and opened the door to find the delivery man had opened the back of his truck. He and his helper were carrying a mattress. "Want to show us where to put this?"

"Unbelievable," she muttered, but gratitude filled her.

Another truck pulled up. Lefty's Glass Company was emblazoned in red across the side of the vehicle. A woman climbed out. She, too, carried a clipboard. "You Haley?"

"Let me guess. Steven sent you."

She looked down, then back up. "Yep."

"Ma'am? This mattress isn't getting any lighter."

"Right. This way." She looked at the glass worker. "You too."

Haley led her workers past her grand-father, who stood in the doorway of the kitchen with an amused look on his wrinkled face. They followed her to her bedroom. Within twenty minutes, she had a bed complete with new mattress, sheets, comforter, and pillows. And new glass in her French door. The evidence techs had taken her old mattress and all the bedding for examination in preparation for a court date, should the perp be apprehended.

The man who'd knocked on her door picked up a bag he'd carried into her room, but hadn't opened. He handed it to her. "He said to give this to you too."

Haley opened it to find a giant bag of M&Ms. She grinned and opened the bag to share handfuls with the workers. "Thanks, you guys."

She saw them to the door, then ran back upstairs to take one more look, trying to convince herself of what had just happened. She stood in the doorway. Her bedroom looked good as new. And while the bedding was different from the ones that had bullets in it, it suited her taste and she loved it.

Simple cream with a splash of blue. For some reason, she thought she might cry. She texted Steven.

> Thank you. It's not my birthday. Why?

You're welcome. Just because.

She drew in a deep breath and went back downstairs to find her grandfather still standing in the doorway. "That was thoughtful of the young man."

"It was. Very." She studied him and ate another handful of the chocolate. "I don't need another DNA test, do I?"

He lifted a thin shoulder in a shrug. "It would be just for your peace of mind. I don't need it. I paid to have it done and it came back a match off of Aileen's hairbrush. I'd had all of her things sealed in airtight containers. The DNA on her brush was still usable."

Haley shifted, thinking and trying to come to grips with the whole situation. She followed him back to the kitchen table and slid into the chair opposite him. She pushed the bag of M&Ms toward him and he helped himself. "Tell me about the relatives I have who are still living," she said.

"First, there's Bridgett. She's a widow and lives a very active life doing charity work. Niall, me brother, is a good bit younger than I. He was born when I was eighteen years old, so I guess that makes him a mere baby at seventy-two now. Unfortunately, he's been very sick and I understand that he might be moved to hospice soon."

"What? Oh no! Don't you need to be with him?"

"I'm where I need to be and he knows it. So no worrying from you. Anyway, he married Darcy and they had two boys, Kane and Peter. They're both pushing late forties and are also married. Kane and Janet have one son, Lachlan, who is married to Maeve. They don't have any children. Peter and his wife also don't have any children."

Haley blinked. "So they're cousins of some sort."

"Indeed. Your father grew up knowing he would take over the business one day. He was excited about it, loved the thrill of it. When he was killed, I couldn't function for a long time, as you might imagine. Niall came to the rescue."

"I'm so sorry," she murmured.

"Niall saved the company. And when I was ready to come back, he moved over and let me do so without a word. He retired a year ago when he started having some health problems and requested I make Lachlan CEO of Burke's Shipping. He's worked hard for the position and I didn't argue. It was a good move." He paused. "But now that I know you're alive, I want you to take your rightful place in the company. Have your inheritance."

Haley caught her breath, her senses spinning. "What? No . . . I . . . I . . . no."

"But sure."

"I can't do that."

He let out a low laugh. "Of course you can."

"I'm not interested in being a part of a company."

"I'm not saying you have to work there. I'm saying you will get half the profits." A smile curved his lips and she had a brief glimpse of the handsome man he would have been in his younger years. "And it's a very profitable business."

"I don't want half the profits."

"Doesn't matter. I've already changed the will."

She froze. "And who knows about this change in the will?"

"My lawyer, of course, and myself."

"That's it? You're sure?"

He scratched his chin. "Well, I believe so.

I haven't gone about discussing the matter. Why?"

"Because if the last couple of days are any indication, it's possible someone is very unhappy with your change."

[16]

Steven read the medical examiner's report that had been emailed to both him and Quinn. He glanced at his partner, who was engrossed in whatever he was reading on his computer. "So the guy in the trunk isn't in the system either."

"No."

"Okay, and no John Does at the hospital matching Carter James's description."

"Right."

"Maybe he's in an out-of-town hospital."

Quinn grimaced. "Or a shallow grave no one's discovered yet." He shoved aside a stack of papers and reached for a pen. "I've got feelers out. Now what are we going to do about Richie? His lawyers are working to get him released as we speak."

Steven's phone buzzed and he glanced at the message.

Haley
Going to see Micah at the hospital around 12:00. Do you
want to go?

He did.

Steven leaned forward. "What kind of il-
legal stuff is he involved in? Surely there's
something else we could nail him on."

"Drugs, guns, prostitution, you name it.
The only problem is, he's a little farther up
the food chain than the ones we bust on a
regular basis. I did a little more digging and
I've got to give the man props for covering
his tracks."

"And his minions are too intimidated —"

Quinn snorted. "You mean terrified?"

"Yeah, too terrified to talk to us." Steven
nodded. "All right. What about his fi-
nances?"

"If I had a reason to check them, I'd get a
warrant. But . . ."

Steven rubbed his chin. "You know, Zeke
said Richie wouldn't hurt his mother because he wouldn't mess up a source of
income."

"What'd he mean by that?"

He gestured to the computer. "The only
source of money I can find for her is government assistance. But it's a lot of assistance.

Like thousands of dollars."

"She's cheating the system and getting more than she should?"

"Yes. Or the money is right, due to Micah's health issues. But it's enough that it would attract Richie's attention."

"Or he's her pimp."

"I thought about that, but there's no record of her being arrested. She's clean, although that could just mean she hasn't been caught yet. A Google search brought up a funeral notice for her mother last year and no mention of a father."

Quinn lifted a brow. "So if he's not her pimp, you think he's taking her checks — or cards or whatever she gets?"

"With Micah being sick, she'd get disability money direct deposited into an account. So, if he's taking it, it wouldn't surprise me. It's several thousand a month. He'd consider it worth his while to take. Although the pimping wouldn't surprise me either — and I'm not saying it's not possible — but she couldn't leave Micah alone all day or all night long. She can't leave him at all, really."

"Unless Zeke is staying with him while she works the streets."

"Maybe, but I don't think so. We sat outside her house all night and she never left it. Didn't have any visitors either. I'm leaning toward the checks."

Quinn lifted a shoulder in a light shrug. "Guess we can ask her."

"Or Zeke."

"If Richie's somehow set this all up, Belinda's not going to say anything. Zeke, on the other hand, might."

"Or we just catch him. But in order to do that, we'd have to follow him, get him on camera either cashing a check she wrote to him or simply using her card at the ATM. Do we have the manpower?"

"Never hurts to ask," Steven murmured as he ran his fingers over the letters in his text back to Haley. "But proving he's coercing her into giving him the money is another issue altogether."

"True." Quinn slammed a hand against his desk and Steven jerked mid-answer. "What?"

"Richie's out."

"Already?"

"I told you they were working on it." He sighed. "You let Haley know Richie's back out and I'll see if I can get someone on him as soon as he leaves the building." Quinn picked up his phone and Steven heard him ask for Captain Thorne.

Steven went back to his text to Haley.

I'd love to come. Want me
to pick you up? Also, Richie
was just released after
making bail.

Haley paced the conference room floor
behind her chair. Olivia stood at the head
of the table while Katie and Maddy sat to
her left. Charlie, Olivia's brother and a
contract employee of the agency, was working with Maddy's current client. Lizzie,
another contract employee, had eyes on one
of Katie's clients. And that's the way it
would remain for now.

Two new faces took up the other two seats
to Haley's right. Christina Sherman and
Laila Rabbinowitz. Haley had met them
briefly before the meeting and had instantly
liked them. Christina, tall, blonde, and
magazine-model worthy, had dark eyes that
didn't miss anything. Laila, a more petite
woman with her dark skin, chocolate brown
eyes, and shy smile, packaged deadly skills
and a razor-sharp mind.

A small sense of relief flowed through her
and she chastised herself for her worry.
Olivia would never bring someone into the
agency who wasn't a good fit for them all.

"Haley?"

Haley jerked at the sound of her name.

235

Olivia was looking at her. "What? Oh, sorry. I was thinking."

"You want to tell us what you need in regard to your grandfather and the Hampton family's safety?"

Haley let out a slow breath and gathered her thoughts. "Yes. As you know, several attempts have been made on my life in the last few days. I'm not sure who or why, but unfortunately, we have several options to speculate on. One, it could be that Richie Derrick, a violent man who I have made angry, could be seeking to hurt me out of spite. Or two, I have a rather interesting past that has just come to light. It could be that someone doesn't want me to come back to life — so to speak. Someone who murdered most of my family when I was five years old."

Her friends reacted in unison. "What?" Katie asked.

"Who?"

"Why?"

Haley held up a hand. "Hang on and let me explain."

They fell silent.

"Who are you leaning toward as the guilty party?" Laila asked.

Haley hesitated. "I hate to guess in case I'm wrong."

Katie reached out and grasped her hand.

Haley squeezed her friend's fingers. "Due to all of the craziness, I haven't been able to really sit down with my grandfather to dig deeper. Maddy, could you cover him just in case? Right now, Quinn has friends watching him, but they have their regular shifts coming up and will need to leave soon."

"Of course."

Haley turned to the new women. "Laila, would you help cover Zeke, Micah, and Belinda at the hospital?"

"Just tell me how to get there."

Haley really liked the soft-spoken, steely-eyed woman and looked forward to getting to know her better. "Thanks."

"And me?" Christina asked.

Haley hesitated. "I need you to have my back."

"You've got it."

Haley turned back to Olivia. "I hope all of this goes away fast. I don't like using almost the entire agency's man . . . er . . . woman-power."

Olivia shook her head. "We're here for you. I've got a few more people on the list to call if I need them to help cover our clientele. This is an unusual situation, but we're a team and we'll roll with it. Everyone just needs to be flexible."

Haley let out a slow breath. "All right. Thank you."

"So what's next?"

Haley looked at her phone and saw Steven's response. "Christina, Laila, and I all head to the hospital."

Steven stood just inside the door to the hospital, where Haley said she'd meet him. He saw her emerge from the covered parking deck, flanked by two other women. She moved with an easy stride across the street, head held high, always watching, ever alert. She spotted him and lifted a hand in greeting. He returned the gesture and held the door for the three of them. "Thanks," she said, then introduced him to the two new members of the Elite Guardians agency.

"Nice to meet you." He focused back on Haley. "Richie's here." Which had derailed his plan to ask Belinda about the checks and if Richie was cashing them — or forcing Belinda to do so and give him the money.

Haley sighed. "Seriously? How?"

"I got a text from the officer on the door. Officer Savakis tried to keep him out, but Belinda insisted on letting him in. Zeke started arguing with her and Richie shoved him out the door and told him to calm down. Zeke is sitting with Savakis now."

Haley's eyes took on a fierce glow, but she simply drew in a deep breath. "All right then. Thanks for the heads-up. Laila is going to stay with Zeke. He's her client for now."

"Good idea."

They walked to the elevator. Once on Micah's floor, Steven and the three women made their way down the hallway to the boy's room. Steven spotted Savakis. Zeke sat in the chair usually reserved for the officer. The teen's eyes were narrowed slits and his fists rested on his thighs. He looked up and spotted Haley and Steven. Steven thought he might have seen a flash of relief before it was covered with a hardness that Steven worried might become a permanent thing.

"He's in there?" Steven asked.

Zeke gave a short nod.

"Zeke, this is Laila," Haley said. "She's going to be hanging around you for a while."

"Why?"

"To make sure you don't get killed in another drive-by."

"Oh." Uncertainty flickered, but he didn't protest.

Haley stepped around him and knocked. Then pushed inside without waiting for an answer. Steven followed. Once inside the room, his eyes went first to Micah, who looked to be sleeping. Belinda sat on the chair next to him and held his hand. Richie stood with his back to the window, hands shoved in his pockets, mouth tight, eyes glaring.

He wasn't happy.

Belinda's gaze jumped to Haley's and the woman walked over to wrap Haley in a hug. "I'm so glad you came."

"How is he?"

"He needs a transplant and soon."

"Where is he on the list?"

Belinda bit her lip. "Not high enough, I'm afraid," she finally whispered.

"What are you doing here?" Richie broke his silence.

Haley glanced at him and Steven crossed his arms, keeping his hand close to his weapon.

"Visiting a friend, Richie. What are you doing here? Couldn't find anyone else to bully?"

His nostrils flared and he took a step toward her. Haley didn't flinch or look away. She simply raised a brow. Steven inched his hand a little closer to his gun.

Then Haley narrowed her eyes. "Relax, Richie. I'm just here to check on Micah."

"He's fine and we don't need you checking on him. So why don't you butt out and go find another charity case?"

Belinda's sharp indrawn breath drew Steven's gaze to her. Anger darkened her features as she stared at her boyfriend. "Really? Charity case?"

"Shut up, Belinda."

"Richie —"

"I said SHUT UP!"

Belinda cringed as if she'd been slapped.

"All right," Steven said. "You want to get arrested again?"

Richie turned vicious eyes on him. "For what? Yelling at my girlfriend?"

"For disturbing the peace."

"For existing," Zeke grunted from behind Steven. "Get out of here."

Richie growled and came at Zeke. Steven simply stepped in front of him.

Richie stopped, turned back to glare at Belinda. "You sure you want to do this?"

Belinda grimaced. "Richie, not right now, okay? I need to take care of Micah —"

"You'll regret this." His gaze swept the room. "All of you." And then he shoved past Steven, shouldered Zeke out of his way, and slammed out the door.

Quiet descended.

"Well, that was intense," Micah said, his

little voice breathless and small.

Belinda whirled and took his hand again. "Don't worry about him, baby."

"Dump him, Mom. You don't need him."

Belinda bit her lip.

"He hits Zeke," Micah said. "You all think I'm too sick to notice anything, but I heard him punching Zeke the other day."

"What?" She swayed, and Steven moved closer to the woman in case he needed to catch her.

Zeke frowned and clenched his fists. "Micah, stop —"

"No, you stop." Micah coughed and closed his eyes, then opened them again. He looked at Haley. "You can make him stop."

Belinda whirled to stare at Zeke, who met her gaze. "He hits you?"

Zeke shifted and hunched his shoulders. "Only a couple of times and I don't let it bother me." He narrowed his eyes at his younger brother. "You shouldn't have said anything."

Micah shuddered. "Yes, I should have. Should have said something before now." He closed his eyes again.

"Why didn't you tell me?" Belinda whispered. "Why?"

Zeke's shoulders dropped. "For a lot of reasons."

Belinda shook her head and Steven could tell she really hadn't known. She dropped into the chair behind her. And wept.

[17]

Haley stepped out of the hospital and into the sun. She lifted her face toward it and paused a moment to soak in the warmth. It wasn't blistering hot yet and it felt good to be outside. Christina had to make a stop on the way out, so Haley stayed behind the large pillar out of sight of the road.

Steven joined her and crossed his arms. "When are you going to tell me about the handler?"

Haley narrowed her eyes. "He was a player. He told me he loved me and that I was special, while he was loving several other special someones." She shrugged. "That's pretty much it."

And she really didn't want to talk about it.

"Jerk," Steven said.

"In a word. He gave me a ring, a very pretty one, and said he wanted to marry me one day. Little did I know he was passing out those rings like they were candy."

Steven winced. She drew in a breath at the memories. Then smiled.

"Why are you smiling?"

"When I told him I never wanted to see him again, he asked for the ring back."

"And?"

"I laughed and told him to go find it. I'd given it to one of the homeless women who hung around the local park sometimes. She cried."

"Oh wow. Bet that went over well."

"Hmm. I thought about flushing it down the toilet, but figured that wouldn't help anyone. At least Kristy could sell it."

"You knew her? The homeless woman?"

"Yes. And I knew she worked when she could and had two children she was desperate to regain custody of."

"Did she?"

Haley shook her head. "But she's completed all the requirements, has a steady job, a clean apartment, and it's looking better for her every day."

The look in his eyes made her want to squirm.

"Don't."

His brows rose. "What?"

"Look at me that way."

"What way?"

"Like I'm some kind of superhero or something. It's . . . weird."

He laughed. A sound of pure pleasure that made her cheeks heat even further. He kept his eyes locked on hers even as his laughter faded. Haley caught her breath and let him study her while she did the same to him. His eyes dropped to her lips, then bounced away.

Christina joined them. Her gaze flitted between the two and she raised a brow.

Steven cleared his throat. "You think Belinda will stand her ground and refuse to let him come back?"

Christina scoffed. "Not likely. Something will happen. Money will get too tight and he'll promise to be her knight in shining armor. She'll give him another chance."

Haley hoped not. "Guess time will tell."

"What now?" Steven asked.

"I want to focus on the case in Ireland," Haley said. "And that means talking to my grandfather some more."

Steven nodded. "Get some more information from him. A list of people from twenty-five years ago that we can look into." He paused. "It won't be easy."

Haley gave him a faint smile. "I don't know how to do easy."

"I'm learning that about you."

She gave him a light punch on the arm and he fake-flinched.

He blew out a slow breath. "It's time for me to head to my parents' house. My father has a doctor's appointment in about an hour and I promised to go with him."

Haley frowned. "Is he all right?"

"No. He has cancer."

"Oh! I'm so sorry."

"I am too."

She reached for his strong hand and squeezed his fingers. "I'll be praying for him."

He looked away and cleared his throat. "Thanks."

"And thank you again for taking care of the mattress and glass door. That was extremely kind. And thoughtful."

He ducked his head and she thought his cheeks reddened a bit. "It was just a couple of phone calls."

"I can pay you —"

He held up a hand and met her gaze. "I did it because I wanted to."

She studied him a moment longer. "Very well then, I'll just say thanks again." She turned to Christina. "Ready to roll?"

"Whenever you are."

Haley pushed away from the pillar. She and Christina headed back toward the parking garage, and Steven took off for his vehicle that he'd left parked in one of the police parking spots.

Haley kept a vigilant eye out for Richie — or one of his goons. She didn't trust him enough not to ambush her or send someone to do it for him. "You see anything suspicious?" she asked Christina.

"No. You?"

"Nothing so far. Does he still have someone watching him?"

"Yes, I'm sure Quinn has someone assigned to him."

"Then he won't try anything during the day where there are witnesses. He'll be sneaky."

Like break into her home in the dark and shoot at the lumps in her bed? Yeah. Probably. Only that still niggled at her. All she could think was "too professional."

When they reached her Hummer, Haley paused and pulled a small mirror from her pocket. Christina did the same and grinned at her.

"Great minds and all that," Haley murmured.

"Exactly." Christina covered the front and the passenger side of the car while Haley examined the driver's side and the back.

"I'm clear over here," Christina said.

"Me too." Haley opened the driver's door and climbed behind the wheel. Christina joined her and Haley backed from the parking spot. "What made you join the agency?"

"Apparently Olivia keeps tabs on the graduates from the academy. My name came up and she asked if I was interested in the Elite Guardians." She shrugged. "I didn't have any offers that intrigued me more, so I said yes."

Interesting answer. She shot a sideways glance at the woman. If Olivia had asked her, she must have exceptional qualifications and skills. Pretty, smart. Deadly. Just like they all were.

Haley drove, her attention focused on the road before and behind her, but was aware that Christina was alert and watchful as well. Thirty minutes later, after a circuitous route to her home and verifying no one was following her, she pulled into her garage and shut the door behind her.

Two police cruisers sat outside her house. As did Maddy's car. But she hadn't had a call, so she was going to assume all was okay.

They entered the house and Maddy met them in the kitchen. "Everything is fine here," she said by way of greeting.

"I figured it would be. Why are the police cars still here?"

"There are different ones coming by at different times. Think they're taking their breaks here."

"Nice. I appreciate that."

"Quinn's well thought of in the department." Maddy gave a small smile. "In spite of his rather vociferous personality."

"Vociferous," Haley echoed. "Ha. Good word."

"I thought so."

"How's my grandfather?"

"Fine. He's been dozing. I think the trip was a little harder on him than he wants to admit. He said he had a bit of a headache and was going to try to sleep it off."

"And his friend? Hugh?"

"Now, he's a character for sure. He's locked himself away with a laptop and says he's working."

"Working on what?"

"Who knows? Something for your grandfather, I think."

"Okay, thanks."

Now that she'd been briefed, she was ready to talk. Part of her longed to spout out the hundreds of questions that swirled in her brain, but the organized, logical part told her to take it one step at a time. One question at a time.

Maddy stopped her with a hand on her

arm. "Steven seems to be a good guy."

"He does, doesn't he?"

"He also seems to be quite interested in you."

Haley gave her a small smile "Are you playing big sister to the guy?"

"Quinn likes him."

"I like him too," Haley said and kept her gaze steady on her friend and coworker.

Maddy held her eyes a moment longer. "Then that's good enough for me."

She left Christina and Maddy talking in the kitchen and went to find Ian Burke. She didn't have to go far and her heart softened when she found him stretched out in her favorite recliner, the television remote resting near his right hand. A baseball game played on the screen, but he had the sound on mute. He looked so natural there, so comfortable. "Grand?"

His eyes flickered open and she nearly gasped at the love that flooded his face and poured from his eyes. "Ail— Haley."

She took his gnarled hand. "You can call me Aileen if it makes you happy."

"The happiest."

"All right then."

He lowered the footrest and she sat on the love seat opposite him.

"Could we talk?"

"Of course." He cleared his throat and took a sip of the water from the glass sitting on the end table. "What do you need to know?"

She rubbed a hand across her face, then rose to grab the laptop she'd left sitting on the end of the couch. She returned to the love seat and opened the device. "I need you to give me a list of names of people from twenty-five years ago who might've held a grudge against you." She absently noted how easy it was to slip into the brogue with him. Hearing it roll off his tongue seemed to bring it out of her.

"It's a long list."

"It's okay."

Her grandfather reached out to touch an aged hand to hers. "You look like your mother, to be sure."

"I do. Duncan showed me her picture."

He fell silent a moment, then cleared his throat and removed his touch. "Well, I suppose we should start with Desmond O'Reilly."

"Why him?"

"His family started a shipping business shortly after my father did. They were competitors. Then one day, one of my father's ships was sunk by pirates and all the cargo was lost. Three men died. The others managed to wait for rescue by holding onto debris from the ship."

"That's awful."

"Truly. My father swore it was one of O'Reilly's sons who was responsible for the deed — whether doing it himself or hiring someone to do it — and thus the feud was born."

"Lasting up until the attack on your — our — home?"

"Lasting up until this very day. Although I haven't had much to do with it lately. But twenty-five years ago, shortly before the attack, I outbid two competitors on a major contract. O'Reilly's Shipping and Shaughnessy Shipping. This corporation decided to go with us for all of their transport. From the gossip that managed to filter down, neither Shaughnessy nor O'Reilly were happy. In fact, O'Reilly was furious, but angry enough to kill my family?" He shook his head. "I wouldn't have guessed it, but who knows? Then again, the gang symbols left on the walls in the castle say Shaughnessy and their shady connections were involved." He spread his hands and shook his head. "Nothing was ever proven one way or the other."

Haley typed a note to investigate the O'Reilly and Shaughnessy families. "What about your staff or the people close to you?"

He shook his head. "Oh no. They were vetted before they were hired. I trust them with my life."

"So you have the same staff now that you had back then?"

"Just Hugh is still with me. I still live in that drafty old castle because it's home, but three-quarters of it is closed off and shut down. I just live in a very small part of it."

"So does Hugh do all the cooking and cleaning?"

"Oh goodness no. I have a cleaning lady who comes in twice a week and a part-time cook who comes four hours a day to prepare food. I generally eat a rather large breakfast and lunch, but have leftovers for dinner. Hugh prepares that for me."

"And Hugh lives in the castle with you."

"He does. His wife and son passed many years ago. I saw how lonely he was — mostly because I was, too — and asked him if he'd like a room. He took it and has been like a son or a younger brother to me ever since. He's twenty years younger than I, you know. Just about the same age as my actual brother, Niall."

Haley nodded, typed in all of the names and shut the laptop. "You've both suffered much loss, so much tragedy."

"It's been our life, our cross to bear, it has. There have been some wonderful moments in there, lovely memories, but the loss, the pain." He ran a shaky hand over his eyes. "Indeed it's been almost too much to bear."

"I'm sorry."

He wiped a stray tear.

"Thank you," she said. "You've given me much to work with."

"Better luck to you than those before you."

Steven tucked the blanket around his father and sat on the couch beside him. His father took his hand. "Thank you, son."

"Of course."

He seemed so frail, so old. Anger gripped him. At fifty-seven years old, his father should be enjoying life. Fishing, traveling, bugging him about grandchildren. Not battling a deadly disease. "Where's Mom?"

"She had an errand to run. I told her I would be fine for the two hours she'd be gone. And I could always call you or 911 if I needed to." He glanced at the clock. "She should be back any minute now."

Steven bit his lip on the words that wanted to roll out. He knew his father was right, but he didn't like the idea of him being left alone.

"My numbers were better today."

"I know." And they were. It was slightly encouraging, but Steven refused to hope too much.

"I feel a bit better too."

He squeezed his father's fingers. "I'm glad to hear that, Dad."

"How's the job going?"

"Busy. Always something going on, a case to solve, a criminal to catch."

"And you're good at that job. Just like your mother was."

Steven looked away, his heart catching at the praise. He never tired of hearing that his dad was proud of him. "Yeah. I used to love listening to her stories about catching the bad guys. Sure did motivate me to go into law enforcement."

"And Michael was the other thing, wasn't he?"

"He was." But he didn't want to talk about Michael.

"Your mother has a big heart, you know?"

Steven frowned. "I know. What makes you bring that up?"

His father sighed. "She has the ability to do things I'm not sure I can but know that I must."

"Dad? You're talking in riddles. You okay?"

His father gave a low chuckle. "I just have

a lot of time to think these days."

"I know."

"You'd be surprised at what I think about."

"You want to tell me?"

His father squeezed his hand. "Maybe. Right now, I'm still processing a lot of things. Like what happened to Michael."

"Don't dwell on that. I can't."

"I don't dwell, I think."

"Well, it's not going to get you anywhere. If it won't bring him back, it's not worth thinking about." He knew he sounded abrupt and borderline rude, but he really didn't want to have this conversation.

"Have you met any nice girls?" A change in subject. His dad wasn't without mercy.

"I've met a lot of nice girls."

"Come on, boy. You know what I mean. Any women you're interested in?"

Haley's pretty face flashed immediately into his mind. "Yes. One," he said quietly. No sense in denying it.

His father stilled. "Really? That wasn't the answer I was expecting."

Steven let out a low laugh. "I know. It's a recent thing."

He told his father a little about the bodyguard who'd captured his interest and then the conversation moved to small talk until his father finally fell asleep sitting up, his head resting comfortably on the cushion behind him. Steven rose and checked his phone. He'd missed a call from Quinn about three minutes ago. He walked into the kitchen so he wouldn't disturb his father and dialed his partner's number.

Quinn picked up. "Hello?"

"Sorry I missed you. I was helping with my dad."

"It's fine. I just wanted you to know we think we might have found Carter James."

Steven straightened. "Where? Is he alive?"

"He is. Barely. I asked a buddy of mine with a search and rescue K-9 to drive the route Carter would have taken to get to Greenville. Told him to let Scout see if he could find anything. It was slow going, but he found him about three hours into the search. Looks like Carter was carjacked at a gas station on I-26. That's just speculation, though, and I hate speculation."

"Sounds like an educated guess to me." He heard the door shut and recognized his mother's footsteps as she came from the garage, through the mudroom, and into the kitchen. She kissed him on the cheek, then walked into the den to check on his father.

"Educated guess. Okay, we'll go with that," Quinn said. "Anyway, Carter was dumped in a field behind the gas station. He's got some serious head trauma and a bullet wound in his back. Poor guy wouldn't have made it much longer."

Steven grimaced. "Ouch."

"Yeah."

"He's at the hospital, I take it?"

"He's there and in surgery. I'm supposed to get a call when he's conscious and can talk. Once they dig out the bullet, ballistics will compare it with the one the ME dug out of our John Doe from the trunk. I'm hazarding another educated guess that the two bullets match."

"I'd say that's a safe guess. I'm just praying the guy makes it. If he does, maybe he can tell us who did this. Did you let his wife know?"

"Yes. She's on her way here as we speak."

"Good."

Steven ran a hand through his hair. "So who was the guy in his trunk? Any progress on IDing him?"

"Nothing yet. And it's not like we can post pictures of him on the news to see if anyone knows him."

"Yeah."

Steven's phone beeped. He glanced at the screen. A text from Haley. "Hey, I've got to go."

"Later." Quinn hung up and Steven pulled up the text.

Haley
Meet me at Starbucks on Two Notch in 30? That's the good part of Two Notch just in case you've forgotten there is such a thing.

Then she'd sent him the address to map. He typed back.

I'll be there.

Steven went to find his mother. His heart nearly stopped when he located her in the guest room sitting on the floor. "Mom? What are you doing?"

She looked up, tears in her eyes and on her cheeks. She gave him a wobbly smile. "Remembering."

He swallowed. "Why? When it hurts so much?"

She bit her lip and looked back down at the photo album. An 8 × 10 of a twelve-year-old Michael grinned up from the page. She used a finger to trace his face. "Because he existed. He had dreams and was so full of life." She gave a tiny shrug. "He deserves

260

to be remembered."

Steven closed his eyes and pinched the bridge of his nose. "I don't want to remember," he whispered hoarsely.

"I know. And that's okay. That's your way of dealing with it."

"It's been twelve years, Mom. It shouldn't still hurt this bad." He slid down to sit on the floor beside her and wrapped an arm around her shoulder. He felt the prick of tears behind his eyes but refused to let them surface. "You know, I have a friend. Well, a coworker. No . . . a friend." He dropped his head with a low half laugh, half groan, then lifted his eyes to meet hers again. "Well, whatever she is, she just discovered that she was presumed dead twenty-five years ago. A few months ago, her grandfather found out she was alive and well. He just flew in from Ireland to see her."

"Oh, how wonderful. The joy he must be feeling. What a reunion."

"I used to dream about that," Steven whispered.

"What?"

"About waking up to see Michael at the foot of my bed with that stupid gorilla mask on. I used to beg God to bring him back to us. Because he's God, right? He could do that. He could undo everything that had been done without even blinking an eye, right?"

His mother didn't answer, but he felt the shudder ripple through her.

"Anyway," he said. "When I saw Haley's grandfather hug her for the first time in twenty-five years, you know what I felt?"

She sniffed and swiped a tear. "You were jealous."

"Exactly. I so wanted that to be Michael and me."

His mother shut the album. "The man who hit him is up for parole."

Everything in Steven froze. A minute passed before he could get his throat to work. "He didn't *hit* him, he *killed* him." She didn't respond. "When is the hearing?" he asked.

"A week from tomorrow."

He gaped. "Why didn't I know about this?"

"I don't know. I got the notice a while ago. They might have sent the information to your Chicago address."

"Probably. So why didn't you tell me?"

"I didn't want to bring it up yet. I've been . . . praying about it. A lot."

He snorted. "Nothing to pray about. I'll be there. He's not getting out."

"Steven —" She stopped, then patted his

hand. "Come on. Help me up." He did and she squeezed his fingers. "I love you, Steven."

"I know you do, Mom. I love you too." He kissed her cheek, then went to find his keys. Meeting Haley was suddenly the one thing he wanted to do more than anything.

[18]

Tuesday, 3:30 PM

Haley arrived early at the coffee shop, got her drink, and chose a seat near the door so she could watch for Steven — and anything else she might need to see. Keeping her back against the wall kept her stress level manageable. Christina stayed in her vehicle watching the area. Which left Haley free to think about her actions.

What had possessed her to text Steven? Why was she so drawn to him? What was it about him that caused her to visualize things like dates and *romance*?

She had to be losing her mind. That was all it was. Having been shot at three times in the last few days had simply caused her to have some sort of brain malfunction, because she'd sworn off men when she'd left G2 and hadn't regretted it one bit since.

Until now.

She pressed a hand to her side where the

stitches pulled when she moved carelessly. That wound was minor compared to the broken heart she'd suffered when Dylan had betrayed her. He'd taken her love and trust and crushed it like a soda can.

The door opened and she eyed the person who entered. The baseball cap hid his features while he looked from side to side, as though casing the store. Haley stiffened, her hand going to her weapon while she watched him. She scanned his clothing, looking for a gun, a knife, anything.

A young twentysomething blonde entered behind him and wrapped her arm around his waist. He leaned over and gave her a light kiss on the lips.

Haley blew out a breath and released her gun. "You've really got to chill," she muttered.

And she would. Eventually.

The door opened again and Steven stepped inside. He spotted her immediately. She lifted her cup and indicated he should go ahead and order. He nodded. Her phone buzzed. She looked down to find a text from a strange number.

The man in the trunk was killed because of you. His name is Gerald Forsythe. Stop your

search into the past or more
will die. Their blood is on your
hands. Enjoy your coffee.

Haley didn't move, didn't blink, didn't breathe. She simply stared at the text. Was he watching the store now? Or had he waited until he'd driven away before sending the message?
She texted Christina.

Do you see anyone sitting in
their car in the parking lot
besides you?

Christina
No. Why?

Forwarding you a text I just
got

She sent it. Then typed a text to the anonymous number.

I'm not drinking coffee.

Steven joined her. "Everything okay?"
She shook her hot chocolate and took a swig. "My stalker has returned." She showed him the text.

266

He pulled his phone from the clip on his belt. "I'll get someone out here."

She reached out and covered his hand with hers. "Don't bother. He's not here anymore. He's just letting me know he's watching." She drew in a breath. "You can run the number and see what it turns up, but I'm guessing it's a throwaway phone."

"Probably, but we'll try it." She gave him the number and he sent it into cyberspace to someone he worked with.

"Also, can you run the name Gerald Forsythe? I could, but I would need to go into the office. I don't have the software on my phone."

"Sure. We can go out to my car and do it."

"Great." They rose and walked out of the coffee shop. Haley kept her attention focused on the area around them, and she knew Christina was watching as well. Steven unlocked his car, then started it, letting the air conditioning wash over them. He pulled the laptop around to him and began his search. "Gerald Forsythe."

"Right."

"There's a Gerald Forsythe who's been reported missing out of Virginia. Says he last checked in with his wife the Saturday before we found the body in the trunk. Officer Gerald Forsythe."

"He's a cop?"

"A decorated one."

"You have a picture of him?"

He turned the screen so she could see it and she studied the man. It was a professional photograph. He sat straight, eyes facing the camera and full lips slightly tilted upward. He looked like a man who could take care of himself. Only someone had killed him. Maybe. "We need to see if we can get a DNA comparison."

"Wait a minute. Look at his left hand," Steven said.

"Okay, what am I looking at?"

"Is that an actual ring on his fourth finger or a tattoo?"

She squinted and moved the screen closer. "I can't tell. Let me call Francisco."

"Oh yeah, the medical examiner. I met him my first day on the job. He's quite a character, isn't he?"

"To say the least."

"He was doing sit-ups when Quinn and I walked in."

"He's moved on from push-ups since he broke the world record."

"Right."

Haley had Francisco on speed dial. She listened to the line ring and got his voice mail. She hung up and dialed his cell phone.

"I've got a spleen in my left hand and a scalpel in my right. You're on speaker-phone."

Relief flowed at hearing him answer. "Thanks for picking up, it's kind of urgent."

"It's always urgent with you people."

"I'll tell your boss you deserve another raise."

"If it's as much as last time, I'm hanging up."

"No, no, don't do that. Is one of your assistants with you?" Haley knew both, but didn't know which one was working with him today.

"Of course. Nan is right here."

"Ask Nan to go check the left hand of the John Doe that was brought in Sunday night. The guy from the trunk. Ask her if he's got a tattoo around the ring finger that would wear a wedding band."

"A tattoo?"

"Yes."

"She doesn't have to check. I remember. His hands were covered in blood when he arrived."

"Well, he had them tucked under his cheek when his face was blown off."

"That would do it. Anyway, once I got him cleaned up, I removed his personal effects, and yes, there's a tattoo there. It's a band and it just says 'Forever' on it."

Haley sucked in a breath and met Steven's gaze. "Okay, then your John Doe now has a name."

"Really? What would that be?"

"Gerald Forsythe."

"Will you be notifying his next of kin?"

"Someone will. Thanks, Francisco."

"I'll be looking for that raise."

She let out a low laugh and hung up. Then turned serious while sadness gripped her. "It's him," she told Steven.

"I gathered." He tapped a few times on his screen.

"Are you letting Quinn know?"

"Yes." He finished and tucked the phone back into its clip on his belt.

"So," she said. "Gerald Forsythe. Who is he — other than a decorated cop? Why was he in South Carolina and why did someone kill him and say I'm the reason he's dead? What's his connection to me?"

"All good questions."

"I hate questions. I want answers." Her phone vibrated and she glanced at the message and gasped. "Maddy said it's my grandfather. An ambulance is taking him to the hospital."

"What happened?"

"She didn't give me details, but I've got to head over there."

"Of course."

His phone buzzed and he pulled it off the clip again. "Uh-oh."

"What?" She paused half in, half out of the car.

"Richie gave his tail the slip."

Steven fell in behind Christina and Haley as they made their way to the hospital. He'd offered to drive her, but she'd already been climbing into her Hummer. His phone rang and he pressed the button that would allow the Bluetooth to activate his speakers. "Hello?"

"Hey, it's Quinn."

"What's up?"

"I've been working on Haley's case."

"Join the club."

A sigh reached him. "You're not going to believe this, but I don't think Richie's behind everything. He could have hired the people to do the shooting, but he's also got an air-tight alibi. He wasn't at Haley's house shooting up her bed, he was caught on video camera knocking over a convenience store. Needless to say, we have a warrant out for his arrest."

"You're kidding."

"Nope."

"Why would he knock over a convenience store? He's got minions who do stuff like that."

"Whatever the reason, he did it."

"All right, then I guess we need to go in another direction."

"Looks like. One other thing, Steven."

"Yeah?"

"I . . . uh . . . did some background checking on Haley's grandfather and Hugh McCort."

Uh-oh. "And?"

"Her grandfather came back clean as a whistle. His friend did too. Sort of."

"What do you mean 'sort of'?" He made a left, then a right, staying on Haley's bumper.

"McCort has used the same bank in Ireland for the past forty-some-odd years. His son banked there as well before his death. Three days before the attack on the castle, someone deposited the equivalent of twenty grand in that account. The son's, not McCort's. While I was investigating the elder McCort, I figured I would just check the whole family. I looked in the investigative report and there was no mention of investigating McCort's son, who wasn't even in the city at the time of the attack.

They checked into the elder McCort, of course, but according to the report, he was cleared two days after the attack."

Steven let out a low whistle as he pulled into the parking lot of the hospital. "How did you get that information so quickly?"

"I have a connection who has a connection."

"So, McCort has a son?"

"Yes, Connor McCort. He was twenty-three years old when the attack happened and he died two days after."

"What happened?"

"Suicide."

"Oh. Whoa."

"Yeah. Two days after that, McCort closed his son's account and a large deposit was made into the senior McCort's account."

"How much?"

"Lots and lots of Irish pounds. The equivalent of twenty grand."

"Wow. Okay, that's a lot of money, especially twenty-five years ago. Can you trace where it was spent?"

"No, and don't have to anyway. It's been sitting there since the day he deposited it."

"You think McCort's son had something to do with the attack after all? Then, out of remorse and guilt, killed himself?"

"It's possible. I think Hugh McCort's the

only one who knows for sure."

"Then we need to ask him."

"You want to tell Haley or you want me to?" Quinn asked.

Haley parked in one of the law enforcement slots that provided the most protection for her to make her way into the building. Steven pulled behind her. He watched her check the mirrors. "I'll tell her. She'll want to be the one to talk to McCort. He'll probably be here with Haley's grandfather."

"Good enough. I'm going back to it."

"Later." He hung up and climbed out of his car to join Christina, who was using binoculars to scan the area across the street.

After a moment, she nodded to Haley, and Haley slid out on the passenger side closest to the entrance. They made their way into the hospital and Haley paused just inside the entrance. "I want to check on my grandfather, then let's look in on Micah."

"I heard from Quinn on the way here. Got an update for you," Steven said.

"I'm very worried about what Richie's going to do next. I need to make sure Belinda understands the seriousness of his actions. And then there's Duncan."

"Yes. And then there's Duncan."

She went straight to the information desk with Christina hovering nearby. "I need to know the status of a patient who was brought in," Haley said. "His name is Ian Burke."

The woman turned to her computer. After a few clicks, she looked up. "They are running tests on him right now."

"Okay. Thank you."

She turned away and pressed her fingers to her eyes. "Want to check on Micah now?"

"Sure."

On the elevator ride up to Micah's floor, Steven told Haley and Christina about his conversation with Quinn, covering Richie's alibi and warrant, then briefly touching on Hugh McCort and his son. Haley let him talk without interrupting, even as her expression got tighter and tighter. When they stepped off the elevator, she shook her head. "All right, we'll deal with that little bit of information about Hugh shortly. Let's take care of one thing at a time."

They walked down the hallway to Micah's room. The officer at the door checked their ID and waved them in. Belinda sat next to Micah holding his hand while Zeke reclined on the window seat watching television with Laila beside him. Zeke sat up when they entered.

"How's he doing?" Haley walked to the

bed and ran a hand over his head. He didn't move.

Belinda sighed. "Not good. He's sleeping a lot more. I think he's really running out of time. The doctor told me he wouldn't be leaving here until he had a new heart or . . ." She swallowed and looked away.

Or he died. Steven understood the unspoken words.

Zeke stood and paced to the door, then back to the window seat. "I want to go to the center today. You think that would be all right?"

Haley hesitated, then said, "Laila, you go with him. Christina can stay here with Belinda and Micah. I'll try to stop by the center soon."

"Of course," Laila said. "Let's take the back stairs."

"Why?" Zeke asked.

"Precaution."

She and Zeke walked out of the room. Belinda's shoulders sagged. Steven met Haley's eyes and she tilted her head toward the door. He got the message. "I'm going to grab a snack," he said. "I'll bring you guys something."

Christina opened the door. "And I'll just be out here with the officer keeping an eye out for Richie."

"Thanks," Haley said. "I won't be but a few minutes and then I want to check on my grandfather." She paused. "Actually, do you mind seeing what you can find out about him?"

"Sure," Steven said and shut the door behind him. He turned and came face-to-face with Richie, now sporting dreadlocks.

"Richie Derrick, fancy meeting you here. You're under arrest." Steven reached for his weapon.

Richie's hand shot out to grab a young woman who had the misfortune to choose that moment to exit the room nearest Micah's, then pulled a gun from behind his back and aimed it at his startled hostage's head. "Get out of my way, cop."

Haley heard Richie's order just as the door clicked shut. Next she heard screams and a heavy crash.

Micah's eyes fluttered open. "What's going on?"

"It's okay, baby," Belinda said. She looked at Haley and raised her brows.

"Put the weapon down, Richie! Let her go!" Steven's command came from the hall.

She heard Belinda's startled gasp. "Richie?"

"Call 911," Haley ordered and pulled her

277

weapon. "He's not getting in here."

"Zeke," Belinda whispered.

Haley dared a quick glance at her phone. "Laila didn't call or text, so they missed him by seconds. Zeke's safe."

"You don't know that. Maybe she couldn't text or call. Maybe he's already killed them."

She rushed to the door and Haley caught her arm to pull her back. "Don't. Please. Trust Laila to do her job and protect Zeke. Get back and stay near Micah." Belinda's nostrils flared and for a moment Haley feared she'd ignore her. "Please," Haley said. "Trust me. Trust us."

Belinda did as requested and Haley walked to the door.

"Belinda!" Richie called out. "You come out here!"

"Put the gun down!"

"Put it down!"

Steven and Christina were shouting orders and Richie was obviously not obeying.

Haley stayed ready at the door. They would take him down out there or she would do what she had to do if he managed to get the door open.

It was a standoff. Steven held his gun steady on Richie, who had his back against the wall. Richie clutched his weapon in a deadly grip against the trembling woman's temple, using her as a shield. If Steven had had a clear shot, he'd have taken it, but Richie had moved fast and Steven simply couldn't take a chance that he'd miss.

The dreadlocks wig, dark sunglasses, and long sleeves to cover the tattoos had effectively disguised him and allowed him to slip past those looking for a bald man covered in tattoos.

"Richie, think about this," Steven said.

"I already thought about it."

"What's going on inside you right now? I want to help."

"Help?" He laughed — and actually seemed amused. "Dude, the only thing you want to do is end this."

"Well, sure, that would be nice."

Richie grinned. "But you ain't getting what you want. Right now, it's all about me."

"It's not too late. You haven't hurt anyone." He wouldn't mention the convenience store robbery again. No sense in reminding him. "All right, it's all about you. Tell me what I can do so that no one gets hurt."

Richie grinned at him again, his eyes hard, cold black pits. "You think I care if anyone gets hurt? You think I even care? Belinda, get out here! Now!" He focused back on

279

Steven. "No woman treats me like Belinda and gets away with it, you understand?"

He understood, all right. Richie had no intention of letting Belinda live to see another day. He had no doubt this was a murder-suicide in the making, so what did he care if he took a few more innocent lives in the process? "Richie, I'm sorry, but she's not coming out here. She has a bodyguard right next to her and you know there's no way she's going to be allowed to come out that door."

Security burst onto the scene and Richie didn't even spare them a look. "Belinda!" The woman struggled against him. "Be still!" He popped the gun against her head hard enough to make her cry out but not go unconscious.

Officers converged and started clearing as many people as they could from the area. "I'm not going. I got patients to take care of," Steven heard one nurse say. "He's not interested in me. He wants someone named Belinda." Her voice faded as she was escorted from the area along with everyone else.

Richie continued to holler her name and cast threats against her children if she didn't "get your sorry self out here."

Steven prayed Haley would be able to

keep the woman inside until Richie could either be talked down or contained. Or killed. He kept an eye on Richie's trigger finger. It hovered too close for comfort. One wrong move, too much pressure, a slip of his finger, and the woman would die. He met her terrified gaze. "What's your name?"

"L-Lisa."

"Richie, that's Lisa you've got there."

"You think I care about her name?"

He didn't. That was the problem. He had one goal. To kill Belinda and whoever got in his way of doing so.

"All right, Lisa," Steven said, "just stay calm, okay?"

"Shut up, cop," Richie said. "I'm giving the orders around here."

"Of course, Richie. But Lisa didn't do anything to you. She never knew you existed until this moment." He looked at her. "Do you have children?"

"Y-yes. Two. A boy and a girl," she whispered.

"Richie, you hear that? Lisa's a mother." He used her name as much as he could, hoping she would become a real person to Richie, not just a means to an end.

"Of course I heard that, cop. I'm standing right here. Now shut up. Belinda!"

He pressed the gun harder against his

hostage's head, and she winced, her frantic gaze locked on Steven's.

Richie took a step away, then another, keeping his back against the wall. He stopped. "I don't care who I hurt right now. Enough talking. You're starting to make me mad. Get Belinda out here. Belinda!"

Steven spared a quick glance around the now deserted area. Cops were hidden, the hostage negotiator on the way, the sniper probably searching for the best shot. He glanced down the hallway. Yeah, a sniper would have a chance with the window at the end. It would have to be some kind of amazing shot, but it was doable. And that's where the shot would have to come from.

Steven drew in a steadying breath. He had to keep him talking until they managed to get a negotiator on the scene. "Richie, think about this."

"I told you, I done thought about it. Now move! Belinda!"

"You have kids?" Christina asked, her voice soft, almost soothing.

Richie blinked. "What? No, I don't have kids." He smirked. "I was going to adopt Micah and Zeke, wasn't I, Belinda? Was going to treat them like my own. I even called them my sons. But not anymore!" He directed his shouts to the room that held Belinda. Then turned his sneer back on Christina. "What does that have to do with anything?"

"Do you believe in God? Or a higher power?"

Richie froze. Steven let her take the lead. As long as Richie was talking, he wasn't hurting anyone. Although his hostage might have a nasty bruise where the barrel was gouging into her head, he figured she'd be all right with that. A bruise was better than a bullet.

"Why you want to know that?" The sweat on his forehead ran down his temples and dripped from the side of his jaw. "You think you going to send me on a guilt trip?"

"No, just curious. I do. Believe, that is. I mean, I didn't used to, but once I started seeing a lot of people die, it sort of made me rethink things. Rethink God."

Richie eyed her like she was crazy, but Steven could tell she'd captured his interest. "Who'd you see die?"

"My targets."

Richie huffed, still ignoring the police presence, still with his back against the wall, and still holding the weapon like he meant business. "What targets?"

"I was a sniper for a special ops group. You wouldn't have heard of it."

"A sniper?" He laughed. "Ain't no women snipers out there."

"Of course there are. Google it. But it doesn't matter. What does matter is that I have no doubt that a sniper has a bead on you even as we speak. This is your last chance to give it up before you die."

Steven winced. He wouldn't have said that. It was antagonizing, pushing the man. Had she pushed too far?

Richie's eyes darted to her, then back to the door. "I'm in a hallway with a hostage. No one's going to shoot me. Now stop talking. Belinda! I'm going to start killing people if you don't get yourself out here now!"

"Richie! Stop! Just stop." Belinda's voice came from behind Steven. He darted a quick glance at her and saw Haley picking herself up off the floor, a dark look on her face and a hand pressed to her still-healing side. Belinda pushed past Steven and he caught her. She jerked away from him and Steven caught her again in a tighter grip.

"I can't let you go to him," he said.

"You can't stop me."

Richie's lips curved in a grimace of evil that made Steven want to pray.

"Belinda, get back in the room and shut the door," Haley said.

"No," she whispered, "I can't. I can't let him hurt someone else just because I've been stupid. I've made a lot of bad choices in my life and all I do is hurt people."

"Belinda," Steven said, "now isn't the time. Let us handle Richie."

"You heard him, he's going to kill her. He's going to kill my boys."

"He's going to kill you both if you don't get back."

"Get over here, Belinda," Richie said. "You get over here and I won't shoot this nice lady." He took the gun from her temple and pointed it at Steven. "Let go of her or die, cop."

"I'm sorry," Belinda whispered with an agonized look between Haley, Steven, and the madman with a gun. "Take care of my boys for me." She tried to pull away from Steven once again, taking another step toward Richie when the window at the end of the hall exploded and Richie's face disappeared in a mist of red.

[19]

Belinda screamed and dropped to the floor. Haley darted to her side and fell to her knees. "She's been shot!" Richie's gun had discharged as he'd gone down and the bullet had struck Belinda in the chest.

Officers descended, medical personnel rushed forward. Haley pressed against Belinda's bleeding chest. The woman who'd been Richie's hostage sat on the floor, covered in blood and brain matter, weeping. Haley would have loved to comfort her, but right now, she was doing her best to make sure Belinda didn't bleed out. "I need a doctor here, now!"

A woman in her midthirties dropped beside Haley. "I'm Katherine Green. I'm a surgeon. Keep the pressure there." She looked back over her shoulder. "I need a gurney!" Two orderlies raced down the hall. She glanced at the still-crying woman. "Is she hurt?"

"No," Haley said, "just traumatized."

And then Christina appeared from no-where to grab Lisa's upper arms and gently propel her to her feet. "Come on, we'll get you cleaned up."

Steven stood near Micah's room, his phone pressed to his ear. His eyes snagged Haley's for a brief moment and a silent message of support passed from him to her. She nodded.

Dr. Green's gaze dropped to Richie's face-less body. She grimaced and turned back to Belinda. "Hang on, honey, we're going to get you some help."

Belinda's eyes flickered, then settled on Haley. "Take care of my boys for me."

"I will until you're back on your feet."

Belinda reached for her hand and Haley let her grab it. "If I don't make it, you take care of them."

"*Not* making it's not an option."

Her eyes fluttered, her lips moved.

Haley leaned closer. "What?"

Belinda whispered again and Haley did her best to hear her. She finally squeezed the woman's hand as they lifted her onto the gurney. "Fight, Belinda, fight for your boys, you hear me?" Blood bubbled from her mouth and Dr. Green pushed Haley aside.

And then they were rushing Belinda down the hall toward the elevator that would take her to surgery. Haley looked down at her bloody hands, dropped her chin to her chest, and uttered a prayer for Belinda.

And her grandfather.

She made her way to the sink, slathered her hands in the sanitizing soap, and scrubbed. And scrubbed.

Gentle hands settled on her shoulders, then one reached around her to pull paper towels from the holder. She took them from Steven and dried her hands.

"I told Christina I had you covered," he said. "She's staying with Micah."

"There's really no need to keep Micah's family covered now, is there?"

"You never know."

"Richie's friends?"

"Maybe. Probably not, but I think we should keep an eye out for a few days."

"Yeah. You're right."

"As for you . . . the threat of Richie is gone, but I'm not so sure you're in the clear too."

"I know."

"Richie had an agenda. He wasn't about to give up Belinda, and I believe he would have killed you to get you out of his way, but —"

"But it's possible he wasn't the only one interested in seeing me dead."

"Yeah."

"Right." She drew in a deep breath and then let it out slowly as she nodded.

"About your grandfather . . ."

She stilled. "I don't know why they brought him in."

"Maddy said he had come down to tell her he had a migraine and asked for some more medication. She went to get it, and when she came back, he was on the floor, having convulsions. She hollered for Mc-Cort and called 911. When they got him here, they did a brain scan and found a small tumor on his brain. Apparently he hasn't woken up yet."

"Oh no," she whispered. She pressed her palms to her eyes. "I haven't even had a chance to get to know him. I really don't want to lose him."

"Come on, I'll take you to him."

She shook her head. "No, if he's unconscious, I need to do what I can do. I just need someone to let me know when he wakes up. Until then, I want to go see Zeke and tell him about his mother."

"At the teen center?"

"Yes."

"All right. I'll take you there, then bring

you back."

She looked him in the eye. "Why?"

"Why what?"

"Why do you seem to care so much?"

He brushed a strand of hair away from her face. "You make it easy to care." He shrugged. "I just do."

She held his gaze a moment longer. "Thanks." She stayed put for another few seconds, then nodded. "All right, then. Let's check on Duncan, then we can go."

Ten minutes later, relieved that Duncan was improving with each passing hour, she pulled the keys to her Hummer out of her front pocket and tossed them to him. "You can drive. I've got to think about how I'm going to tell Zeke I let his mother get shot."

After checking the vehicle for any explosive devices, Steven crawled behind the wheel and let the engine purr to life. He had to admit, at any other time, driving the big tanklike vehicle would have thrilled him, but he was worried about Zeke's reaction to the impending news. He knew Haley blamed herself for having to deliver it. "How did she get past you?"

"She took me by surprise. I had my back to her with my attention on what was going on outside the room and watching the door in case Richie got past you guys. She simply came up behind me and gave me a hard shove. I bounced off the wall and slipped to the floor. And out the door she went." She shook her head. "I haven't made a dumb rookie mistake like that in . . . forever."

"You had no reason to believe she would try to leave, did you?"

"I did at first. She was worried about Zeke, but I thought I had her convinced he was all right and that Laila would make sure nothing happened to him."

"She didn't come out because she was worried about Zeke. She was worried about Richie's hostage."

"And you."

"It's not your fault."

She shot him a tight smile, then glanced back out the window.

"My brother died when he was twelve," Steven said. "I was eighteen."

Her head whipped around. "What?"

"For a long time I blamed myself, but time has allowed me to come to the conclusion that there wasn't anything I could have done to prevent it. It doesn't lessen the hurt, of course, and the guilt still manages to creep up on me. But in my head, if not my heart, I know it wasn't my fault."

"What happened?"

"We were out riding our bikes. I was eighteen and supposed to be watching out for him." He gave a little shrug. "We grew up in a middle-class neighborhood with sidewalks that led out to the main road. We were riding down to the corner drugstore when a man lost control of his Suburban, going an estimated eighty-seven miles per hour, and crashed into my brother." He took a deep breath. He'd seen it happen and couldn't do a thing about it. "That man blew a .15 on the Breathalyzer."

"Drunk."

"Plastered. My brother had gone ahead of me, daring me to a race."

"Just a boy being a boy," she whispered.

"But I used to think it should have been me."

"You still do, don't you?" she asked quietly.

He grimaced. "Sometimes. If I think about it too long." Which he made sure never to do.

"And the driver walked away?"

"With a broken wrist and twenty-five years in prison."

"I'm so sorry."

"I am too." He drew in a deep breath. "He's up for parole."

"Are you going to fight it?"

"With everything in me. He's a murderer. He's staying where he belongs."

Steven stopped talking, wondering why he'd confided that. It wasn't that he kept it a secret, he just didn't talk about it. Ever. But Richie's death and Belinda's getting shot wasn't her fault and he wanted her to feel better. If talking about Michael would help, he'd do it. That fact alone was something he was going to have to do some serious thinking about. It meant he cared about her.

"Why do you suppose God lets things like that happen?" Haley whispered.

"That's one question I don't ask. I just have to focus on the fact that God is perfect and sovereign in every way. And that in the end, he will serve justice to those who deserve it. It's my job just to believe that. And trust it." He fell quiet a moment. "Doesn't mean I have to like it, though."

He pulled into the parking lot of the teen center and pulled to a stop. With a glance around, Haley climbed from the Hummer and quickly made her way inside the glass doors. Steven walked in behind her and immediately his mood lightened. Teens were everywhere. Laughter, music, and sheer *fun* emanated from the place.

"Haley! Haley's here!" A young girl threw

herself at Haley and was caught up in a hug.

"Hey, Madison, how's the dance routine coming?"

"We are killing it. And guess what?"

"What?"

"Some rich dude that Donnalynn knows paid for us to leave a day early and come back two days late so we can tour New York and not just get there, perform, and leave. We're leaving early Friday morning instead of Saturday!" She grabbed Haley's hands and jumped up and down. "We get to see a play on Broadway! And go to the Statue of Liberty and see Times Square and . . . and . . . *everything.* And the school is letting us go and they got us a chartered bus to ride on that has a bathroom and every—"

"Madison, girl, let Haley get a word in." Michelle bustled over and gently took the girl by her shoulders and moved her out of the path. "She'll get back to you in a minute. I'd like to have a word with her."

"Madison?" The blasting music had stopped and a woman peered around the edge of the door that was obviously the dance studio. "Where'd you go? Come on, honey, we need to run through the number again."

Haley gave Madison another hug. "I want to hear all about it, but I need to talk to

Cupcake here, okay?"

"Oh sure. You're still coming with us, right? Even though we're leaving early?"

Haley hesitated. "I'm going to do my very best to be there."

Madison bit her lip, then a smile bloomed across her face. "You'll be there. I know you will. I need to get back to practice. See ya. Coming, Donnalynn." She darted away, her enthusiasm shimmering around her.

"All right, baby girl, what's wrong and who is this?" Michelle asked.

Steven was impressed by her ability to read body language and pick up on tension. Haley looked up at him. "This is Detective Steven Rothwell. He's . . . a friend. Steven, this is Michelle Cox, also known as Cupcake."

"Cupcake?"

"She loves them. And she wants to die in a vat of frosting."

Steven raised a brow and looked at the woman. "You want to die in a vat of frosting? Why?"

She patted his arm. "It's a long story, darlin'."

He shrugged. "Not a bad way to go when you think about it."

"I agree." She looked at Haley. "I like him. Now, what's going on, hon?"

"I need to talk to Zeke," Haley said. "Is he in the gym?"

"Zeke's working his magic with the little ones. They love him. That boy's got some mad basketball skills. Does he play with his high school?"

"I'm not sure," Haley murmured. "Might be a good thing to find out." She drew in a deep breath. "Speaking of a long story, I just came from the hospital. Zeke's mother was shot and is in critical condition. I came to take him to be there when she comes out of surgery."

Michelle gasped. "Oh no. I'll gather the others and we'll have a prayer for her. But you go get him now and take him over there."

"Thanks."

Haley truly didn't know how he was going to take the news of his mother, but she knew she didn't have a choice. She had to tell him.

Zeke ran over to her, sweat glistening on his forehead, his shirt rimmed with wet around his neck. "What's up? Is Micah okay?"

"Micah's all right for now. Zeke, your mother's been shot and —"

"Shot?" He stumbled and Steven grabbed

his upper arm to steady him.

"She's still alive," Haley hastened to reassure him, "she's just in surgery. I came to get you — you'll be there when she wakes up."

Zeke gripped his head with both hands and paced in a circle. "I don't believe this." He dropped his hands and spun to face her. "It was Richie, wasn't it? He shot her, right?"

"Yes." She'd spare him the details for now. "Come on and we'll take you to her."

"Thought you were going to keep her safe."

Haley winced. "I —"

"It wasn't Haley's fault," Steven said. "Richie had a hostage in the hallway. Your mother pushed around Haley to try and talk to him. The sniper got Richie and his gun went off, wounding your mother."

Of course Zeke would want to know who shot her. She sent Steven a grateful look.

Zeke swallowed hard and looked at the floor. "I'm ready."

Haley stood with Zeke while Steven checked the Hummer before nodding. "All clear." He held up her keys as she walked closer. "You want to drive?"

"No, you can."

She climbed in the passenger seat, fastened her belt, and shut her eyes. A headache was forming behind her eyes, her side ached with a renewed fervor, and now she had to drop Zeke at his mother's side and check on her grandfather. It was a fifteen-minute ride to the hospital. She rummaged in her purse and found the ibuprofen. She took two, then checked her phone. No messages. She sent a text to Maddy.

> Any news on my
> grandfather?

Maddy
Still the same

came the immediate response.

> What about Zeke's mother?

I checked on her ten minutes
ago. Still in surgery. Micah is
sleeping and Duncan is fine.

She told the guys the latest and heard Zeke sigh.

Her hands were tied for now. There was nothing else she could do at the moment. Haley leaned back against the headrest. The only way to keep the headache from blooming into a full-blown migraine was to shut her eyes until it eased. "Are you watching the mirrors?" she murmured to Steven.

"Yes."

"Is it okay if I close my eyes for the ride?"

"Of course. I'll be able to warn you if anything seems off. I've got you covered."

"Thanks."

She immediately slipped into a light doze, having trained her body years earlier to rest when she had to. Sometimes she could still do it. Sometimes not. Today she had no trouble doing so with Steven and Zeke's soft conversation flowing around her.

When the Hummer pulled to a stop, she opened her eyes and noted the time. He'd given her twenty-five minutes. She caught his gaze.

He smiled. "I got Zeke's permission. We called and his mom's still in surgery and will be there for a while. He and I agreed that a few extra minutes wasn't going to change anything."

True enough. "Thank you." Haley had to admit she felt refreshed. Much to her relief, the headache was almost gone.

He'd parked in the law enforcement spot close to the entrance. He climbed out of the Hummer while she scanned the area and saw nothing that worried her.

She checked her mental to-do list: (1) Get

Zeke to his mother's side. Or at least in the waiting room. (2) Ask Maddy for another update on her grandfather. (3) Find Hugh McCort and get answers about the money in his son's account. (4) Check on Duncan and see how he was feeling. (5) See if she might be one step closer to solving her own cold case.

[20]

Steven made sure Zeke was settled in the waiting room with Laila at his side. Her presence probably wasn't needed, but he wanted to be sure before they pulled her off of him. An officer was still on Micah's room, the crime scene cleanup crew still scrubbing up from the incident earlier. He checked in on Duncan and found the man sitting up in bed, looking much better than the last time he'd seen him. "Do you have a moment?"

Duncan waved a hand to the chair and Steven took it. "All I have are moments right now. What do you know?"

Steven decided he would fill the man in on what they'd learned about McCort. Christina had followed Haley to the post-op waiting room where he figured she would stay until her grandfather was out of surgery.

"We've learned a few things," Steven said.

"What's that?"

He explained about the money.

Duncan sat back with a wince. "Have you talked to McCort?"

"No, getting ready to do that in a few minutes. Haley's with him now, I believe."

"Will you talk to him, then come back and fill me in?"

"Of course."

Steven left and went to find Haley. He found her just where she said she'd be.

Sitting next to Hugh McCort. She caught his eye as his phone rang. He saw that it was his dad and answered the call. "Hi, Dad."

"Steven, is it a good time to talk?"

"Uh . . ." He looked over at Haley and saw her talking to Hugh. "Sure, Dad. What's up?"

"I need to tell you something, but I don't want you to tell your mother I told you."

Now his dad had his full attention. "All right. What is it?"

"Walter Phillips is up for parole."

"I know. Mom already told me."

He heard his father sigh. "Did she tell you anything else?"

"No. Like what?"

"Like the fact that she supports his release."

Steven froze. Then finally found his

tongue. "I'm sorry. I don't think I heard you right. Could you repeat that?"

"You heard me."

Steven found a chair away from the others and lowered himself onto it. Haley caught his eye and raised a brow, but Steven looked away. "How . . . why . . . what . . ." He stopped and pulled in a breath. "I don't understand. Is she having some sort of mental breakdown?"

His father laughed. Low and without humor. "No. When he was up for parole two years ago, the two of you fought hard to keep him behind bars."

"And we succeeded."

"Your mother has since had a change of heart."

Steven rubbed his eyes, his brain spinning. "She's been visiting him, hasn't she?"

"Yes. Once a week."

"Why?"

Haley whipped around to stare at him once more, and he realized he'd shouted the word.

He turned his back. "Why?" he asked again, more controlled this time.

"He asked . . . no begged . . . for her — our — forgiveness and she gave it."

"And what about you?"

"I'm . . . still working on it."

Steven couldn't believe it. He had to be in the throes of a nightmare. "Dad, he killed Michael."

"Son, he was a kid himself. Barely nineteen years old. Just a stupid kid," he whispered. "Doing stupid stuff nineteen-year-olds do."

"No, not all nineteen-year-olds. I never did that. You never did that."

His father fell silent, then he cleared his throat. "Yes, that's true. But . . . son, he made a horrible mistake. He went to prison at nineteen. He's been there for twelve years. Should he have to pay for a mistake for the rest of his life?"

Familiar rage rose up in him, clawing its way from his gut to his throat. Steven stood and paced to the window. He kept his voice low and even. "Killing Michael wasn't a mistake, Dad, it was murder. And I'll never forgive Walter Phillips as long as there's breath in my body." He wanted to hit something. No, he wanted to pound on Walter Phillips until the man was as bruised, bloody, and broken as his brother had been when Steven had raced to his side and held him, knowing it was too late for him to do anything. Too late for *anyone* to do anything.

His father hadn't responded to Steven's

heated vow.

"I've got to go, Dad. I'll talk to you later."

"All right, son. I understand."

He hung up and let his chin touch his chest as he gathered his anger and hate and tucked it back into the neat little box he'd kept it in for the past twelve years. Then he turned and walked over to slip into the chair beside Haley.

"Are you all right?" she asked in a low whisper.

"Yes." He paused for a beat. "No." Another pause. "It doesn't matter." He leaned forward and nodded to Hugh. "Any news?" he asked softly.

"No." Hugh shook his head and dropped his face into his hands.

Haley stared at him a moment longer but didn't push him. Steven was grateful for that. The waiting room held three other people. They sat on the opposite end, so their area was fairly private.

"Hugh," Haley said softly, "I need to ask you something."

The man looked up at her. "Of course."

"Did your son have anything to do with the murder of my family twenty-five years ago?"

The old man paled. Alarmingly so. "Why would you ask me that?"

305

"Because we've discovered a money trail that leads to him — and on to you," Steven said.

McCort shut his eyes. "Twenty-five years. I wondered when this moment would happen."

Steven saw Haley's eyes widen and anger flash. But she drew in a breath and fell silent. He figured she was choosing her words.

"So, he had something to do with their deaths?" she asked.

"Indirectly."

"What did he do?"

Hugh swallowed and looked away. Steven wanted to push him, but Haley sat statue still, just watching the man.

Steven shot Haley a look, but she didn't blink. Hugh met her eyes, then looked away again. "He never expected them to die." His shoulders rose and fell. He met her gaze once more. "You have to believe me. He never knew what they had planned."

"Please explain," Haley said, her voice soft. Lethal.

"About two weeks before the attack, my son came to me. He was living in Dublin at the time, but drove to see me. He arrived about midnight and spent the night. The next morning he explained that he was

306

heavy in debt to a bookie. Many thousands of pounds."

"The equivalent of twenty thousand dollars?"

He blanched. "That's the amount. I didn't have it, of course. I had a nice little savings account, but not that much." He paused as though gathering his thoughts. "My wife and I lived simple lives," he finally said. "She stayed home with Connor, our son, when he was a wee one and never went back to work. She didn't want to and I didn't see any reason why she should. So, I gave Connor what I could and told him to tell them that he would get them the rest a little later. I was just trying to buy him some time. Buy me some time so I could figure out what to do, how to get the rest of the money."

"Were they satisfied with that?"

Hugh let out a watery, humorless laugh. "Well, they didn't kill him, but they broke his arm and his nose, a few ribs, and knocked out three teeth. He was in the hospital in Dublin for a few days, and during that time I got a phone call from him saying he needed my help."

"Help with what?"

"He wanted me to leave the door open to the Burke castle because he had some friends who were going to rob the place.

Just take enough jewelry or whatnot to pay off his debt. The Burkes had insurance, he argued, they had plenty of money and would never miss it. And he could pay me back what I'd already given him."

"What did you say?"

"I refused. Flat-out refused. I loved my job, I loved that family. I'm an honorable man." Tears clouded his eyes, but he blinked and he shook his head. "He screamed at me. He said they were going to kill him if I didn't comply. He said they had someone at the hospital at that very moment ready to kill him. So I said I'd do it, but —"

"But?"

"But I couldn't. Once my son was released from the hospital, I went to Dublin, picked him up, and took him home."

"And?" Haley asked.

"And then I told him he needed to run. Run as far away as he possibly could and start over. I even offered to purchase him a plane ticket to anywhere he wanted to go."

"And he agreed?"

"That he did. To my face. But apparently, they not only wiped his debt clean but paid him another $20K on his assurances that the door would be open."

"Then there was no turning back for him," Haley murmured.

"To be sure. There was no turning back. I later figured out that he had stolen my keys, made an impression of them, then returned them to my dresser. I never knew. But he left the day before the attack. He'd called a cab and just disappeared. I thought he'd taken my advice and run."

"But he hadn't?" Steven asked.

Hugh pressed his fingers against his eyes. "Here's where things get a bit fuzzy for me. He left in a cab and I'm not exactly sure what happened after that. I've pieced it together as best I can. The only thing that makes sense is that he dropped the key off to whoever he owed the money to. I didn't hear from him until after the murders. He just showed up in our kitchen, weeping and muttering about being responsible for the Burke family's deaths." He rubbed a shaking hand down his wrinkled cheek. "I can't tell you how I felt when I heard about it. I insisted that he go straight to the Gardaí, that he turn himself in. I said I'd go with him, help him confess what he'd done." He swallowed and swiped a tear that had trickled onto his cheek. "What I'd done," he whispered.

"What had you done?"

"I'd kept silent. I didn't warn them, but I thought . . . I really thought he had run. I thought it was just all . . . *talk.* That he was just desperate, that once I told him I wouldn't help him rob the family, he'd decide to run. And then the next thing I know . . . they're dead and he's weeping on my kitchen floor." He rubbed a hand across his eyes. "I wanted to confess to the Gardaí that I was guilty. As guilty as if I'd carried a gun myself. Connor said he would go confess the next morning. When I woke the next day, he was gone."

"Where?"

"I thought he'd run away. I thought . . ." He rubbed his head. "I thought a lot of things, but they were all wrong. My son had gone to his home. He'd committed suicide two days after the attack. At least it looked like suicide. There was no note, nothing. My wife —" He choked up and his throat worked before he could gather control to speak once again.

Steven glanced at Haley. Her blank face told him nothing of what was going on behind her green eyes. "Go on," she said.

"My wife was inconsolable. Connor was our only child. She was worried about him because he hadn't answered our calls and drove to Dublin to see if he was all right. He'd hung himself in his closet and she found him. She had to be sedated for weeks, and even after she was weaned from the drugs, she wasn't right. She kept looking for him to come home."

"To your home?"

"Yes. 'Twas like she'd put the entire thing out of her mind and he was just off somewhere working. By the time I could even get myself together to think straight, the investigation had come to a halt. The authorities blamed it on the mafia, who appeared to have a score to settle with Ian, and I . . . just . . . never told them what I knew. Instead I dedicated my life to taking care of my wife and Ian, doing my best to make up for something that can never be made up for." He swallowed. "I saved his life, so I did," he whispered.

Haley shifted, her hands clasped tightly in front of her. Steven wondered if it was so she wouldn't strangle the old man. If only he'd said something . . .

"When someone later tried to kill him?" Haley asked.

" 'Twas a couple of weeks after the funerals. He was at the office. He didn't like to drive, so I chauffeured him everywhere most of the time. He said he was ready to leave and I went to get the car. When I went around to open the door for him, I caught a glimpse of someone on the roof across the street. A wink of the sun off something. Maybe it was my military training, maybe it was just paranoia after everything, but I shoved him in the car, slammed the door, and hit the ground just as the bullet plowed into the space where Ian had been standing."

Haley stood and paced away from them, then back. She stood in front of Hugh. "You saved him and I'm glad, but that doesn't bring them back. If you had only told my grandfather —"

Hugh shook his head. A lone tear coursed down his cheek. "I know. I think about them every day. I see them in my dreams, begging me to turn myself in, to do the right thing. I can't live with this anymore." He shuddered. "I'll tell Ian as soon as he wakes."

"If he wakes," Haley murmured.

"True. If he wakes." He looked at her. "Do you hate me?"

Haley bit her lip and Steven squeezed her hand. She rubbed her eyes with her free hand, then dropped it to her lap. "I think you miscalculated and that miscalculation, that lapse in judgment, had extreme consequences that you couldn't foresee. Then again, if you'd spoken up immediately after the deaths, you may have been taken into custody and not had the opportunity to save him. Who knows?" She looked away for a long minute, then sighed. "But no," she said softly. "I don't hate you."

She didn't, she really didn't hate him, but the anguish ran deep. Even if he hadn't believed his son would actually do anything, if only he'd told someone what Connor had said, threatened —

But no. She knew what it was like to make a stupid decision and have it blow up in your face. And have someone, several some-ones, die because of it.

Christina stood at the door watching them. Haley caught her eye and shook her head. She nodded and turned her attention back to the hall while Haley kept looping the conversation with Hugh through her mind.

She wished he'd done things differently, but he hadn't, and what happened had hap-pened. She couldn't change the past, but what she knew could possibly change her future. Haley sat and watched the minutes tick past. Hugh leaned his head back and dozed. The fact that she'd said she didn't hate him seemed to free him of something.

She rose and paced, then she sat and checked her email. She requested an update about Gerald Forsythe and got nothing more than she already knew. She walked over to the desk to check in on Belinda, then paced back to the chair next to Steven and dropped into it.

"How is she?" he asked.

"She's through surgery and is in post-op ICU. She's in critical condition — the bullet punctured a lung and did some other damage. The fact that it happened here in the hospital with no wait time for an ambulance saved her. She's got a good medical team and she's fighting."

"Her last words were for us to take care of her boys. She thought she was going to die."

They fell silent for a moment, then Haley sighed. "She's made some rotten mistakes, but she learned from them. She was trying to do better. Zeke told me she was doing online school. She wants to become a nurse." She drew in a breath and ran a hand through her hair. "Have you checked on Carter James?"

"I have. My mother's been keeping in touch with his wife and texted as we walked into the waiting room. He's improving and his wife hasn't left his side."

"They set him up."

"What?"

"Whoever carjacked him. They didn't want him found for a while. Why?"

Steven gave a slow nod. "Because they didn't want us to know the man in the trunk wasn't him until it didn't matter anymore if we knew or not."

"He's taunting me. He doesn't want me to find out what really happened twenty-five years ago. He wants to guilt me into letting it go." She rubbed her eyes. "And maybe I should."

"No, you shouldn't."

"Too many innocent people have been hurt already. Carter James, Duncan —"

"You."

She lifted a shoulder in small shrug. "I don't want anyone else to get hurt."

"But you sure don't want him to get away with killing Gerald Forsythe or shooting Duncan. So what's the alternative?"

"There isn't one." She closed her eyes for a moment. When she opened them, she focused on the far wall. "Carter James was convenient, an easy target. That's the only reason they picked him. And they needed a rich man's fancy car to make the dead body in the trunk look like all the other incidents. They took the keys and parked the car in a poor area."

"Just like the others so they could go

about with their intended agenda without raising any red flags."

"Yeah. Targeting me," she said. "But they didn't have to kill someone to do that. So why Forsythe? They obviously didn't want anyone identifying him for a while." She pursed her lips and stood, hands on her hips. "Unless . . ."

"Unless?"

"The text said Forsythe was dead because of me." Sorrow pierced her, but it wasn't her fault. Mentally, she knew that. She just hated that an innocent man had gotten caught up in whatever deadly game this killer was intent on playing.

"So, what's the connection?"

"It's suddenly obvious and I feel rather like an idiot for not seeing it sooner."

"What do you mean?"

"Okay, everything started going wonky when Duncan began looking for me, right?"

"Apparently."

"Do you remember that he said he hired someone to find me here in the States, and once he got word that I was found, he told the guy not to contact me, but instead hopped a plane and took over following me?"

"Right."

"So, who was the guy he hired?"

"You think he was Forsythe, the guy in the trunk?"

"It's plausible, don't you think? I mean, I get a text from some anonymous person telling me who the man is and that it's my fault he's dead. It's the only possible connection I can think of."

"They needed to kill Gerald Forsythe because he'd found you and they didn't want him telling you." Steven stroked a hand across his jaw. A nice firm jaw that showed strength and character.

Haley blinked at her thoughts. Now was not the time to notice anything about him, but sometimes random thoughts happened as though protecting the brain from what it didn't want to think about.

"I think you're probably on to something," Steven said. "If it's him, he left the car at the airport for Duncan."

She straightened. "So where did he go after he left the airport?"

"And who did he go with?"

"You think there's some security footage at the airport?" she asked. Renewed energy perked her up.

"I think we need to find out." Steven texted Quinn and asked him to look into it. Then he looked at Haley. "Want to go find

Duncan and ask him about Gerald Forsythe?"

She hesitated and glanced at the lightly snoring Irish man beside her. "You think he'll leave or run or . . . anything?" she asked softly.

"No, but I can't guarantee it, of course."

"He thought it was just crazy talk. He thought his son was just desperate and wouldn't act on his words."

"Yes." Steven tilted his head and studied the man who was oblivious to the conversation. "He's lived a quarter of a century blaming himself for keeping quiet. He could have prevented their deaths and . . . he didn't."

"He didn't know. At least I don't think he did. I'm not sure if he truly didn't know or not. He may have thought his son would steal, but . . ." She stopped, a deep sadness invading her.

"What can I do to help you?" he whispered.

She looked into his eyes and the compassion there nearly undid her. She wanted to embrace what she read there. Wished she could just let him hold her and be her shelter from it all right now. But she couldn't. "His remorse is genuine and the regret he feels, the guilt and self-recrimination . . . it's all there."

"What do you think your grandfather is going to say?"

"I . . ." She shrugged. "I couldn't even begin to guess." She paused. "Then again maybe I can. He'll probably feel betrayed and betrayal is a hard thing to get past."

[21]

Steven left the waiting room and made his way back to Duncan O'Brien's. Haley decided she'd better stay with McCort. And besides, she'd said, she didn't want to leave and take a chance on missing the doctor when he came out to talk to the family. Namely her. So he'd left her texting someone at the teen center about the trip that had been moved up to Friday.

Steven flashed his ID to the officer still on the door, then knocked.

"Come in."

He pushed the door open and stepped inside.

Duncan still looked pale, but his eyes were bright. "Back already?" He frowned. "Is Mr. Burke all right?"

"He hasn't woken up yet, but I'm assuming he's still all right." He settled in the chair next to Duncan so the man didn't have to strain his neck looking up at him. "I have a question for you."

"Of course."

"What was the name of the man you hired to find Haley?"

"Gerald Forsythe, my cousin. He's a police officer."

Steven blew out a low breath. "I see. When was the last time you heard from him?"

"Shortly before I arrived. We arranged for him to leave the rental car at the airport for me. I wired him the final payment and that was it. Why?"

"I'm sorry to tell you this, but he's dead."

Duncan blanched. "What?"

"I'm really sorry."

"Oh, it can't be so." He raised a hand and covered his eyes for a brief moment. "He has a family."

"They've been notified."

"Tell me what happened."

Steven did, then waited a few more minutes to let the man process the news. "Are you going to be all right?" he finally asked. "I want to get back to Haley."

"I'll be all right. I prefer to be alone right now anyway." He cleared his throat. "Ye'll let me know how Mr. Burke is?"

"Absolutely. And . . . again, I'm really sorry about your cousin."

"Thank you."

Steven left and made his way back to the waiting area, where he found Haley and McCort speaking with the doctor. Haley glanced at him and shook her head. Steven's heart sank. Had he died? He stepped closer. "We'll keep him comfortable, but if he has any other family, you should notify them."

"Of course," Haley whispered.

Hugh simply looked stunned, his face a mask of harsh regret. "It can't be so," he said. "There's no hope he'll wake up?"

"It's possible he'll wake up and surprise us all," the doctor said. "As far as I can see, everything looks fine with his brain despite the tumor. The tumor itself looks very small and will need to be biopsied at some point if he wishes to do so."

"So the tumor caused his seizure?"

"Yes, that's what it looks like."

Haley planted her hands on her hips. "Doctor, what's wrong with him? Why won't he wake up?"

He drew in a breath and spread his hands. "I'm not sure, to be honest. His vitals are good, but he's not responding to stimuli. Let's just watch him for a while."

"So he's in a coma?"

The doctor hesitated. "I'm not sure I'd call it a coma. Yet. Let's just give him some time and see what happens. Of course, at his age —"

"Of course," Hugh murmured. "You really think I should call the family?"

"I would, just to be on the cautious side. Like I said, at his age, you never know."

Haley turned to Hugh. "You know who to contact, of course?"

"I do."

"Then I'll leave that to you."

Steven shook his head. What had happened in the last few days? How had he become embroiled in such a mess? A mess he had no intention of letting Haley go through alone. He watched her struggle to contain her emotions and process the news.

And how had he come to care about her so much in such a short period of time?

It didn't matter. They'd been through some intense times together. Times that had brought them closer than the average dinner-and-a-movie date would have.

While Hugh got on his phone, swiping a stray tear in the process, Steven pulled Haley to the side. "Forsythe is the man Duncan hired to track you down. They were cousins."

She didn't even blink. "All right then, at least that's one question answered. And we know the people you're after haven't struck again."

"No, but it's getting close to the time that they will." He raked a hand over his head. "We'll worry about that in a bit."

"What's next on your agenda?"

"I need to check on Zeke's mother, then figure out a way to catch the killers before they strike again."

Katie appeared in the doorway and Haley waved her over. She approached, her eyes roving. They settled on Hugh McCort, then bounced back to her. "How is everything?"

"Interesting. I'm ready for boring."

Katie slid into the chair beside her. "I talked to Quinn. The bullets from the man in the trunk and the one they dug out of Carter James match."

"I figured they would," Haley murmured. "Has Quinn been able to talk to Carter?"

Katie shook her head. "They're keeping him sedated for now. He has quite a bit of swelling on his brain."

Hugh cleared his throat and Steven raised a brow at the man. He tucked his phone into his pocket. "The family is on the way."

"Who?" Haley asked.

"Not all of them, of course, but five of them you'll get to meet."

Haley's half-stunned, half-panicked expression tugged at him. Steven reached out and closed his hand around hers. He figured she was feeling a bit shell-shocked at the fact that she was going to meet her family in a few hours.

"I'm supposed to be getting on a bus to New York in a few days." He released her hand and she sank into the chair. "What do I do? I can't leave and I can't *not* leave."

"You don't have to worry about that yet. Let's give your grandfather some time to wake up."

She gave a slow nod. "You're right." She stood and rubbed her palms down her jeans. "I want to see him."

Haley's brain spun and she paused at the door to her grandfather's room. Members of her family were coming in from Ireland. And she would meet them all. *Overwhelmed* didn't come close to describing the emotion running through her. There was also a mixture of excitement and curiosity.

Her grandfather lay still in the ICU bed. She walked to his bedside while a nurse typed something into the computer. "How is he?" Haley asked.

"It's hard to say. He's the same as before, really. He just needs to wake up."

Haley reached for his hand and curled her fingers around his. "Hi, Daideo," she whispered.

His fingers flexed and Haley jumped. "He just squeezed my hand."

The nurse turned and pulled the stethoscope from around her neck to insert the ends into her ears. She listened to his chest, then straightened. "It's possible it was just a muscle spasm." She glanced at the heart monitor. "His heart rate is up a bit, though. Keep talking to him. He might be able to hear you."

Haley kept her grip on the man's hand. "Daideo, I need you to wake up. Maybe it's selfish, but I'm not ready for you to go on to heaven. I just met you and I want to get to know you more." This time her words produced no response. "I have something I really need to talk to you about too." She sighed. "Anyway, apparently our entire family is on the way to see you and I'll admit, I'm a wee bit nervous."

Still no response. She reached behind her to pull the chair next to his bed and sat down. Still holding his hand, she rested her head on the mattress and closed her eyes.

Haley had no idea how long she slept, but the sun climbing into the sky and peeking through the blinds awakened her. She looked into her grandfather's face and was disappointed to see that he appeared the same as he had last night.

"Haley?"

She turned to see Steven in the doorway. "Hey."

"You okay?"

"I think so. What did I miss?"

"Nothing too exciting, thank goodness. It's been quiet."

"Have you been here the whole time?"

He shook his head. "I went to the office, then home and got a shower, talked to my dad a bit, and came back about thirty minutes ago."

"Did you tell Quinn about McCort?"

"I did."

She stretched gently, wincing at the pull of the stitches still in her side. "How's it healing?"

"It's fine. It only hurts when I move wrong. Which includes stretching. How's Hugh?"

Steven settled into the window seat. "Still beating himself up. He's very sad."

"I expect so."

"Why don't you hate him? He could have stopped the murder of your family if he had just said something to your grandfather or the police."

"Hold that thought." She rubbed her eyes and stood to walk to the sink. One glance in the mirror had her regretting that she'd looked. She grimaced and rinsed her mouth, then drank her fill from the sink. Haley pulled the hair tie from the ponytail and ran her fingers through her hair. Once she had the ponytail redone, she felt halfway human again. "Want to walk down to the cafeteria? I'm starving."

"Sure."

She walked out of the room and Steven followed her. Once they were seated at the table with food in front of them and, most importantly, coffee, she took a swig of the dark liquid and let out a little sigh. "Okay. In answer to your question, I don't hate him because I can't. I've come to realize that we're all human, Steven. We make mistakes, we have moments of bad judgment, but it doesn't mean we're evil people. It just means —" she tilted her head and offered a slight shrug — "we're human."

"So you're okay with him keeping his mouth shut?"

"Of course not," she snapped. Then took a deep breath. How did she explain? "Do I wish he'd made a different choice? Of course I do. But he didn't. Sometimes you know the right thing to do, but you hold off doing it out of fear or with the thought that you're protecting someone — or something. Whatever the reason, you don't act and someone gets hurt — or dies because of it."

"Who died on your watch?" he asked softly. "What mistake did you make?"

She flinched, glanced at the clock, and then back to her half-eaten breakfast. She pushed it away, not hungry anymore. "When I was with G2, I found out another operative was going to retire. He was tired of the game, but he was determined to finish his last assignment. I tried to talk him out of it because I knew there was something wrong with him. He insisted he was fine. He told me to back off, pushed past me, and said he had to catch a bus home. I reminded him that he'd driven to the office. That morning, we'd spoken and walked into the building together. He froze, got on the elevator, and went down to the parking garage. I followed him a few minutes later and found him wandering the garage looking for his car."

"Dementia?" Steven asked softly.

"Sudden-onset Alzheimer's. But I didn't know that until later. He admitted he was stressed out and some things going on at home had him not thinking clearly. I found his car for him and he drove off. Still not feeling right about the whole thing, I searched his office."

"Whoa."

She rubbed her eyes and drew in a deep breath. "I know it sounds awful, but I worked with him. Lives depended on him being able to do the job. If there was something going on that would hinder his abilities, I needed to know it. Anyway, I found a medical file and it had his diagnosis in it. I took the file, went to his home, and confronted him. He was furious and even took a swing at me. Once he calmed down, I told him I was going to let our handler know that he wasn't fit for duty. He broke down, made me promise not to say anything. He also promised to go to our supervisor first thing the next morning and tell him himself. I said he could have until then, but if I found out he didn't go, I would."

"What happened?"

"He left that night on a mission. I went to my supervisor immediately, but by then it was too late. The team was dead," she whispered. "All of them."

"Haley, I'm so sorry."

"I wasn't on that mission because I'd requested three days of leave."

He winced.

"I was furious with him —" She waved a hand as though in dismissal. "I was blazing mad at Brendan for being so stupid as to put everyone at risk and getting them killed because he *forgot* what he was supposed to do — and overwhelmed with guilt that I hadn't said something to my supervisor immediately. I hated myself for a long time, but I had to finally realize that hate is a very destructive emotion and I want it to have no place in my heart." She drew in a deep breath. "So, no, I can't hate Hugh for doing something so similar to what I myself have done. He's human, he made a tragic mistake, and he wishes desperately he'd made a different choice. I get that. I feel that to this day. But no one can change what happened and hating him doesn't hurt him, it just hurts me."

"What if he wasn't sorry? What if he didn't care that he'd caused their deaths. Would you hate him then?"

She hesitated. "I don't know. It's hard to say what I would or wouldn't feel. I know what I would hope my reaction would be, but . . ." She shrugged. "I can't say. I *can* tell you this. My ex-boyfriend didn't care that he hurt me, that what he did was wrong. He used me and laughed about it — even bragged about it around the office to his buddies. Hating him felt good at first. It consumed me. I wanted revenge, to destroy him and his career. And I was close to doing it simply because I could."

"But you didn't."

"No."

"What stopped you?"

"The thought of who I would become if I did it. The truth is, he's a good operative, he's just a lousy person. I saw the signs but ignored them because I wanted something in my life besides work, so I have only myself to blame for that. But when it was all over, I realized I never really loved him. I loved that he was in the same business as I and we could talk about our jobs and not have secrets from each other." She gave a wry smile. "Turns out he was keeping secrets anyway." She gave a slight shrug. "So I had to let it go. It wasn't easy. It was definitely a daily thing and sometimes an hourly thing, but eventually, it got easier. And then one day I realized that I had truly released the hate and he had no more power over me. No kind of hold over me at all. I don't really know how to explain it. It was like the heart that had held so much hate and anger and bitterness had been removed and a new one had taken its place." She gave a soft chuckle at his skeptical expression. "I know it's hard to take in. I can only credit God with it. Without his help, I'd still have a heart full of hate."

[22]

Steven stepped out of the room, her words battering his soul like a canoe caught in a hurricane. *Betrayal is a hard thing to get past.* She'd spoken those words in reference to her grandfather and Hugh, but she might have been talking about him. He felt betrayed by the people who were supposed to be the most trustworthy, the ones who would fight for justice for Michael, not let his killer go.

With these thoughts in mind, by the time Haley had finished speaking, he'd felt bruised and raw. He battled with the hate he'd yet to let go of for the man who'd killed his brother, and wished he was as strong as Haley.

On impulse, he called his mother. He'd ask her what she thought she was doing, demand she stop visiting that man in prison, and leave well enough alone. Her phone went to voice mail and he left her a message to call him when she could. The door opened and he turned. Haley walked out and let the door shut behind her.

"What next?" he asked.

"I want to go see Belinda and Micah. Then I need to decide if I'm going on the trip on Friday." She rubbed a hand across her face and the fatigue etched there struck him.

"Come here."

"What?"

He grasped her upper arm and pulled her to him in a hug. She held herself tense against him for a moment. He raised his hands to her shoulders to massage them and the tension slowly lessened. She rested her head on his chest for another long moment, then drew in a deep breath. "Thanks."

"You're welcome. Are you ready to see Belinda?"

She lifted her head and met his gaze. He wished he knew what she was thinking, but her eyes were shuttered, her thoughts her own. "I think so."

"All right then, come on."

She stepped away from him. Reluctantly, he thought. He instantly missed the feel of her in his arms and vowed it wouldn't be the last time he held her.

Christina stepped up next to them and

Steven felt his face flush. He supposed she'd witnessed that moment. Then he decided he didn't care.

Together, the three of them walked down the hall to the elevator and made their way to Belinda's room. The nurse was just leaving, shutting the door behind her.

"How is she?" Haley asked.

"She's holding her own. She's awake, but very weak."

"Is it all right if we speak to her?"

She hesitated. "I think so. Just don't stay long."

"Of course."

"I'll stay out here," Christina said.

"Thanks."

Steven held the door for Haley and she slipped past him and into the room. She walked to the bed and looked down at the woman who'd sacrificed herself so Richie wouldn't kill an innocent person. Or people. Zeke and Laila were nowhere to be found. Steven assumed Laila had taken him down to the cafeteria or to get some air.

Haley took Belinda's hand in hers and the woman's eyes flickered open.

"Hi," Haley said.

"Hi," Belinda whispered.

Steven hung back. The two women had bonded over Belinda's children, and he was just in the way at the moment.

"I hear you're going to be okay," Haley said.

"Yeah, that's what they tell me. How are my boys?"

"They're fine for now."

"Micah? He's still . . ."

"Yeah. He is."

Belinda drew in a breath and grimaced. "Hurts to breathe."

Haley frowned. "Let me get a doctor."

"No. Not yet." She swallowed and closed her eyes.

Steven slipped out the door and located a nurse. "Belinda's in pain. Can you do something for her?"

The young man nodded. "Let me check her chart and see what she's ordered."

"Thanks."

Haley leaned in and stared at the wounded woman. "What did you say?"

"I want you to take my boys. If I die."

"You're not going to die." Haley ran a shaky hand over her ponytail. She wasn't sure she could promise to do as Belinda had requested. "You just need some time to heal."

Belinda closed her eyes and a tear leaked down her cheek. "Haley, you're a good woman. I can't think of anyone who would have bought Micah's medicine for him. But you did." She squeezed Haley's hand — or Haley thought she tried to. Her strength was fading.

"Just rest now, Belinda. I promised not to tire you out."

"No." She opened her eyes. "I need to know someone's watching out for them."

Haley hesitated. "What about your family?"

She shook her head, restless and agitated. "No. Parents are dead. One brother who's a drug addict. There's no one. Promise me you'll take care of them."

Haley squeezed her hand. "That's a promise I can make. I will definitely make sure they're taken care of. But you're going to be fine."

They sat in silence for a few moments with Haley still holding her hand. "I believe in God, you know," Belinda said, "and Jesus. I believe what the Bible says."

"I do too."

"I haven't been very good at living it, but I've asked his forgiveness for everything I've done wrong."

"Then you're forgiven."

She coughed and grimaced. "By his grace, yes, I believe it. My mother always said that being poor is no excuse for being dumb. I've been dumb." She drew in a labored breath and Haley frowned in concern.

Haley rose. "Let me get the doctor."

"In a minute." Another harsh breath. "My purse. There's an envelope. Get it."

"Now?"

"Yes, please."

Haley moved to do as she asked, but pressed the call button to bring medical personnel. She didn't like the way Belinda looked or sounded. Haley rummaged through the old brown bag and found a crisp new envelope. She held it up. "This?"

"Yes. I just wish I could do everything all over."

"We all have regrets, Belinda. I don't know anyone who goes through life without them. It's part of being human."

"Maybe so. But I have one thing left that I can do. I love my sons very much. I would have given up long before now if I didn't have them. I love them so much." She fell silent again as though she needed the break to regain her strength.

"I can tell, so no talk of giving up, okay? They love you very much too, and they need you."

Belinda's eyes remained closed and Haley wondered if she'd fallen asleep. The heart monitor blipped consistently, but her oxygen levels seemed to be dropping. Haley started to rise to get the doctor, as she uttered a prayer for her new friend.

Steven stepped back into the room and caught her eye. "The nurse is checking with the doc."

"Good, I called for someone as well."

Almost before she finished her sentence the door opened again and the doctor, followed by the nurse, entered. Belinda lay still and pale. Haley stood to get out of the way, but Belinda's hand tightened around hers.

"The doctor is here to check you out," Haley told her. "I'm just going to step outside."

Her eyes opened and locked on Haley's. "Give him my heart," she wheezed.

Haley froze and looked at Steven, then the doctor to make sure she'd heard right. "What did you say?"

"Make them. Give Micah. My heart." Her eyes closed and her grip loosened.

The doctor shoved Haley out of the way and she stumbled back into Steven's arms. "Belinda?"

"Haley," she rasped, her voice pained and breathless. "Promise me."

The doctor's orders flew past her ears, but

she caught the words "blood clot in her lung."

"I promise, Belinda. I promise."

The woman's eyes opened and locked onto Haley's and then closed, her dark lashes fluttering against her cheeks.

Soon the room filled with medical personnel and Haley and Steven were ushered out into the hall.

Haley gripped Steven's hand. "She can't die." Steven's arms closed around her and she buried her face in his chest. "I promise," she whispered. "I promise."

[23]

"We did all we could, it just wasn't . . . enough. I'm so sorry for your loss."

The words echoed in Steven's mind as he stared at the floor. Just like his brother, Belinda was gone. Her boys were orphans. Zeke was slumped into the chair next to Haley. He hadn't let go of her hand since the doctor had appeared in the hallway and announced Belinda's death.

Christina and Laila stood to the side, sipping coffee and talking in low voices.

Katie, Olivia, and Maddy stepped off the elevator and made their way over to her. Haley stood and the three friends wrapped her in a group hug.

"So sorry," Katie said. She moved to Zeke and squeezed his bicep. "I'm sorry for you too, Zeke."

He nodded, but kept his eyes downcast. "If he wasn't dead, I'd kill him."

Steven knelt in front of the teen, who

lifted his eyes and met Steven's gaze. The dark hatred in his eyes pierced him, but he understood it all too well. "There are others just like him out there."

"What do you mean?"

"Just what I said. Guys like Richie are one reason I became a cop."

"What are the other reasons?"

"A drunk driver killed my brother. I vowed to get as many drunks off the road as I could. To keep other people from having to go through the pain that my family went through."

Zeke's eyes widened. "Oh. I'm sorry."

"Yeah, I am too."

He felt Haley's hand rest on his shoulder and give it a slight squeeze. Appreciation for her support rocked him. He cleared his throat.

"Richie is just one of many thugs out there," he said. "Dangerous and deadly to innocent people. We need good officers fighting to get them off the streets and away from people like you and Micah and your mother. And we need people fighting to keep them behind bars."

Zeke frowned. "You saying I should become a cop?"

"I'm saying you should think about it. Every woman you save from a Richie will be in honor of your mother. Every drunk I get off the streets is in honor of my brother. And it does help heal the hate." Or it had. Shame gripped him, but he kept his expression encouraging. After the conversation with his father, a fresh serving of hate had just filled his heart to the very top and he wasn't sure how he was going to purge himself of it.

Zeke swallowed and looked away.

The doctor appeared in the waiting room once more. "Excuse me. Are you Micah Hampton's family?"

Haley stepped forward and lifted her chin. "We are."

"We need you to sign some paperwork. He's getting a new heart."

"My mom's?" Zeke whispered. Haley had told Zeke of his mother's pleading last words. Even in her pain, her desperation to save her child — her children — had been her priority.

The doctor turned kind eyes on the teen. "Yeah, son, your mom's." He turned his attention to Haley. "I need proof that you have the legal right to represent Micah."

Haley blew out a short breath and swiped the tears on her cheeks. She reached into her back pocket and pulled out an envelope. "It's right here. Belinda had a will, believe it or not. It's even signed by her lawyer and a witness. For some reason she felt led to give me guardianship of her boys the day after she met me." She cleared her throat and looked around. "I guess we know why now."

The doctor gave a slow nod. "Then let's get the paperwork done and get this boy his new heart."

He left and Haley slumped into the chair.

Maddy sat beside her. "What are you going to do about this weekend?"

"I don't know. My grandfather is still in ICU in a coma and his family —"

"Your family too."

"Yes," she said slowly. "My family too — that's going to take some getting used to — is coming in." She rose and paced, then looked at each of her friends and coworkers. "But I promised I'd go on this trip."

Olivia frowned. "This is kind of an extreme circumstance, though. I would think they'd understand if you had to back out."

"Yes. Of course they would, but I don't want to." She pressed her fingers against her eyes. "No. I have to figure out how I can be on that bus when it pulls out Friday morning. That's two days away. Hopefully things will be much different between now and then."

■ ■ ■ ■

He hadn't forgotten her; he'd simply been biding his time, waiting and watching. The killer reached into his pocket and felt the reassuring presence of his weapon. Ready to use it when he had the chance. She was just hard to get to.

With her practically living at the hospital, his options for how to take her out were limited. Not to mention the fact that she was constantly surrounded by people. Professionals, if his judgment hadn't failed him.

So, he was just going to have to get creative in how to complete his assignment.

He let go of the gun and flipped the page of the magazine as he listened to the conversation behind him. The doctor had just told her that her friend was dead. *What a shame. Not.*

He continued to listen and began to plan once more. The possibility of collateral damage had never stopped him before. And it sure wouldn't now.

With Haley surrounded by her friends and coworkers, Steven left the hospital and checked in with his mother on the way to the precinct. When she didn't answer, he called his aunt Sadie. "Hello?"

"Hey, I was just looking for Mom. Is she with you?"

"She had an errand to run. I'm here with your dad."

"Is he all right?"

"Seems to be doing pretty well today. I got him to eat a piece of chicken and some mashed potatoes, so I consider that progress."

"Where'd she go?"

"I . . . uh . . . she went to visit someone."

Sadie's hesitation sparked his curiosity. "And who would that be?"

"Someone who she decided needed her help."

Steven huffed in exasperation. "Aunt Sadie, why are you being so evasive?"

"Oh dear. I think your father needs his tea refilled. I'll get your mother to call you when she gets home. Love you, dear."

And then she hung up.

Steven scowled at the device as though his aunt could see his expression. She was at the prison. He knew it as well as he knew he wanted to hit something. Deciding to talk to his mother as soon as he could, he made his way to his desk and found Quinn pacing in front of it. "Hey."

"Hey."

"What's going on?"

"This case. We think we might have a connection on the rich guys getting killed and stuffed in their trunks."

Steven sat in his chair and booted up his laptop. "What's that?"

"All of the victims were in the same area of downtown right before they were killed. Different restaurants, a hotel, but all within a three-mile radius."

"Interesting."

Quinn checked his phone, then pushed it aside. "Exactly. And it looks like they all disappeared on a Friday night, but were killed on a Saturday."

Steven studied the whiteboard attached to the easel where Quinn had laid out the timeline. "The houses were all broken into on Saturdays just after midnight. Guess that would technically be Sunday, but you know what I mean." He frowned. "But wait a minute. This one." He jabbed the picture of the second victim. "He wasn't downtown."

"Actually, he was. We'd discounted them having the downtown thing in common because we didn't think he'd been there the night he was snatched. But apparently he'd picked up a client at the hotel and spent about an hour there before leaving."

"How'd you figure that out?"

"His wife said her best friend mentioned seeing him. She called me because she thought it might be important."

"And we're just now learning this? Why didn't the best friend come forward with this when you were investigating his death three months ago?"

Quinn cleared his throat. "Apparently, she hesitated to because she thought he was having an affair."

"Was he?"

"I don't know. That's not my concern. What I care about is we've got him in the same area as the others — discounting Carter James."

"Yeah, but he's not a victim of these guys," Steven said. "He's got his own killer."

"Exactly."

Steven rubbed a hand down his face. "It's about time for these guys to hit again, isn't it?"

"That's what I was thinking."

"So, we need to set up a sting."

Quinn's eyes gleamed. "That's why you're almost as good a partner as Bree. We're going to set it up for this Friday night — and every Friday night thereafter until we get them."

"It's a long shot."

Quinn sent him a thin smile. "Not with the car that I'm going to be driving."

[24]

Thursday evening, Haley stood outside her grandfather's room and watched the family walk toward her. She braced herself. She'd done her research. She knew who they were and what they looked like. If they were going to be visiting her grandfather, she was going to know everything about them she could. After all, someone had tried to kill him and that someone was possibly still out there. Christina and Maddy had insisted on securing the floor. Haley knew they were there, along with several other friends, but would stay out of sight, letting Christina be the only one visible — which hopefully wouldn't come across as protection. Instead, she would be a friend, nothing more. Which she appreciated. The security allowed her to focus on the people who'd just arrived at the hospital.

She'd admit she was anxious to meet them. All her life she'd wanted a family. The homeless people on the street had been her family for as long as she could remember, but secretly she'd wanted someone who had the same blood running through her veins. Haley knew it was silly. She and Olivia had discussed the fact that family was made up of those who loved you, not your blood type. She got that, she really did, but the insecurity of not belonging to anyone was still there. The five people walking toward her had known each other all their lives. She was the new girl. Would she be accepted or would she be the odd person out once again?

"Guess it's time to find out."

"What's that?" Christina asked, walking up beside her.

Haley shook her head. "Nothing."

"They look friendly enough, if concerned."

"I understand — and agree with — the concern," Haley murmured. "Let's hope you're right about the friendly."

From their pictures, she recognized each one immediately. The older woman, Haley's aunt Janet Burke, spotted her first. Her eyes widened and she stopped. Janet's husband, Kane, broke away from the group and hurried toward her. He wrapped her in a hug. "Aileen."

"It's Haley, Dad," the young man next to him corrected.

The older man drew back and she saw some of her grandfather in him. His eyes, especially. "Right. Haley." He spoke to his son, but his eyes never left hers. "Thank you for the reminder, Lachlan." He gave her a smile that seemed genuine. "This is my son, Lachlan."

Lachlan cleared his throat. "When Hugh called us, we were stunned."

She noticed he didn't say thrilled, or glad to meet her, just that it was shocking news. But she'd give them the benefit of the doubt for now. "Thank you."

Lachlan eyed her. "I guess we're cousins of a sort."

Haley turned her attention to him. He was about her age, with dark hair and green eyes. He was good-looking and knew it, she decided. There was a certain arrogance in his face, a shuttered look to his eyes that she couldn't read.

He shrugged. "Welcome to the family, I suppose I should say." He motioned to the man behind him. "This is our uncle Peter. His wife, Ciara, didn't come, and beside him is my wife, Maeve."

"Pleased to meet you, Maeve. Peter."

They were eyeing her. Summing her up,

she was sure. As well as questioning her grandfather's sanity?

Probably.

"My father, Niall, couldn't come," her uncle Kane said. "He's having some health issues, but he sends his love and prayers to Ian."

"I'm Janet. How is Ian?" Janet seemed to have recovered from her initial shock in seeing Haley and her warm voice expressed her concern for Haley's grandfather.

"He's still in a coma," Haley said. "There's been no real change, but sometimes I think he hears me when I talk to him." She noticed Janet eyeing Christina. "This is my friend, Christina. She's been a big support through everything."

After appropriate nods and quick smiles, Kane clasped his hands together. "Can we see him?"

"Of course, but you'll have to go in just a few at a time, I believe."

"Fine. Janet and I'll go in, then we'll let the others have a turn."

"The waiting room is outside the double doors at the end of the hall," she told the others.

Kane took his wife's hand and together they slipped inside his uncle's room. Haley watched the rest of the family walk toward the waiting room.

Christina planted herself outside the door, her stance alert and protective. "A bit reserved, but that's to be expected. At least they were outwardly friendly."

"At least." Haley took a deep breath and followed her uncle and aunt into her grandfather's room.

Just as she shut the door, her phone buzzed. A text from Madison, the teen from the center.

I'm so excited about tomorrow!!!!! I don't want to bother you, but I wanted to tell you how much I appreciate all you do for us at the center!! You keep saying how much God loves us in spite of our circumstances . . . well, I just want to tell you I believe you because God put you in our lives. I've been thinking a lot and you said God always keeps his promises and so do you. I didn't think anyone kept their promises or were worth believing in, but you've changed my mind!! So . . . thanks. See you in the morning!!!! P.S. Sorry for the long text, but I just wanted to tell you that. I love you, Haley!!!!!!

Haley wanted to burst into tears. Instead she simply closed her eyes for a brief moment to collect her runaway emotions. Yes, she'd keep her promise. *Please let me keep my promise, God.*

The knock on the door brought her head around. Steven stepped inside. Her heart pounded her happiness at his presence.

"Hey," he said softly.

"Hey." She stood to the side and he walked over to place a hand on her shoulder. She made the introductions and the three of them shook hands.

Kane frowned. "I hope he wakes up soon. We have business to take care of."

"Kane!" His wife stared at him, her appalled expression matching Haley's feelings exactly. But she kept her mouth shut as she figured his wife would take care of him.

He snapped his lips shut, then grimaced. "Sorry, I didn't mean that how it sounded."

"Of course you didn't," Haley said. Janet pulled him from the room and Haley glanced at Steven with a raised brow. "Huh."

"Yeah."

She touched her grandfather's hand. "I'll

be back, Daideo."

His fingers twitched, then lay still. She waited to see if he would do anything more, but after several minutes passed with no more movement, she moved toward the door. Steven followed her out and they came face-to-face with Lachlan and Maeve.

"We wanted to see him," Maeve said. "Is it all right?"

Haley hesitated, feeling strangely protective of the man she'd only known existed for a few days. But these were his family and they'd come a long way to see him. That had to count for something, right? "Of course." She looked at Steven. "I'll be there in a minute."

"Don't let us keep you," Lachlan said.

"You're not keeping me." But she wasn't leaving him alone with her grandfather. Someone had tried to kill him twenty-five years ago, and while she may share blood with these people, she didn't know them. Lachlan raised a brow. His wife frowned at her but said nothing as she stepped through the door Haley held open for her. Her gaze snagged Christina's and the woman gave her a small nod.

Haley hung back while the two of them stood at his bedside and talked to him briefly. Maeve touched his hand and leaned over to whisper something in his ear. Then she turned and walked from the room.

Lachlan turned to her. "Who are you really?" he asked softly.

Haley blinked. "What?"

"Oh, you've done your homework, I'll give you that, but no one really believes you're Aileen, you know."

Haley had wondered what they'd truly thought about her and Ian's claim that she was his granddaughter. Now she knew. "So you've come en masse to make sure that I'm not swindling your great uncle?"

"Something like that."

"He found me."

"So he explained in his letter."

"What letter?"

"The one he left, letting us know that he was off to South Carolina to get his granddaughter and bring her home so that she could take her rightful place in Burke's Shipping."

"I see. Well, he did say something to that effect."

Lachlan looked back at the man in the bed. "So what did you do to him?"

Haley blinked. "I did nothing. He has a tumor. It's not very big, but apparently it's been there for some time."

"And it just now decided to make its presence known?" He scoffed and turned to her. "He's a good man. He's loved me like my own grandfather — more than my own. Uncle Ian had time for me when Grandfather didn't. If I find you had anything to do with him winding up in this bed, I'll make you pay, you understand?"

He loved him and was hurting to see him like this. Haley relaxed her guard a fraction. "Sure, Lachlan, I understand. I mean him no harm, I promise you."

"Your promises mean nothing to me. I'm watching you."

He swept from the room and Haley let out a breath. *Wow.*

Micah's surgery was over and declared a success. Steven shook his head. It was hard to believe that kind of surgery took only about four hours. Micah's had been done in four and a half. He was in recovery and Zeke was there with him, waiting for him to wake up. Laila continued to update them via texts.

Steven tried to remember the last time he'd spent so much time in a hospital waiting room and couldn't come up with it. He had permission from his captain to continue the investigation into the shooting that had wounded Haley and placed Duncan in the hospital. Carter James was expected to be able to talk soon, and Steven wanted to be there when he woke up.

He had his laptop and could work, so that's what he did. He'd taken it upon himself to find out everything he could about each one of Haley's family members. He and Maddy sat side by side at the table in the waiting room and worked. She was in touch with one of the legal attachés in Dublin, and together they were getting the background they needed on each person.

Haley slid into the chair beside him. "Anything?"

"One thing strikes me as interesting," Maddy said.

"What's that?"

"Ian's brother, Niall, is in hospice. He's not expected to live much longer."

"What? Ian didn't tell me that," Haley said. "Someone — Kane — mentioned Niall had his own health issues, but nothing about the fact that he was dying."

"So don't you find it interesting that practically his entire family left his side to come to Ian's?"

Haley rubbed her eyes. "That's just weird. Isn't it? And somehow wrong?"

"Niall's wife, Darcy, is with him." Maddy shot her a tense smile. "I called hospice to see who was there. And the nurse told me there was a sister, Bridgett, who was staying with him and Darcy almost round the clock."

"So what are the rest of them doing here? I mean, I can see one or two coming, but all of them? Especially Kane . . . that's his *father.* Ian is his uncle."

"Who knows, when it comes to family dynamics," Steven said.

Haley blew out a breath and rose to pace. "I leave tomorrow." She shook her head and dropped her chin to her chest. "I can't leave tomorrow. I'm going to have to break my promise, and for as long as I can remember, I've never broken a promise."

"They'll understand, Haley," Steven said.

Maddy nodded her agreement.

"They'll understand, but they'll be disappointed." She pursed her lips. "I'll see them off on their trip. It's probably better that way. Whoever tried to kill me has been awfully quiet. I don't want to risk him taking a shot at me with a bunch of kids on the bus." She ran a hand through her hair. "I could drive separately. Or fly in and meet them."

"What day is the performance?" Steven asked.

"Sunday afternoon."

"Then that's what you should do. Fly in,

watch the performance, then fly back."

Her forehead cleared. "Exactly. I can do that." She grabbed her phone. "Let me tell Michelle and Donnalynn about the change in plans."

She stepped into a quiet corner and made her call. Steven watched her, wishing he could do something to ease her worry, make things easier for her.

"Are you going to ask her out?"

Steven lifted a brow at Maddy. "Is it that obvious?"

"To me."

He turned his eyes back to Haley. "Think she'd go out with me?"

"Probably. Especially if you have a bag of M&Ms with you."

"I can arrange that."

The minutes ticked past. Steven heard Haley on the phone with Michelle, and Hugh sat talking to Ian's family on the other end of the waiting room. The older man's face looked strained, and Steven wondered if he was telling them about his son's part in the deaths of their family members. He hoped not. Now probably wasn't the time to mention it.

Maddy looked back at her computer and let out a low whistle. "Well, that's interesting."

"What?"

"Lachlan and Maeve Burke have been in the States for the past two weeks."

"Really?" Haley stepped to look over Maddy's shoulder.

Steven crowded in as well.

"Got a hit when I checked their passports. They went through security in Atlanta."

"What are they doing here in the States?" Steven asked.

"Probably something work related," Haley said. "I guess that explains why he and his wife would come on to South Carolina when he got word about his uncle."

"True," Steven said. "I'd like to ask him, though."

Haley stood. "Come on. I'll introduce you and you can ask some questions."

She crossed the floor to where the family sat.

Steven followed so he could listen in.

Lachlan stopped talking midsentence and looked up her. "What is it? Is there more news?"

"No, nothing," Haley said. "I just had a question for you." She introduced Steven as law enforcement.

"All right."

Steven cleared his throat. "We found out that you and Maeve have been in the States

362

for the past two weeks. What were you doing here?"

He frowned. "You're spying on us?"

"It's all part of the investigation," Steven said.

"What investigation?"

He gave them the short version, watching their faces. They all appeared genuinely stunned. "So, when this information turned up, we thought we'd ask. That's all."

The man's forehead cleared slightly. "I've been here on business," he said, confirming Haley's guess. "Maeve decided to come with me. When Hugh called and told me about Ian, we came right away and picked up the others at the airport."

Easy enough to confirm.

"What kind of business?" Steven asked.

Lachlan cleared his throat. "I'm sure you know we're in shipping. We have a lot of business with companies here in the States. I was closing a deal with a company that deals in airplane parts. Some of the parts are too big to fly in, so they ship them. I wanted them to use Burke's Shipping and they agreed to do so. I was walking out of the meeting when I got Hugh's call."

Haley seemed satisfied with the answers. Steven wasn't so sure. All this time, Lachlan was in the US. He made a mental note to send a text to Quinn and ask him to check the man's story. As well as his phone records. "So, you know Ian was looking for Haley?"

Lachlan stilled, glanced at Haley, then back to Steven. "Yes. He said so in the letter. And I knew he'd hired someone to find her. I . . . saw the invoice from someone named Gerald Forsythe for car rental reimbursement and for 'investigative services' into Aileen Burke." He used air quotes as he said the words. "I asked Hugh about it and he told me while swearing me to secrecy."

"And did you share that information with anyone else?" Haley asked.

"Of course not. I mean, just my father. He said he didn't know anything either but told me not to worry about it, that it was just —"

"Just what?"

"Just Uncle Ian being delusional, that he'd never gotten over — or rather accepted — his family's death. I kind of forgot about it after that. Until I got the call to come to the hospital."

Steven noticed the rest of the family members remained silent and allowed Lachlan to be the spokesperson. His wife, Maeve, sat beside him, her perfume wafting his way every time she shifted. She was a very pretty woman, he decided, but she held herself aloof. He didn't know if that was because she was just stuck up or because she was an introvert. Only time would tell. Kane and Janet held hands and she rested her head against his arm, listening.

Haley stood. "Thanks for the information."

Steven took his cue from her and they headed back to rejoin Maddy at the table. "Did you get your trip worked out with the kids?" he asked Haley.

"Yes, I think so. This is better. If whoever is after me decides to strike again, then the kids won't be in danger." She rubbed her temples. "I guess if I have to break a promise to protect someone's life, then I can live with it."

"That's a good perspective." He looked across the room again at the family and frowned. Were they concerned about the sick man in the hospital bed? Or the fortune that would be doled out upon his death?

[25]

Early Friday morning, Haley and Christina stayed a good distance back from the idling bus and watched the students load onto it one by one. Haley's heart lay heavy with the fact that she wasn't going with them, but pride swelled. They were great kids, talented kids, and they'd do well. And she'd be there on Sunday to watch them perform. She waited until the bus pulled away and then climbed back into her Hummer.

Christina slipped into the passenger seat. "Are you okay?" she asked.

Haley nodded. "I'm okay as long as the kids are okay."

She patted Haley's shoulder. "I think they're okay. Are we headed back to the hospital?"

"We are." Haley cranked the car and turned in the direction that would take them there. "I probably should start paying rent, I'm there so much."

"How's Micah doing?"

"I saw him last night. He's doing great."

"Does he know about his mom?"

"No," Haley said. "Not yet. Zeke didn't want to tell him until he was a little stronger."

Christina picked at nonexistent lint on her khakis. "So . . . uh . . . I mean I know it's none of my business, but are you going to keep them? The boys?"

Haley shot her new friend and coworker a glance before checking the mirrors and the road in front of her. "I don't know," she said softly. "I haven't had time to think or process a lot of things going on in my life right now."

"No one would blame you if you didn't."

"I know. And for what it's worth, I don't really care what other people think. I'll make the decision based on what's best for them. And me."

"Of course."

Haley drove in silence for the next few minutes. Then cleared her throat. "What would you do if it was you?"

Christina let out a low laugh. "My situation is totally different from yours." She shook her head. "I don't know. My parents were fostering kids from the time I was ten. They still take in some occasionally. I'm single with no real attachments to anyone or any place." She sighed. "It's easy for me to say I'd take them in, but if I was really faced with your decision?" She shrugged. "Truthfully, I don't know that I'd want to be tied down like that. Then again, it would be nice to have someone else in the house besides just me." She rolled her eyes. "That sounds pathetic, doesn't it?"

Haley laughed. "No, I understand, to be sure." She turned into the hospital parking lot and made her way to the area reserved for the police. She placed the card on her dash, glanced around the area, then climbed out when nothing set off her internal alarms. There'd been no attempts on her life over the last two days. In her opinion, that was good news and bad news. Good news that she wasn't dodging bullets. Bad news in the sense that she knew the person who wanted her dead hadn't gone away.

So what was he up to and when would he strike again?

The killer noted that Haley had not gotten on the bus like she was supposed to do. He was only slightly frustrated, as he'd planned for the possibility that she might choose not to ride with the teens. However, he *had* thought she might follow in her car and had planned accordingly. Unfortunately, she wasn't going to do that either. He grunted. She was scared that her presence would put her precious teenagers in jeopardy.

His phone rang and he grimaced when he saw the number. "What?"

"Is it done?"

"It will be by the end of the day."

"I need her alive."

The killer stopped. "What?"

"Circumstances have changed. I need her alive. Don't kill her yet."

"My price is still the same."

The person on the other end swore. "That's fine. You can kill her eventually. I just need something from her before you do it."

The bus rolled away. "What did you have in mind?"

The killer listened to the plan and rolled his eyes. Unbelievable. It was a horrible plan. But the money was amazing. He'd make it work. He hung up.

"So, we'll go with plan B," he murmured. He thought about it and decided he could work with what he already had in motion. Just a few slight tweaks and all would be well. Haley would be dead, and he'd have his money and a nice cottage in the Caribbean. Finally. Never in his career as an assassin had he had so much trouble eliminating a target. Well, his strategy was about to change. Instead of going to his target, he was going to convince the target to come to him.

Steven sat in his office and stared at the screen of the laptop. He'd just come back from the hospital after attempting to talk to Carter James. The man had gotten so upset they'd had to sedate him, so Steven had texted Haley that he'd be in his office.

He wanted to sit down and really do some digging into her family. Steven didn't want to believe they were bloodthirsty gold diggers, but he had to check. He'd requested the case file from the Gardaí and it had finally landed in his inbox. He opened the pictures of the crime scene and started going through them.

A paper airplane landed on his keyboard. He looked up to find Quinn staring at him with one raised brow. "Earth to Steven."

He blinked at his partner. "What?"

"I've been saying your name for the last ten minutes."

"Oh. Sorry. I've been reading."

"No kidding."

Steven steepled his fingers in front of him and rested his chin on his thumbs. "What do you need?"

"Your help in the sting tonight."

"Of course. What time?"

"Five o'clock. As near as we can calculate, these guys disappear around eight, but I'm willing to bet that they're watched first."

"I'll be there."

"How's your dad?"

"He seems to be doing okay right now. He goes back to the doctor in about a week."

"Good." Quinn shook his head. "No luck with Carter James, huh?"

"Nope. We'll have to try again later."

"What's up with Haley's family?" His partner leaned forward and placed his elbows on the desk. "*Are* they her family?"

"Looks like it."

"So, she's an heiress, huh?"

"Um. I guess."

Quinn smirked. "So, you think she'll go back to Ireland and don her tiara?"

"Why don't you suggest that she do that?" Steven couldn't believe he actually got that question out with a straight face.

Quinn looked horrified at the thought. "No way. She's got a mean right hook."

"I bet she does." Steven fell quiet. "Hey, you mind if I ask you something?"

"Sure."

He'd already asked Maddy her opinion, now he'd see what Quinn had to say. "You've known Haley a while now. What kind of guy does she go for?"

Quinn raised a brow. "Why? You interested?"

"Maybe."

"Let's put it this way. If she were to go out with you, then I'd know what kind of guy she'd go for."

Steven stared at him.

Quinn shrugged. "I've never heard of her going out on a date for as long as I've known her. She doesn't trust men when it comes to the romance department."

"Or she doesn't trust herself," Steven murmured.

"What?"

"Nothing."

"What is it that you like about her? Besides her looks and sunny disposition?"

Steven recognized sarcasm when he heard it. He let it roll over him. "She's smart. She cares about others more than she does herself. She has a good heart."

"No. She has a new one."

He'd posed as a road construction crew member and flagged the bus down barely fifteen minutes into the trip. When the driver had stopped, he'd approached the bus, his yellow hard hat pulled low. The driver had opened the door and the guy had shot him, pulled him out of the seat, and thrown him onto the floor. "That's to show you I'm serious. Sit down and shut up."

Screams echoed through the bus, only to fall silent when he stood at the front of the bus and waved the gun. "You move, you die, understand?" He knocked the hard hat from his head and handed it to Donnalynn. "Collect the phones. All of them."

Donnalynn rose to do as he demanded. Michelle took a chance and slipped hers into the pocket of the seat in front of her. As Donnalynn moved from seat to seat, Michelle felt a slight pull on her seat back and Madison whispered in her ear. "What are we going to do, Cupcake?"

"We're going to sit and wait. When he gets what he wants, he'll let us go." Michelle spoke but couldn't stop the slight tremble in her voice.

After Donnalynn handed him the hat and he set it on the floor without counting the phones, Michelle let out a small breath of thanks.

"Now, I'm going to drive a little ways and if you know what's good for you, you'll stay seated. Anyone stands up, I'll shoot. Nod if you understand."

Nods all around.

"Now place your hands on the seat in front of you and don't move them. And do not try to talk to me. I'm not interested in hearing what you have to say."

No one had argued. Or talked.

When they stopped, they all waited in tomb-like silence. He allowed them to eat and to drink and to take turns using the restroom at the back of the bus, but as soon as they finished, they were ordered to place their hands on the headrest of the seat in front of them. And there they sat. He didn't talk, he didn't move.

When the sun began its slide down past the trees, he started the bus. From the dirt road where he'd parked them hours earlier, he drove, taking them past mounds of stone, dirt, and mulch. Michelle looked into the rearview mirror, and his eyes met hers with cold indifference. Chills pebbled into goose bumps. She glanced out the window, her mind spinning prayer after prayer to the only One who could help them now. The bus turned and hit an old gate, pushing it open. Metal scraped against metal as they went through.

Michelle didn't know what his plans were or why he was attacking them, but she knew they needed help. It was time to take a chance, because she had a feeling time was running out for them. The last person she'd talked to had been Haley. Without taking her eyes from the man, she slid her hand into the pocket of the seat in front of her and pulled out her phone. With a trembling thumb, she swiped across the bottom of the screen, then held it to the home button. She flicked a glance down, then back up.

The bus jerked to a stop and he stood.

"The bus is running. You will be comfortable. You don't have to worry about suffocating. The exhaust will be pumped out. Now it's time to take a short nap."

Their attacker pulled a can from his pocket.

And it was leaking.

Panic swirled in her chest.

He was going to gas them. *Oh Lord, help us!*

He pulled a gas mask over his face and looked at her. "When you wake up, do not try to escape. The doors are rigged with bombs. Do you understand? Nod if you do." His voice sounded odd, but she could hear him.

The gas filled the bus quickly and Michelle felt her arms growing weak, her eyes closing. She thought she managed to nod just before she leaned into the window. She let her eyes close and held her breath, desperate for a few more seconds of consciousness.

She peeked at the screen and hit the green button.

He left, shutting the doors behind him.

She heard Haley's voice. Her lungs strained. "Haley . . . we've been kidnapped. Help." And then blackness.

The morning had given way to the afternoon and the afternoon to the evening sooner than Haley would have liked. She'd spent the time getting to know her new family and holding Micah's hand for most of the day. He didn't understand why his mother hadn't been in to see him, and the doctors still didn't want him to know about her death. Not just yet.

She'd been sitting with Micah when her friend Nathan had texted her to let her know he was sick with the flu and wouldn't be able to make it to care for the horses for a few days.

She and Christina had arrived at Haley's home about an hour ago. "Thanks for helping," Haley said as she finished mucking out another stall. She shut the door, then moved to the next one.

Christina looked up from unwrapping the hose. "Of course. Two makes the work go faster."

Haley led Comet from his stall and tied his lead rope to the hook on the wall of the barn.

"Where did you learn to take care of horses?" Haley asked her.

"I ride every once in a while. My brother has a barn in Kentucky. When I visit him and his family, we always go out on a trail ride with my niece and nephew."

"Is that where you're from? Kentucky?"

"I'm an Army brat. I'm from all over."

Haley's phone buzzed and she pulled it from the back pocket of her shorts. "Hello?"

"Haley . . ."

"Cupcake, good to hear from you. Are you all almost there?"

". . . been . . . help . . ."

"Michelle? You're breaking up." The call dropped and Haley dialed the number back. It went straight to voice mail. "Cupcake, call me back. I couldn't understand what you were saying." She hung up and stuck the phone back in her pocket. She frowned.

"What's wrong?"

"I don't know. That was Michelle. One of the trip chaperones. I mean, I think it was her. She must be in an area with a really bad signal."

Haley stroked the brush down Comet's side while Christina held the hose over the bucket in the stall. She filled it to the top, then set the hose aside, swiped the sweat off her forehead with the back of her wrist, and placed her hands on her hips. "You think they're okay?"

"I don't know. I heard the word 'help.' It makes me nervous." She dialed Madison's number. It went straight to voice mail. She tried a few more and got the same response. "I don't like it."

"Let's try tracking her number."

Haley dialed Steven's number and got no answer. Then she tried Quinn's. "Hello?"

"Hey, I need you to see if you can get a location on a phone for me."

"Sure. What's wrong?"

"I don't know. I'm hoping nothing."

"Hold on, I'm almost to my desk." She heard rustling and then the click of the keyboard keys.

"You still there?" she asked.

"Yeah, it's going to be a long night. Steven and I have a sting set up to see if we can catch our killers in action. All right, give me the number."

Haley did.

More keys clicking. "I'm not getting a

location. She's off the grid."

Haley's stomach tightened. "Try this one." She gave him Donnalynn's number.

"Same thing," he said.

"Something's wrong." They tried five more numbers with the same results and Haley's panic level shot up. "Something's not right, Quinn."

"Well, we're not able to track them through their phones."

"What about the bus? Track the bus."

"Give me the name of the company."

She did and Quinn said, "Hold on."

Haley bit her lip. *God, keep them safe, please.*

"What are you thinking?" Christina asked.

"That I need to find them. I want to ride the route they took. See if we can see them. Find out why we can't reach them."

"And I said track the bus, now!" Haley flinched at Quinn's bellow. "If I have to come down there, I'm going to arrest someone, understand? This is an emergency."

Somehow that's how Quinn got results, so she didn't chastise him about catching more flies with honey.

He came back to her. "They're getting it." His voice faded again as he spoke into the other phone. "Yeah? Yeah. Okay. That's what I needed to know . . . Haley?"

"Yes."

"They said the GPS was disabled. There's no way to track it."

"I'm going to drive the route."

"I'm on the way."

"No, I'll let you know if I need backup. Right now, it could be nothing. Christina's with me."

"I don't like it. I'm going to send an officer to go with you."

"Fine, but they'll have to catch up to me."

"Haley —"

"Gotta go, Quinn." She hung up and turned to Christina. "Let's go."

They checked the Hummer and found it clean. The two of them climbed in and Haley cranked the powerful vehicle. She pulled out and headed down the drive, waving to the police officer sitting at the entrance to her property. He waved back and stayed put. His orders were to make sure no one set foot near Haley's house whether she was home or not. Haley didn't bother to ask him to follow her. She wanted him there in case Hugh or someone decided to come to her house. She sure didn't want anyone walking in on a killer.

Haley headed for I-20. Christina was texting and letting the others in the agency know what was going on and what they were doing.

"Maddy agreed with Quinn and thought you should wait for some backup."

"I don't know if we even need backup for anything. This is just a scouting mission."

"All right," Christina said, "messages sent." She paused. "You know this could be a trap, right?"

"The thought occurred to me."

"Okay, just checking." A short pause. "Because right now, it's just you and me."

"And the officer on the way." Haley blew out a low breath. "Do you want me to let you out?"

"No way. This is my job and I don't mind doing it. I was just pointing that out."

"Thank you. We'll be careful." Her phone buzzed. "Take a look at that, will you?"

"Sure. It's a text from someone named Madison."

"Madison? She's one of the teens. What does it say?"

Christina lifted her eyes to Haley's, then back to the phone.

I have them. I will kill them.
Come alone. Come now. You
have fifteen minutes to get
here. If you're not here at the

appointed time, they die. If you
have anyone with you, they
die. If I see any cops, they die.
If you text or call anyone, they
die. I've hacked your phone,
I'll know. It's very simple.

Haley swerved to the side of the road.
"Fifteen minutes. What time is it?"

"7:15."

"Okay. It's time for you to go."

"There are pictures." Christina held the
phone out so Haley could see.

Solemn, scared faces in a dark bus stared
back at her. She swiped. Another picture.
This time of the door of the bus wired shut
with what looked like a bomb attached. And
the last picture was of the emergency exit.
Another bomb. Her heart pounded. "I've
got to go. Get out."

"I'll lie down in the back."

"He'll check. Get out now. Track my
phone. Track the GPS on my car, but get
out."

"He'll kill you if you go alone."

The vivid image of him coldly firing three
shots into her bed flashed. "He'll kill *them*
if I don't. I'm running out of time. Now
go!"

Christina gave Haley's phone back to her,

then pulled her own phone from the clip on her belt. "He doesn't know you're with anyone. You can use my phone to communicate." She laid her phone on the center console.

"Perfect. Thanks."

Christina slipped out of the car and slammed the door. Haley responded.

> I'm on my way, but I don't know where I'm going.

Yes you do. Just follow the signs. And tell your friend to get back in the car and to throw her phone out the window. Now! Thirteen minutes.

> What signs?

12 minutes. Tell her to get back in the car.

He could see them. He was watching. But how? Haley scanned her dash, the area around the mirrors. No cameras. That meant he was watching from a distance. She rolled her window down. "Christina, come back!" The woman turned and Haley motioned her back. While Christina was quickly retracing her steps, Haley slid Christina's phone off the console and sent a group text to Steven and Quinn.

911. Help. I-20 toward NY.
Bus rigged to explode.

She snapped a picture of her phone's screen with the three photos and hit send. She was surprised her fingers cooperated, but her adrenaline was flowing, her mind sharp, and her fury boiling. She was taking a chance that he could see what she was doing, but she had to do something.

The passenger door opened and Christina looked in. "What?"

"He knows you're with me, get in."

Christina climbed in.

Her phone buzzed again.

The clock is ticking. Throw her
phone out.

"Throw your phone out the window."

Christina grimaced but did so.

Haley put the Hummer in drive. "He said to follow the signs, but I don't know what signs."

"It's close by. He gave you fifteen minutes."

384

Haley glanced at her phone. "Which is now ten minutes." Her fingers flexed on the wheel. "Follow the signs," she muttered. Her eyes landed on the orange and black detour sign just ahead. She took the exit ramp, praying she was right.

[26]

Sluggish but awake, Michelle shuddered as the events played through her memory. She wanted to sink back into the blessed oblivion, but she had kids to take care of. She pressed a hand to her head. It pounded with a fierce throb, but she ignored it as she took in the situation and did her best not to panic. The bright interior lights reflected on the windows, showing only a dark red hue beyond them. The attacker was gone and the bus was still. But they had light until the battery died — or they ran out of gas.

Her phone said they'd been out for about an hour.

She looked over the silent, scared kids who'd woken one by one to discover their situation, then back at the driver who had yet to open his eyes. She leaned over, placed her fingers over his wrist, and felt his pulse beating steady if a bit slow. "I need to get this bleeding stopped or this man is going to die," she said.

"What do you need me to do?" Donna-lynn asked.

"I need something to tie around his chest to hold this shirt in place." Fortunately, instead of putting their suitcases under the bus, they'd just put them in the empty seats. Michelle had dug into hers and found the white T-shirt she was using to hold over the man's wound.

Donnalynn stood. "I have just the thing. They're in my suitcase."

"He said there was a bomb," Madison said.

"I know what he said, baby. There are two bombs. One on each door. We can't do anything about that, but we can pray, so get to it, okay?"

"Okay," the girl whispered. "But I'm scared. And my head hurts."

"Mine does too. Why don't you look in my purse and get some ibuprofen?"

"Okay." Madison didn't move. "What does he want?"

"What?"

"You said that once he got what he wants, he'll let us go. What does he want? And who can give it to him?"

"I don't know. For now, we're pretty comfortable, we have a bathroom, and we have food." But a lot of that food was under the bus. She hoped they wouldn't be there long enough to need it.

"Here," Donnalynn said. She pressed a soft cloth into Michelle's hand.

Michelle looked at what she held. "Compression stockings? Perfect."

"Well, I knew we were going to be doing a lot of walking, so I threw them in."

"Here, help me tie this around him." Together, they worked and got the makeshift bandage in place. The stockings did the job. Michelle sat back and wiped the sweat off her face. "Whew." She slid into the seat opposite Donnalynn. "He's still alive. Let's pray he stays that way until we can get him help."

"I'm scared. I want out of here."

"Madison, shut up," Terry Lee said. "We been kidnapped." He looked at Michelle. "And we need to figure out how we going to get out of here. Ain't no one riding in on a white horse to rescue us."

Three of the other teens stood in the aisle. "Yeah, Cupcake, Donnalynn. We've got to do something."

Michelle exchanged a glance with a terrified Donnalynn, then closed her eyes and prayed for guidance. What to do? She had to think and not give in to the fear clawing at her. She opened her eyes and looked more closely out the window. "It looks like we're wedged between two walls of red mud."

"It stinks too."

"That smells like mulch," Donnalynn said.

"I noticed that," Michelle said. She considered their limited options. There would be no breaking or opening the windows and climbing out. Even if they could get the windows open, she didn't know how far they were buried under whatever was surrounding the bus. The running bus.

The exhaust! It would kill them. For a moment, she froze. Then his words came back to her. He'd said it wouldn't. There must be some ventilation she couldn't see.

Only the door in front held black space beyond it, but she didn't dare try to open it. She could clearly see the bomb on it. The interior lights and the air were still on for now. But that would only last as long as the gasoline and the battery. She thought about the man who'd just thrown them into the middle of terror. He hadn't worn a mask. He didn't care that they saw his face. Which meant that once he got what he wanted, they would all die. So why worry about the exhaust backing up and killing them?

Because he was keeping them alive for a

reason. For now.

Steven set his soft drink on the bar and stood. They'd only been at this for a couple of hours and he was ready to give it up. He hoped Quinn had made some headway on their stakeout. Steven's personal problems were distracting and he couldn't afford to be distracted while trying to catch a killer.

Adding to his inability to focus was the fact that his phone had been buzzing all evening with texts from his mother, asking when they could talk and when he would be willing to visit the prison with her. Apparently, his father had confessed to his loose lips. He thought about ignoring the phone. If he didn't read it, he didn't have to acknowledge it. Instead, he groaned and pulled his phone from his pocket to check for any messages. Only to find he'd missed a call from Haley and texts from Christina. As he read the texts, he shot to his feet. Where was Quinn?

Quinn burst through the front door and Steven caught his eye. His partner waved him over in a gesture that said something was very wrong. He caught up to his partner. "You got the texts?"

"Yes."

"I'll drive." Steven held the door and the

two of them raced to his car.

Haley continued to follow the road off the exit until she came to another detour sign. He'd led her off the route sufficiently enough that the officer who had been trying to catch up with her wouldn't have any idea where to go. "Why would he take the chance that I wouldn't be able to find it?"

"Because he expects you will."

Haley continued to follow the detour signs, noticing several cars in front of her doing the same. "How can this be right?"

"Just keep going."

Haley's phone rang. She picked it up and saw Steven's number flashing at her. She didn't dare answer it. *He* would know.

She let it go to voice mail.

The phone immediately buzzed an incoming text. "What does it say?"

Christina looked.

Very good on not answering. You've bought yourself three more minutes. Hurry, they're six feet under right now and probably need you to bring a shovel.

Haley gritted her teeth. She hated flying

blind, so to speak. And then there were no more signs. She pulled to a stop.

What now?

She waited. No return text.

Hello?

"He's not answering me. He's talking in riddles and wants me to figure it out. Why not just tell me?" She pounded the steering wheel, frustration zipping through her. She now had four minutes.

"He doesn't want to take a chance that you'll be able to tip someone off as to where you are," Christina said.

The pictures of the kids and the bus flashed in her mind. "The bus was dark."

"They're in a building somewhere?"

She opened the pictures back up on her phone. Madison's teary eyes grabbed her heart. She was terrified. Haley was terrified for her. "Look at the windows. There's something on the outside. Looks like mud or dirt to me. What do you think?"

"Could be mud or dirt, sure."

Haley glanced around. "Do you see any mud?"

"No, but I see another sign."

392

"Where?"

She pointed. "There."

"Harry's Mud and Mulch?" *Six feet under and need a shovel?* "That works." Haley pulled away from the side of the road and headed straight for the place. She stopped at the gate and got out.

"Careful," Christina warned.

Haley planned on it, but a sense of urgency pushed her. She pulled her weapon and held it in front of her as she walked to the gates. "They're locked." The place had probably closed a few hours ago and was quiet as a graveyard. She shuddered at the analogy. "What now?" She was down to about a minute.

She started walking the fence.

Christina got back into the Hummer and followed her, keeping the vehicle between her and the road.

Haley walked all the way around until she was opposite the gate. She walked up to the back entrance and found the gate lock cut, part of it lying on the ground. She pushed against the gate and it swung inward.

Christina pulled up beside her.

Haley stepped inside the yard and took in the mounds of dirt, gravel, mulch, and sod. Piles of it everywhere. Two Bobcats to her left stood silent, just waiting for someone to crank them and put them to work. She glanced around and spotted no cameras, nothing to record whatever happened in the next few moments.

"I'm here!"

Christina shot her a perturbed look.

Haley ignored her. "I made it with —" she glanced at her watch — "three seconds to spare! Now where are you?" She pulled her weapon.

Christina did the same, staying in the vehicle with the window down. "I can always run him down," she murmured.

"Good idea. He's got to come out in the open first, though." She let her gaze bounce from area to area. "The six feet under and needing a shovel crack was a message. He buried them, Christina. We need to find a pile that's big enough to bury a bus — and do it in a hurry."

"This was way too easy to figure out," Christina said.

"Because like you said, he wanted me here but didn't want to take a chance on us letting someone know where we were going." She turned in a slow circle. "Hey! I'm here!"

She started walking again, looking for the bus, keeping an eye out for someone who might have a bead on her. Christina continued to drive, keeping one side of her covered. She did her best to keep the piles of mulch and other materials to her left. There were hills and valleys. So many places to hide a bus.

"Keep coming, Haley!"

She froze at the sound and listened but couldn't tell where the voice was coming from. "Why are you doing this?"

She kept her weapon ready as she covered the area, then walked forward, staying next to the Hummer, using it for protection. They rounded a corner and she saw a dark SUV parked to the side. She glanced at Christina. "You think it belongs to him?"

"Could. But he's not in it."

"No, he wouldn't be."

Her brain spun, seeking a way to save the kids and get this guy at the same time. Fear pounded through her — not the fear of dying, although she didn't want to, but the fear of failing. She kept it controlled, knowing she'd only get one chance, possibly only one shot. But he couldn't die until she knew where the bus was.

"Who are you?" she called out.

Something caught her eye. Something out of place. Sort of.

"Christina, look at that mound next to that embankment. About twenty yards in front of the SUV. Does that look different

395

than the others?"

"It does. Like it was shoved off the hill above it?"

"Exactly." She walked toward it.

"Or he did that on purpose to lead you in the wrong direction," Christina muttered.

"Maybe, but we need to find out."

Christina stayed with her.

Haley wanted to know who she and Christina were up against. Two against one could seem like pretty good odds, but he had a bus full of people held hostage that could be killed with the press of a button, so he had the upper hand. For now. "Come on, I'm here! Show yourself!"

He stood up from behind the protection of the SUV, a gun leveled at her. "Toss your weapon out where I can see it. If you hesitate, they will die."

Haley didn't even think about it. She knew this part had been coming. With only a slight wince, she gave her Sig Sauer a toss.

"Very nice. Now tell your friend to throw her weapon out of the passenger side window."

"Do it," Haley said.

"You don't have a weapon and I won't have one if I do this."

"Just do what he says. He'll kill them."

Christina blew out a breath, then rolled

the passenger window down. She removed the clip and tossed the gun. Haley heard it land with a thump.

"Good job. Now both of you, walk toward me."

Christina didn't move. Neither did Haley.

"Where's the bus?" Haley asked.

"Get in the car and I'll tell you."

"Tell me where they are first."

He stood with one hand behind his back, the other held the weapon in a rock-steady grip. "You want your friends to die? I said walk this way."

Her stomach clenched, but she held firm. "I want to know where the kids are. As soon as I know they're safe, I'll go anywhere you want me to, cooperate fully."

Christina stayed quiet while Haley talked.

He pulled his other hand from behind his back and Haley noted the small device tucked beneath his fingers.

A detonator switch?

"Get in the car," he said.

"Why?"

"We're not having a discussion. Get in the car or I blow up your friends. You have five seconds to make up your mind. One . . ."

"Don't do it, Haley," Christina said.

"I have to. Do whatever you have to do to stay alive to rescue them. He plans to kill you — and everyone on that bus."

"Four."

"I'm coming." She stepped away from the safety of the Hummer and walked toward the vehicle he wanted her to get into.

Christina climbed out of the Hummer. "Haley —"

"Stay behind me. Don't give him a clear shot. He wants me alive for some reason if he wants me to go with him." She continued to put one foot in front of the other, desperate to find a way to avoid getting in the SUV without putting the lives of the people she loved in jeopardy.

Christina walked slightly behind her. "If she's going, I'm going too," she called.

Haley watched his eyes, and a slight shudder went through her as it always used to when she was in G2. The man's eyes flicked to Christina, then back to Haley. His lips tightened a fraction. He'd figured out Haley had made herself a shield.

She stopped in front of him, the hood of the SUV between them. She finally got a good look at the man who wanted her dead. He was handsome, with his dark hair and blue eyes, and he stood about six feet tall. He was built like someone who was a frequent visitor at the local gym.

"How does she stop the bus from blowing

up?" Haley asked.

"I'll let your friend figure that out. But she'd better move fast. Time is running out."

"How much time?"

In a sudden move, he tossed the item in his hand at Christina, dove across the hood to grasp Haley's bicep, and pressed the muzzle of his weapon against her head.

With the gun still at her temple and his fingers wrapped around her upper arm, he slid from the hood and landed on his feet in a catlike move that even she couldn't emulate. "Get. In. The. Car."

Haley knew this was no ordinary assassin. But she was no ordinary hostage.

His grip would leave bruises, but that was the least of her worries. He shoved her toward the vehicle. Then something slammed into them. Haley grunted as they hit the ground and rolled, catching a glimpse of Christina's face next to hers.

A shot sounded and Haley froze for a split second. Long enough for him to get a punch into her wounded side. The pain arched through her and the breath left her lungs.

Another crack sounded and she flinched. He was shooting at Christina. She pressed a hand to her side and prayed her stitches held.

She rolled onto her back and saw Christina on the ground under the SUV.

He aimed at Christina again and Haley swiped a foot into his right knee. Their attacker cried out and went down with curses. Christina rolled out from under the SUV to the other side and dove behind a smaller pile of gravel. Haley wasn't sure a bullet wouldn't travel right through the gravel, but at least Christina appeared to be safe for the moment.

He turned the weapon on her. "That's it," he growled. "She just killed her friends."

"They're not her friends!" Haley scrambled to her feet. "They're mine and I've done everything you said."

"Except bring help with you."

"She was in the car already and you know it. You told me to bring her!"

He pulled her around to the passenger side and opened the door. "Get in, you're driving."

Haley held a hand to her side and drew in a deep breath, then crawled across and slid behind the wheel. The keys were in the ignition.

He kept the gun on her while he planted himself in the passenger seat and shut the door.

"Where am I going?"

"Get back on the highway and head back

toward town. I'll give you directions as you drive."

"Did you kill Gerald Forsythe?"

"I did. Now drive."

[27]

Steven and Quinn drove the route the bus had planned to take. "There's no way we're going to find them this way," Steven muttered. He spun the wheel and took the next turn a little too fast. He braked and wished he could slow his racing heart as easily.

"She said I-20. Just keep looking." Quinn held his phone to his ear. "Yeah, I left the car at the restaurant," he said. "I had an emergency to take care of. Get someone out there ASAP to take our place. We still need to have someone trying to catch these guys. Yeah. Thanks."

Quinn hung up and Steven's phone buzzed. He took the call with his Bluetooth speaker. "Yeah?"

"This is Christina. I need a bomb squad and an explosion detection dog at Harry's Mud and Mulch off I-20," she panted.

"What? Where are you?"

"Had to find a phone. He made me toss

mine. Listen up. The guy buried the kids and chaperones in a bus at Harry's Mud and Mulch off I-20, you got that?"

"I got it." He exchanged a worried glance with Quinn.

"Not sure exactly where he buried them," Christina said, "but there's an area that looks different. If you can get a dog over here, he can confirm it or find the right place. Probably need a Bobcat driver to remove the debris he dumped on the bus. And someone needs to call the owner."

"Okay, slow down. Hang on." Haley's students had been kidnapped? His heart thudded even while he noticed Quinn going to work with the information.

"Christina," Steven said, "where's Haley?"

"I don't know. It's a long story and I tried to stop him, but he forced her into his black SUV, plates GKS555. Probably stolen. But I managed to toss her cell phone through the window. I'm pretty sure it hit the back seat, but I don't know how long you have until he finds it."

"You get that, Captain?" Quinn listened, then nodded at Steven. "He said they're working on it now."

Steven took the exit ramp.

"That Mud and Mulch place is about five miles back," Quinn said. "Let's get back there and make sure no one shows up and accidentally stumbles on the right pile and blows everyone up."

Steven nodded. "We need people out there looking for Haley."

"As soon as we get a hit on her phone."

Haley drove with gritted teeth. Her side pounded out a new rhythm of pain that she fought to ignore. Christina was alive. She'd escaped, so there was hope.

He took her off the highway and through back streets she'd not gotten around to exploring since living in Columbia. "Left at the stop sign."

"Why are you doing this?" she asked.

"I don't get into the whys of the job, I just do it."

"Money."

"Lots of it."

"All right. Who hired you, then?"

"Doesn't matter."

She snapped her head sideways to look at him. "It might not matter to you, but he's the one who wants me dead."

"Then he can tell you. You're going to see him shortly."

"He wants me dead — and you were hired to kill me. But now you've kidnapped me, so now he needs me alive," she muttered.

"Why does he want me alive?"

"Shut up and drive."

He wasn't going to tell her anything. She flexed her fingers on the wheel and thought about running the vehicle into the nearest solid object. After several seconds, she decided against it. She simply couldn't afford to take the risk. She followed his directions and realized he was taking her on a road she'd already been down. They were driving in circles. But why?

To kill time?

He'd glanced at his phone several times but hadn't texted or called anyone.

He was waiting for instructions.

She watched the clock even as she formed and discarded one plan after another.

But the added time was good. Each minute that passed gave Christina more time to figure out how to find her and her kidnapper. Because Haley had a feeling when they arrived at their ultimate destination, she was going to be in for the fight of her life.

Steven's phone buzzed and he snagged it before the ring ended. "What?"

"It's Captain Nelson. Our tech guy got back to me about Haley's phone and I wanted to call you myself."

"And?"

"Her GPS is turned off."

"What? No."

"I'm sorry, son. We'll keep trying in case she comes back online, but we're going to have to figure out another way to find her."

Steven drove into the mulch yard, spotted Christina waving at them, and pulled up beside her. Quinn got out of the car.

Steven didn't move for several seconds as he listened to his captain lay out his plan, including searching traffic cams. "All right, thanks, Captain. I'll let Quinn know."

"Keep me updated."

"Will do." He hung up and frowned. Then he pushed his door open with a grunt and stepped into the muggy air.

Quinn stopped midsentence with Christina. "He find Haley?"

"Her GPS isn't on."

"He hacked her phone," Christina said. "I didn't have time to do anything but throw it in the car before he started shooting at me. We couldn't call for help because he knew every move she was making on it."

"The captain is on it," Steven said. "He'll figure it out. He's also got someone searching the traffic cameras."

"Pull over under those trees right there."

"Where?"

406

"There!" He jabbed her temple with the weapon. "Pull over!"

Haley winced and glared at him, then drove the car onto the shoulder of the back road and put the gear in park.

"Keep your hands on the wheel. If you move them, I'll blow you away." He pulled cuffs from the side of his black cargo pants and slapped one on her right wrist. "Slide out the passenger door after me."

Haley obeyed. Self-defense moves flicked through her mind, but she knew if she killed or escaped her current captor, another would just come after her. She let him drag her out of the vehicle, only to be surprised when he opened the back door, shoved her onto the back seat, and cuffed her to the door handle.

"Try to get out before I'm ready and your friends die. I still control the bomb strapped to the bus. You understand?"

"I got it." She thought they had traveled way too far for him to be able to detonate the bomb, but that didn't mean he didn't have someone close enough to do so — or that it couldn't be detonated by phone. She couldn't take any chances at the moment.

"Now lie down."

Haley swung her feet up on the seat and did as ordered as best she could with her hand cuffed to the door. She scanned the back seat while her captor went around to the driver's side and climbed in. He shut the door and pulled back onto the road. Haley's pulse pounded. She wouldn't deny she was afraid, but she was also angry. Very, very angry.

Someone had been behind the deaths of her family twenty-five years ago and, as a result, changed the course of her life.

"You are one tough chick, you know that?" he said.

"Thanks." The sarcasm slipped out before she could bite it off.

"You have more security and are harder to get to than a celebrity," he said.

So he'd figured out her weak spot and exploited it. She bit her lip and prayed for the safety of the kids and chaperones. He didn't seem to expect a response from her, so she stayed silent, hoping if she didn't respond, he'd keep talking.

The back of the vehicle was clean. No stray paperclip to unlock the cuffs, no ballpoint pen, no hairpin. Nothing.

He made a sudden left and she held on to keep from sliding off the seat. He didn't seem inclined to say anything further, so she said, "Christina will find me. You know that, right?"

"She'll be too busy rescuing your friends from the bus."

"But I have other friends who'll be looking."

"Let them look."

"Why haven't you killed me?"

"Because I was told not to. Yet."

His words chilled her and she glanced around once again. An object tucked just under the driver's seat caught her attention. It hadn't been visible only moments before. He turned again, another left, and the item slid further toward her.

Her phone! But how . . . ? Christina. That's why the woman had taken the risk and tackled her and her kidnapper. It had allowed her the time to toss the phone in the window. She'd wanted to give Haley a fighting chance if she could actually get the phone. Or a way to track her if she couldn't. That meant help was on the way!

But being handcuffed to the back door on the passenger side wasn't going to allow her to grab the device. She stretched and placed her foot over it and slowly started dragging it toward her.

He spun the wheel to the right and braked. Her foot slid off the phone and she nearly groaned in frustration. She pressed her foot back onto it and slid it further, then reached down to grab it, when her door opened and pulled her arm. She gave the phone a quick kick and knocked it back under the seat. There was no way she wanted him to find it.

She'd have to find a way to get to it later. She didn't think he was going to leave. Instead, she had a feeling he was planning to finish the job once he had the green light.

He unhooked the cuff from the car and shoved her toward the building. A log cabin overlooking the lake behind it. She had no idea where she was.

That could be a problem.

But she took note of her surroundings and the dark sedan sitting in the gravel drive. Older pines gave the area a private feeling — a sense of seclusion.

That could also be a problem.

He continued to hold the weapon on her as he gripped the loose cuff hanging from her wrist.

Her heart thudded in her chest. Whoever was on the other side of that front door was responsible for the deaths of her parents, her younger brother, for her life as she knew it. And he'd paid a hit man to take her out.

"Open the door."

Haley twisted the knob and the door swung inward. She immediately noticed the den area connected to the kitchen. A true open-concept layout, the den held a comfortable leather couch that faced a brick fireplace. Above the mantel was a large flat-screen television that played a national news channel. French doors led to the back deck that overlooked a green yard and a wooden dock floating on the placid water. Footsteps to her left caught her attention and she turned to see a figure in the hallway walking toward her. Their eyes connected and Haley felt the breath leave her but refused to show her emotion.

Instead, she raised a brow. "You?"

[28]

"A traffic cam picked up the vehicle," the captain said.

Steven watched the explosion detection dog sitting, alerting the bomb squad to the bomb beneath the large pile of mud and mulch.

"Our tech guy is following it from camera to camera. Looks like he took the exit for Lake Murray. After that, we're not sure. He hasn't been able to pick him back up."

"Okay, at least we have something to work with. Can you have units ready to stand by once we locate her?" *Please, Lord, let it happen and happen soon.* He couldn't stand the thought of something happening to her. He was just getting to know her, and for the first time in a very, very long time, he wanted the option of a relationship to continue.

"Of course."

He hung up only to have his phone buzz

again. Katie. "Hello?"

"I was talking to your buddy Hugh. Did Haley tell you that her grandfather changed his will the day after he found out she was alive?"

Steven paused. "No, she didn't tell me that. How does Hugh know?"

"He knows everything about that family."

"Except who killed three of them."

"Well, yes, or so he says."

"You don't believe him?"

"I don't know. I can't read him as well as I would like. He sure comes across as sincere. But he left a little while ago and hasn't come back."

Steven frowned. "Where'd he go?"

"I'm not sure."

"All right, let me know when he shows back up. What about the rest of the family?"

"They've kind of scattered. Said they were going to the hotel to rest. Lachlan said he needed to work, but that they would all be back as soon as they got word Ian was awake."

"Okay, thanks."

"There's more."

"Tell me."

"My contact from Scotland Yard called me. She looked into the investigation of the murders and said that while Niall Burke was initially cleared of any wrongdoing, he was noted to have ties to the mafia."

"What? Why are we just now learning this?"

"Because the FBI wasn't a part of the original investigation — the local Gardaí handled it. This comes from our field office. It's a shame. We had information to share and didn't know we needed to."

"Communication back then wasn't quite what it is today."

"I know."

"Anyway, Niall isn't answering any questions right now. He's hovering at the edge of death."

"And his family is here." Steven drew in a breath and continued watching as pile after pile of dirt was removed by the bomb squad. Robots and humans. The humans wore their protective suits and were digging by hand, careful not to accidentally set off any explosive device. It was going to be slow going. Steven stayed well back while he talked to Katie. "It doesn't make sense. So, Ian changed his will."

"Yes."

"Who is going to be the most affected by the change?"

"Kane and Lachlan. Kane is Niall's son and Lachlan is the grandson, just to refresh your memory."

"Right. So they're the ones with the most to lose."

"Hugh said they'll lose half."

"And Lachlan's been in the States for the past two weeks."

"You think he's the one who killed Gerald Forsythe and tried to kill Haley?"

"No, I think he hired someone to do it for him. I'm going to send someone to the hotel to pick up him and his father. I have some questions for them."

Haley stared at the woman in front of her. Maeve, Lachlan's wife. Surprised, and yet not. "Does Lachlan know about this?"

"Of course not. He's very much like his father and grandfather. Too weak to take the necessary steps to ensure the fortune stays in the family."

Haley *was* part of the family, more so than the woman in front of her, but she didn't think it wise to remind her at the moment. "So you took it upon yourself to do so."

"I did."

Hard hands shoved her into the wooden chair, and her captor snapped the cuffs around the side of it. The chair wobbled slightly and creaked when she leaned back. An old, flimsy chair. "But you were just a child twenty-five years ago, just like me," she said. "You didn't have anything to do with the murders."

"True enough," a voice to her right said, " 'twas my mother-in-law, Darcy." The second woman shut the door behind her and faced Haley full on.

Haley gaped. "Janet?" Kane's wife. Her gaze snapped back to the younger woman. "Maeve? The two of you together are doing this?"

"That's right." She motioned to the man behind her. "Put your mask on and hold the gun to her head."

He did so and Janet snapped a picture with her phone, tapped a few keys on the keyboard, and then lowered the device.

"Why?" Haley asked. "After twenty-five years?"

"Because you were found."

"So I need to die?"

"Exactly." The older woman stepped toward her, the gun a comfortable weight in her hand. "Only you can't die yet. Unfortunately, I've only just learned that your grandfather changed his will the moment he learned you were alive, and he will have to sign a paper saying he is reverting back to the old will. Until then, you will have to keep us company."

"Because I'm the bait."

"He signs or you die." She waved the phone. "I just sent him the picture. The papers have been delivered to his hospital room."

"By whom?"

"It doesn't matter."

The only other person who could possibly be involved was Peter, Kane's brother and Niall's other son.

"You're not going to let me live whether he signs the papers or not," Haley said.

"True." She pointed the weapon at Haley's forehead. "Can't have you talking now, can we?"

"Of course not. And then you'll make sure my grandfather has an accidental death as well, won't you?"

Janet gave a slight shrug.

A blinding rage swept over Haley and she drew in a deep breath, blinked, and allowed a cold calm to invade her to the depths of her soul. Did this woman really think Haley would just sit calmly by while she threatened to kill her and her grandfather? "Darcy had them killed, you said."

"It couldn't be helped. Niall was going to walk away from the business. He said he was tired of working for his brother." She let out a short laugh. "Can you imagine?

Walking away from all that money? The *ee-jit.* He was going to branch out, do his own thing, live off the land like paupers if they had to, he said. Darcy was livid and having none of it."

"So your mother-in-law hired the hit men, who used Hugh's son, and made it look like a Mafia attack?"

"She did. It didn't hurt that Ian had just outbid a Mafia-owned company. The time was all right for everything to happen. Ian was supposed to die as well, but in the end it didn't matter. Darcy got what she wanted."

"Niall staying with the company while his brother grieved." Haley didn't bother trying to work her wrist out of the cuff. Instead, she let her mind continue to flick through escape options. Ones that would allow her enough time to reach her phone.

"Which is what she wanted," Janet said. "With Ian dead, Niall would have taken over, but he possibly would have decided to sell out at some point to chase his silly dream."

Haley flinched at the scorn in the woman's voice. She felt sorry for Niall, Kane, and Lachlan. How had they been so deceived by such treacherous women?

Haley worked her hand around so that she

had a good grip on the chair. The way her hand was cuffed to it, it would just look like she was trying to find a more comfortable position. She rocked back a bit and felt the wood give slightly. "So while Ian and his wife managed to survive, the death of his family had the same result. Niall in charge." She kept her eyes on the woman, but her senses were very aware of the man just behind her to her right.

"Exactly. He couldn't let down his precious older brother, you know. Or at least I knew that."

"And used it to your advantage."

"Of course. He took over the majority of the business until Kane could graduate with his degree and step into his father's shoes. Niall was glad to hand the reins over to Kane, and eventually Lachlan, who was also happy to take them."

"What was Ian's part in all of this?"

She gave a ladylike huff. "He wasn't even in the picture for a long time. He signed what was necessary for Niall to make decisions for the company without having to consult him on each and every one. By the time he was ready to come back and take over, Niall was doing so well, Ian left things as they were. He was older and ready to go into a partial retirement anyway. He kept his finger on the pulse of the company, but Niall and Ian are so much alike — and do business very much alike — that the two never really had anything to butt heads over."

"So how did you find all that out? I mean, that's not something that you just talk about around the dinner table."

"My mother-in-law and I were very close. Two minds working as one, you might say. I came across some correspondence in Niall's office one afternoon when I was . . . dusting."

Haley laughed, a sound that was harsh to her own ears. "Sorry, but you don't look like you've ever dusted anything in your life. I think you mean snooping."

She shrugged. A lazy lifting of her shoulder. "Whatever. I asked my mother-in-law about it and she asked me what I would do if I thought the family fortune was in danger."

"And your answer?" The longer she kept the woman talking, the longer someone had time to find her.

"I told her I would do whatever it took to ensure that it was protected."

"Including murder?"

"Including murder."

Haley flicked a glance at Maeve, who'd

stayed silent during the entire exchange. She looked bored with the whole thing. Were none of them born with a conscience? Or did the love of money simply allow one to block it out completely? "And you, Maeve? You're just fine with all this?"

Maeve lifted her blue eyes to connect with Haley's. "We must do what must be done." She sounded like she was quoting someone. Probably her mother-in-law.

"Is that what she's convinced you of?"

"All right, enough chitchat," Janet said. Her eyes flicked to the man still standing silent behind her. "Lyle, go pick up the papers and let me know what he says."

Wait. He was leaving? She had to get to her phone. She still had the one cuff on her right wrist, but her left hand was free. True, the older woman looked like she knew how to use a weapon, but Haley couldn't take a chance on her abductor leaving with her phone.

Haley flexed her fingers around the side of the chair once more to make sure she could do this one-handed. She had no choice. Before she could think twice about it, Haley tightened her grasp, spun out of the chair, and slammed it into the man's face, making sure she connected the edge of the hard seat with his much softer nose. She heard the bones crunch, his scream of agonized pain, and Janet's harsh yell for Haley to stop. A piece of the chair fell to the floor while the rest of it dangled at odd angles.

Haley ignored the order, prayed Janet had bad aim, and bolted for the door. She held the chair with one hand and twisted the knob with the other, then shot outside onto the porch.

No one fired at her, but she heard Janet and Maeve shouting at her captor to not let her get away.

She kept going, straight for the vehicle. Keeping it between her and the house, she opened the passenger door and snagged her cell phone from the floor.

"I'm going to kill you!"

Haley looked through the back window behind the driver's side to see her kidnapper bearing down on her, blood streaming from his broken nose, eyes already blackening like a raccoon. Haley swung the chair against the back of the SUV and it broke the rest of the way, leaving the cuffs still around one wrist.

But at least now she could run.

Steven kept an eye on the monitor. He'd moved from his vehicle to the bomb squad's van while Quinn consulted with Katie, Maddy, and Olivia, who'd all shown up about twenty minutes ago, then spread out to look for the vehicle Christina had described. Choppers were also in the air.

And, according to Hugh McCort, Ian Burke had just woken up at the hospital. Steven texted the man back.

> He has coverage on his room. Watch who goes in and out. Don't let anyone in the family be in there alone with him.

Why?

> I'll explain later.

Steven's phone buzzed yet again. He looked at the screen and his heart skipped a beat. A text from Haley.

Ping my phone.

> GPS is off.

Steven waited anxiously for another text from her. He spun around and waved at Quinn. His partner jogged over. "I just got a text from Haley to ping her phone. She didn't realize her GPS was off. We need someone trying to track her down now."

Quinn got on the phone.

Steven's phone dinged again.

On a lake.

Name?

DK

"She's on Lake Murray, but we don't know which inlet," he told Quinn. "We need a chopper if we're going to get to her fast enough."

"Have to know where she is first."

"We'll find her. Once we're in the air, we'll be able to get to her faster. I'm trying to cut out as much time as possible."

"I hear you." Quinn got on the phone while Steven paced and prayed. He turned when Quinn called his name.

"Text the others," his partner said. "The chopper's almost here."

No sooner had he said the words than Steven heard the *whomp whomp* of the blades carrying the craft their way.

A cheer erupted from behind him and he turned to see teens streaming from the bus. Michelle brought up the rear.

"Thank you, God," he whispered.

Now to find Haley.

Haley kept moving from tree to tree, watching the man come after her. She'd made him angry. Very angry. If she gave him a chance, he'd kill her, regardless of what his employers wanted. She'd made it personal. She dared another glance at her phone. She had to get the GPS turned on, but she didn't have the time to go through the steps to do it.

She turned to look and froze. Where had he gone?

Haley turned and pressed her back to the nearest tree while she scanned the area. Not good. She had a signal, she could call out, but calling wouldn't do her any good if she couldn't tell anyone where she was. And they couldn't track her. As quick as her shaky fingers would move, she turned on the GPS signal, glancing up and around with each tap on the screen.

And still she didn't see him. Not in front of her. Not behind her. So where?

She went back to her phone and texted Steven again.

GPS on. Janet n Maeve r behind everything. Peter, 2,

I think.

U just popped up on the
screen. UR at Lake Murray. On
the way.

Hurry.

So what now? *Think. Think.* Okay, she was
somewhere on Lake Murray. She'd lost
track of her captor. Her side was killing her.
It was three against one. Her best option
would be to lay low and wait for help.

But there was no way she was going to let
Janet and Maeve get away. They'd head
straight to the airport.

No, Steven had their names. He'd make
sure they couldn't catch a flight.

The faint sound of a helicopter reached
her ears. Could that possibly be help?

She drew in a deep breath, looked behind
her, then back toward the direction of the
road. Just in time to see Lyle step out from
behind a tree and raise his weapon. Haley
shot for cover behind the next tree when
she heard the crack. The bullet smacked
into the trunk, sending bark and wood flying.

"She's not going to pay you if you kill me!"

"I don't care!" Another shot sounded, this

time from behind her.

Janet was marching toward them, her arm extended, weapon pointed at Haley. "You can die now. He signed the papers."

Janet behind her, Lyle in front of her. Her only hope was to swim across the lake. She darted for the water. Gunshots followed her, and she was actually shocked that none hit her. The water was cold enough to take her breath, but not frigid enough to keep her from diving under. Silence surrounded her.

She swam as far as she could underwater before her lungs screamed at her for air. She kicked out and broke the surface, dragging in deep breaths.

The sound of a hard splash behind her spun her around. Her heart thudded at the sight of Lyle swimming like a fish to catch up to her. Haley struck out for the opposite shore. If he caught her, he'd drown her. He was stronger and her wound had weakened her.

The chopper now hovered almost directly overhead, stirring the water, the spotlight on the action below.

A hand clamped down on her arm and yanked her under.

[29]

"He's trying to drown her!" Steven pointed to the two figures thrashing in the lake. "We have to act fast! What do you want to do?"

Haley resurfaced and Steven saw her land the heel of her palm on the guy's cheek. His head jerked back and he grasped her hair and shoved her back under the water.

And held her there.

Steven ripped off the headphones, tossed Quinn his phone, and jumped.

The impact ripped through him, but he'd landed feet first. He sank for a moment, then kicked his way to the surface. His head broke through and he spun, looking for Haley and the man trying to kill her.

Both were underwater. Steven dove and opened his eyes. They thrashed just ahead of him. The chopper made the water rough, but he swam toward them. They surfaced once again and so did he. Steven looked up to see Quinn holding on with one hand and leaning out of the chopper, his weapon aimed at the scene below.

Steven knew what he had to do. He stroked harder toward the fighting duo and saw that Haley was losing. Neither one had noticed him yet. They spun in the water and Steven's heart nearly stopped. Haley had her hands wrapped around the man's wrist. A knife hovered just above her chest.

Steven launched himself at the attacker and wrapped his arm around the man's throat. Haley's eyes widened and she gasped. The knife swung Steven's way as the man stabbed blindly in his direction. Steven managed to dodge the weapon but knew he had to do something or his face was going to be filleted.

Haley gave a cry, rose in the water, and threw a right punch directly into the man's nose. He gave a bloodcurdling scream and the knife sank into the water.

The man went limp in Steven's grasp.

"Can you swim?" he yelled at her.

"I'll make it," she gasped. Her breaths came in quick pants and her face held no color.

"Are you sure?"

"I'm sure. We still have two more to round up."

She struck out toward shore and Steven

followed, his arm still around the unconscious man's throat. He was tempted to squeeze a little tighter but resisted and continued to stroke toward the shore. His feet found the bottom at the same time Haley's did. They stood and slogged the rest of the way to shore.

Haley collapsed and touched her side. Her hand came away with a tinge of red.

"Broke your stitches open?" he asked while he cuffed the unconscious man.

"No, this is the other side. He got me with the knife before I could dodge it. It's not too bad, though, just a graze." She sucked in another deep breath and stood. "Time to find out about the kids on the bus and to arrest the ladies of the house."

The words had no sooner left her lips than the chopper swerved off and law enforcement descended from the front of the home. "We've got them!"

"Hope someone got Peter," she muttered.

"The kids and their chaperones are safe. They were freed from the bus moments before I left to come find you."

"Oh thank you, God."

He thought she might cry, but she simply sniffed and shoved the heels of her hands against her eyes.

"All right. I'm ready when you are," she said.

Steven stood and with Haley's help managed to hoist the murderer onto his shoulders in a fireman's carry. Another officer hurried down the slight embankment and took part of the load.

The three of them and their prisoner headed back up and around the side of the house to find several ambulances, numerous law enforcement vehicles, and the two women in handcuffs.

Maeve looked bored with the whole process. Janet, however, glared at Haley. "You're going to pay for this."

"No, Janet, you are." She looked at the officer. "Get her out of my sight."

He obliged.

"I've got to get to the hospital to see my grandfather."

"I'd take you," Steven said, "but I don't have transportation."

A car pulled into the drive and Haley smiled. "That's all right. Katie does."

"Perfect timing," he said.

"And I'm guessing she's got a change of clothes in there for me."

He studied her. "Is that Maddy's shirt? The one she brought you in the hospital?"

She looked down. "Yes." And groaned. "And it's got a rip in it from the knife. Rats." Then shrugged. "Well, she said she wanted it back with no bullet holes. I can do that."

Steven laughed and took her hand. Then pulled her into a hug. Haley went still, the feel of his heart beating next to her ear doing strange things to her emotions. Things she'd sworn she wasn't ever interested in feeling again. Because feeling them meant being vulnerable, opening herself up to someone. To pain. She felt his hand under her chin as he lifted her head to look into his eyes. "Will you go out with me?"

She blinked. "Like on a date?"

"Yes."

"Oh." She thought about it. Thought about what it would mean to go out with him. To let him know she found him as attractive as he seemed to find her.

"The pause isn't doing much for my self-esteem here, Haley. I'll bring M&Ms. Will that help?"

She pulled his head down so she could capture his lips with hers. She felt him smile against her lips, and then he kissed her with a gentleness that made her heart soar. A sweet exploration that let her know without a doubt that he was the kind of man she was interested in. And besides, he'd just saved her life at great risk to his own. That counted for a whole lot.

He lifted his head, and while his eyes were tender, the smoky sweetness stirred her senses. "I'm going to take that as a yes."

"Good. That's another point in your favor."

"I didn't realize I was earning points." He paused. "What did I just earn a point for?"

"You're not only good-looking, you're smart too. I didn't have to say a word and you knew I was going to go out with you."

"That was a pretty good 'yes, I'll go out with you' kiss." Another pause. "Let me be sure of one thing, though."

"Okay."

"You think I'm good-looking?"

Haley laughed, a real laugh from the depths of her belly. Yes, this was the kind of man she could go for. Then she sobered. "Let's go see if Katie will take us to the hospital. I really need to see my grandfather."

"He woke up."

"I figured he did. Janet said he signed the papers on the promise that I wouldn't be killed."

"Let's go ease his mind."

She ran a hand through her wet, tangled

mess of hair. "I'd better clean up first."

"We can do that on the way to the hospital. I'll want some dry clothes myself."

"Katie!" Haley called.

Katie looked up from her phone. "Haley! You're all right." She ran to her and threw her arms around her in spite of the sopping, slightly bloody clothes.

Haley hugged her back. "I'm fine."

Katie drew back and looked her up and down. "Oh, you're in one piece. I'm so glad."

"Thanks."

She eyed the red-stained hole at Haley's side. "Is that Maddy's shirt?"

"Yes."

Katie touched the hole and lifted a brow.

Haley frowned. "It's not from a bullet. You heard her. She only specified bullets."

"Hmm." Katie hugged Haley again. "As long as you're in one piece, that's all that matters. Come on, I'll take you to see your grandfather."

One hour later, after a quick stop at the local mall, Haley and Steven sported dry clothing, new shoes, and for Haley, a light dusting of makeup as they returned to the hospital.

Haley pushed open her grandfather's door and stepped into his room. She walked farther in and found him sitting up in bed, eating a banana.

"Haley!" He set the fruit aside and held out a hand.

She grasped it and squeezed. "How are you feeling, Daideo?"

"Better." His eyes twinkled with gladness at seeing her and the love there seared her. Then he sighed and sadness stared back at her. "I had no idea my shenanigans would place you in danger."

"Shenanigans?"

He looked away, then at Steven. "For twenty-five years, I had a feeling one of my family members was responsible for the deaths of your parents and John." He shook his head. "I had no idea the extent of their evil, I promise."

"Go on."

"When I came to see you and you were being targeted, I knew I had to figure it out. The seizure was simply the tool I used to do so. After I had the seizure, I woke to hear the doctors talking. They were concerned I was still unconscious. And that's when the idea was born."

A smile tugged at her lips. "You faked it."

"That I did."

"And everyone came over because they were worried about you."

"Well, some of them anyway. Peter came in and sat beside me and whispered you would die if I didn't wake up. He said that he had some papers to sign that would save you, but I had to wake up to sign them."

"I don't understand. Did he think you wouldn't figure it out? That signing papers to revert to your old will wouldn't clue you in?"

He patted her hand. "I don't think I was supposed to live long enough for them to worry about it."

"Yeah." She sighed and rubbed her eyes. "Where's Hugh?"

"I sent him on back to your house. He's been here nonstop and was exhausted. I had to remind him he wasn't a young man anymore."

"At least he's safe there now."

"Indeed." He paused. "I know you're not interested in running the family business, but will you at least come visit me occasionally?"

Haley leaned over and kissed his cheek. "Every chance I get."

Steven marveled at Haley's strength. She'd almost been killed several times and yet she hadn't let that slow her down. Her own family had turned on her and she refused to let the anger or hate overtake her.

They entered another room at the hospital. Micah still lay in the bed, but even Steven had to admit the boy looked better. He actually had some color in his lips and cheeks.

Zeke sat on the window seat playing a video game on his phone. Laila sat in the chair next to Micah, her feet propped on the side of his bed, eyes shut. They opened at their entrance and she stood. "I'm just going to grab a bite to eat."

"Thanks. And you don't have to come back. The danger's over."

"Cool." She fist-bumped Zeke and touched Micah's hair. "I'm glad the danger's over. Doesn't mean I'm going to be a stranger to you guys, though, right?"

"Absolutely," Zeke said.

Laila disappeared and Zeke turned his game off. "The danger's really over?"

"Yeah, they got the person trying to kill me."

Zeke frowned. "I thought that was Richie."

"I did too, at first. Turns out it was someone else." She'd explain it all to him later.

"Is that why you haven't been around much?"

"Yes. I was afraid that someone would try something and you would be hurt."

He nodded. "I thought that might be it. That's what Laila said anyway."

"I'm glad she explained it to you." She sat beside him. "Does he know yet?" she whispered.

"Yes," Zeke said. "He kept asking. The doctor told me to go ahead and tell him because he was getting more and more upset that she wasn't coming in."

"Haley?" Micah's voice whispered across the room to her, and Steven watched her face soften.

She stood and walked over to him. "Hey, guy, how're you feeling?"

"Better. I walked yesterday."

"That's great."

He used the power button to lift himself into a sitting position. Haley reached for the cup of water and handed it to him.

Steven moved to the other side of the bed and sat in the chair. "I'm sorry about your mom, kiddo."

Tears leaked onto his cheeks and he swiped them away. "I am too." He pressed a hand against his chest. "But everyone says she's always with me."

"Exactly."

"I get out of here in a few days, you know."

"I know."

"Are you going to adopt us?"

Haley drew in a deep breath. "Do you want me to?"

"My mom wanted you to."

"Yeah, but how do you and Zeke feel about that?"

Steven watched Zeke out of the corner of his eye. The kid couldn't hide his yearning. But he gave a nonchalant shrug. "I'm okay with it, I guess." His eyes met Haley's. "I think you like us."

"I do."

"And I think you would treat us fair."

"I would."

"Could we do it on a trial basis?"

Steven didn't blame the kid. All of his hard knocks had taught him to trust no one.

Haley pursed her lips, then nodded. "I think that sounds like a great idea."

Steven's heart thudded. Haley was going to be an instant mother of two kids. One of whom would be on medication for the rest of his life. He had to think about this one.

Of course, if she had refused to take the kids, he would still be doing some hard thinking.

But he'd known she wouldn't refuse.

Because that's just the kind of person she was.

He crossed the room and placed a hand on Zeke's shoulder. "Want to shoot some hoops later?"

The teen's eyes lit up. "You bet."

Haley's gaze met his and Steven swallowed at the look there. It almost looked like love.

[30]

One Week Later

Steven pulled in a deep breath, closed his eyes, and decided he really could do this. Maybe.

Haley placed a hand on his arm. "You can do this."

"Right."

"I think you have to."

"I know."

Yes, he had to. Walter Phillips had killed his brother and Steven was going to forgive him if it killed *him*. Not today, though. Today was just a start.

According to Haley anyway. All Steven could bring himself to do was to reserve judgment.

He walked into the prison and followed the protocol that would allow him to face his demons. Personal effects, weapon, et cetera. Haley stayed at his side in silent support.

Together they followed the guard back into one of the private rooms where lawyers often visited their clients or detectives cajoled a confession.

Steven stopped at the door and looked through the window. The prisoner was already there, dressed in the standard orange jumpsuit and seated at the table. Steven paused and simply studied the man for a moment. Thirty-one years old. Twelve years of his life spent behind bars.

And he didn't look like the monster Steven had been expecting. He was thin, but muscled as though he spent a great deal of time in the yard or the gym. His teenage face had morphed into a square jaw that sported a five-o'clock shadow. He was a good-looking man with blue eyes and blond hair. But prison had obviously hardened him. His jaw looked permanently tight and he had a scar that ran from the corner of his right eye to the base of his right ear.

The guard opened the door and Steven stepped inside.

Haley paused. "I can wait out here."

"No." He grabbed her hand. "Please."

"Okay." She followed him in and his pulse slowed a fraction. Now he understood what she'd been feeling the day she'd met her grandfather. Maybe. Her grandfather had never killed anyone.

Steven let go of her hand and slipped into the chair opposite the man who'd changed his whole life. "Hi."

"Hi." He held Steven's gaze, but Steven saw his Adam's apple bounce. "They said you wanted to meet with me."

"Yes. Uh . . . thanks for agreeing to." He wouldn't hate him. He wouldn't. He wasn't going to love him either, though. At least not right now. "You're up for parole again."

"Yes." He folded his hands on the table and Steven noted the bitten nails and scars on the knuckles. But no tattoos that he could see. "And you're going to fight it, aren't you?" The man's resignation resonated.

"Yes. Or I was."

Walter's back snapped straight. "Was?"

Steven rubbed his eyes. This was even harder than he'd thought. "Tell me why I shouldn't protest it — and don't give me the speech you're working on for the parole board."

Walter sat still and stared at the table. "I was stupid. I was nineteen but oh so stupid."

"Agreed."

Walter flinched, but didn't stop. "I'd been to a party that night, of course. I was pretty much partying every night. Harder and harder than the one before. It occurred to me that I might kill myself — and I was okay with that for various reasons. It never really crossed my mind that I might kill someone else."

Steven stayed silent, his heart pounding, blood rushing. He wanted to shut the man up and encourage him to keep going at the same time.

Walter drew in a breath and looked at the door as though he'd like to bolt through it. He cleared his throat. "I've been seeing a therapist, and I've learned a lot about myself over the past ten years. I've found God. But everyone in here finds him when it's time for the parole board to meet, so I won't go there."

Steven was surprised at the statement. "Yes, they seem to, don't they? How did you find him?"

"Do you really want to know?"

"I wouldn't ask if I didn't."

"Your mother forgave me." Tears surfaced and he blinked. "The mother of the child that I killed forgave me," he whispered. "That was the only thing that could have convinced me that God could forgive me too."

Steven sat stunned. Speechless. Grieving. And, if Steven could believe Walter, in awe of his mother. He cleared his throat and shifted in his chair. "That's a pretty speech."

"I'll stay in here if it makes you feel better. I deserve it. No one knows that better than I do. I can never undo what I did no matter how much I want to. What I did was unforgivable in a lot of people's eyes."

"I know." Steven locked eyes on him. "So how do I know you won't do it again?"

Walter didn't answer for a moment. "I don't know. I can tell you I won't, of course. I know that I won't take another drink as long as I live, but" — he shrugged — "I don't know what to say to make you believe it."

"I'm glad you realize there aren't words."

Walter looked down at the table. "Thank you for meeting with me today."

"You're welcome." He paused. "Why did my mother start coming to see you?"

Walter took a deep breath. "I asked her that the other day. I tried to kill myself a couple of years ago and wound up in the hospital."

"And my mother was the volunteer that came to your room."

"Yes."

"She did that before my dad got sick. Visited people in the hospital, prayed for them if they wanted it, took them magazines."

"She knew who I was the minute she saw my name on the door, but she came in anyway."

Steven nodded. "Yes, she would do that."

"Look —" Walter spread his hands — "I know I don't deserve anything but what I've got. I'm not trying to convince anyone that I deserve to be out of here. But I want out. I want a chance to prove myself and make a difference in the lives of other people. Kids who are living like I used to. Kids that haven't killed anyone yet, but might in the future." He rubbed a shaky hand down his cheek, then shook his head. "I truly don't know that any of that will happen. I just want the chance to try."

Steven stood. "Thanks for meeting me."

"Sure."

Steven walked to the door and the guard opened it. He turned back to look at Walter one more time. He simply sat there, his eyes sad. Resigned. Then he slowly stood as well. Steven motioned for Haley to exit first. She did and he followed her.

She slipped her hand into his and he squeezed. She squeezed back. And Steven thought he might be all right.

And so would Walter Phillips.

EPILOGUE

Six Months Later

The party was in full swing by the time Steven arrived. He walked around to the back of the house, his nerves tight, palms sweating. Now that he knew his father was in remission, he had made some kind of peace with his brother's killer — no, the teen who'd caused the accident that resulted in the death of his brother. He'd never forget it. But he was ready to move on.

With Haley. They'd seen each other almost every day over the past six months.

He realized things could change at a moment's notice. Life would have more curve balls to throw at him, but he was ready to deal with those head on.

With Haley.

She'd roped off part of the back pasture and strung lights around the perimeter. Kids danced, adults chatted, and Michelle handed out cupcakes.

Steven walked over to her and gave her a hug. "How are you doing?"

Michelle tilted her head, then pursed her lips. "I have the occasional nightmare," she finally said, "but they're fading. The Lord comforts." She handed him a cupcake. "And these don't hurt."

He laughed and bit into the sugary sweet. "You've got that right."

"She's over there."

"Who?" He made sure he had his innocent face on when he asked the question.

She swatted his arm. "You know who."

"Thanks."

He finished off the cupcake and walked over to Haley, who stood by herself, staring off into the dark. "Not in the mood to party?" he asked.

She whirled and launched herself into his arms.

He kissed her and didn't come up for breath until she giggled. "What?"

She motioned behind him and he turned to find they had an audience. Four teen center kids who'd been standing at the fence feeding apples and carrots to the horses giggled and whispered behind their hands.

He kissed her cheek. "I guess we're entertaining."

"More so than the cupcakes and s'mores

apparently."

Micah appeared and jumped onto Steven's back. Steven caught the still skinny but growing boy and piggybacked him to the lounge chair, where he dropped him. "Take a load off, kid."

Micah's laughter thrilled him. The boy still missed his mother, but he was adjusting. And her heart was beating a steady rhythm of love in his chest.

Zeke looked up from the group he was talking to and waved. "We're adopted!"

"I know! Congratulations!"

Zeke grinned and Steven was excited for him. And for himself. Because if Haley was agreeable, he'd be calling Zeke and Micah "sons" before too long. He was hoping to give this adoption party something else to celebrate.

If he could get Haley alone.

Daniel and Katie, along with Daniel's niece, Riley, were there. So were Wade, Olivia, and their daughter, Amy. It looked like Olivia was ready to have her baby at any moment. Maddy, too, was sporting a baby bump, and Quinn grinned every time his eyes landed on her.

Laila and Christina were already working overtime, and Katie had been teasingly warned she couldn't get pregnant until

Olivia and Maddy were back at work. She'd smiled and said she wasn't making any promises.

Steven slipped an arm around Haley and pulled her to the side. Away from the loud music, the dancing and fun.

"Steven?"

"Come on, I want to pet a horse."

"What? Since when? You're scared of them, remember?"

"Not scared anymore. You've . . . desensitized me."

She laughed. "Okay, come on."

This time she grasped his hand and led him over to Sasha, the gentle mare she'd agreed to take as a rescue last month.

"She's put on weight," he said.

"Yes. She's looking good."

"You look good. In fact, you look down-right beautiful."

Haley's heart thudded at the look in his eye. "Well, thank you. I appreciate that."

"You know what I appreciate?"

"What?"

"The fact that it's no longer ninety degrees in the evenings. I appreciate that you had this place sprayed for mosquitos. And I appreciate —"

She laughed. "You appreciate . . . ?"

"Tradition."

"Oh. Well, cool. I do too."

"Good, I thought you might. That's why I want to do this right."

Haley stilled and the butterfly swarm that seemed to live in her belly when she was around this man came to life. "Do what, Steven?"

He dropped to one knee and took her hand. "This."

"Oh, me."

"I hope that's a good 'oh, me,' 'cuz if it's not, tell me now."

"It's a good one. Keep going."

Relief flooded his face and his eyes crinkled in a grin. He dug into his front pocket and pulled out a small box. "I talked to your grandfather earlier today."

"You did?"

"Uh-huh. I asked him if he thought he might be up to hosting a wedding at his home."

"I see." Her voice thickened and she cleared her throat. "An' whose weddin' might ye be thinkin' he's goin' to host now?"

"Ours if you say yes. I love you, Haley. I was wowed by you from the moment I set eyes on you. But that's just the physical part. There are a lot of pretty women out there, but you have a special heart, a love inside you that just keeps on giving, expanding with each person you meet. It's contagious too. And I love it when you talk in that Irish brogue of yours. I want to hear it every day for the rest of my life."

Tears dripped down her cheeks and she didn't even try to wipe them away. "When did you get so eloquent?"

"I've been working on it."

"I love you too, Steven."

He pulled the ring from the box and slipped it on her finger. Then stood to pull her into a hug. "Like I said, I want to spend the rest of my days with you. Loving you, fighting with you, making up with you, doing life with you . . ." He glanced back toward the festivities. "Raising kids with you. Do you think you can go for that?"

"I can go for it to be sure."

"I have a new outlook on life because of you, a new hope . . . a new heart."

"You're making me cry." She sniffed. "And I'm not a crier."

"I'm not either, but I don't think that's going to stop me."

She laughed. "I love that you make me laugh. I love that you love those boys over there. I'm not as eloquent, sorry. I haven't had time to practice. Can I just say that I love everything about you — except maybe yer tendency to insist on yer own way — and we call it good?"

He threw back his head and shouted his laughter. Then picked her up and spun her around. Sasha snorted and backed up. "Sorry, girl." Steven set Haley on her feet.

"Hey, lovebirds, what are you doing?" Micah called.

"Celebrating life!" Steven grinned down at her. "Haley said yes!"

Micah whooped and he and Zeke high-fived. Their friends gathered around them and the congratulations ensued once again. Haley couldn't stop grinning. She sent up a silent thank-you to the One who'd made everything new. Her gaze slid to a glowing Maddy and Olivia. New life. She looked at Micah and Zeke, a new family and a new start. She gazed at Steven, her beloved.

A man with a new heart.

And a soon-to-be new wife.

She kissed his cheek and he pulled her over to the dessert table. Michelle handed him another cupcake.

"Let's practice." He handed it to her and then took another for himself. They crossed arms and each took a nibble.

She watched his eyes and knew exactly what was coming.

She smashed the cupcake into his face a

mere second before she felt the sticky sweetness cover her mouth and chin.

Laughter surrounded them as he kissed her.

And Haley couldn't wait to see what the future held for them and those she loved.

ACKNOWLEDGMENTS

Many thanks once again to my awesome law enforcement readers who corrected all of my police procedural. You all are amazing and the book wouldn't be the same without you.

A special thanks to Barb Barnes, editor extraordinaire, and Avonlea Krueger, who went above and beyond to make Haley sound believably Irish. ☺

Thanks to the fans for sticking with these awesome ladies of the Elite Guardians. I don't know about you, but I'm going to miss them! I feel a short story coming on . . .

Thanks to Cheryl Van Andel for all four awesome covers for the original publisher's editions. I'll admit, I wasn't sure at first, but they definitely grew on me and I liked each one better than the last. They're my favorites now!

Thanks to everyone at Revell who works so hard to produce an amazing product. You guys are wonderful and I'm blessed to work with you.

ABOUT THE AUTHOR

Lynette Eason is the bestselling author of the WOMEN OF JUSTICE series, the DEADLY REUNIONS series, and the HIDDEN IDENTITY series, as well as *Always Watching, Without Warning*, and *Moving Target* in the ELITE GUARDIANS series. She is the winner of two ACFW Carol Awards, the Selah Award, the Book of the Year Golden Scrolls Award, and the Inspirational Readers' Choice Award. She has a master's degree in education from Converse College and lives in South Carolina. Learn more at www.lynetteeason.com.

The employees of Thorndike Press hope you have enjoyed this Large Print book. All our Thorndike, Wheeler, and Kennebec Large Print titles are designed for easy reading, and all our books are made to last. Other Thorndike Press Large Print books are available at your library, through selected bookstores, or directly from us.

For information about titles, please call:
  (800) 223-1244

or visit our website at:
  gale.com/thorndike

To share your comments, please write:
Publisher
Thorndike Press
10 Water St., Suite 310
Waterville, ME 04901